Image and Theme
Studies in Modern French Fiction

Bernanos
Malraux
Sarraute
Gide
Martin Du Gard

by
Susan M. Keane, Ralph Tarica, John A. Fleming,
C. D. E. Tolton, and John Gilbert

Edited, with an Introduction, by
W. M. Frohock

Published by the Department of Romance Languages and Literatures,
Harvard University, and distributed by the Harvard University Press.

1969

Library of Congress Catalog Card Number 79–95931
SBN 674–44395–0

Printed in the United States of America

CONTENTS

Introduction
    by W. M. Frohock   **1**

Dream Imagery in the Novels of Bernanos
    by Susan M. Keane   **11**

Ironic Figures in Malraux's Novels
    by Ralph Tarica   **38**

The Imagery of Tropism in the
Novels of Nathalie Sarraute
    by John A. Fleming   **74**

Image-Conveying Abstractions in the
Works of André Gide
    by C. D. E. Tolton   **99**

Symbols of Continuity and the
Unity of *Les Thibault*
    by John Gilbert   **124**

Notes   **149**

INTRODUCTION

The authors of these five monographs have in common the Ph.D. from Harvard and an abiding interest in the analysis of fiction. All are, at this writing, Assistant Professors — at Simmons College, the University of Maryland, and the University of Toronto — but they worked together as graduate students, discussed recurrent problems and experienced similar frustrations and satisfactions, so that while perhaps no two of them, and even less all five, would accept any single adjective ending in "-ist," it is not surprising that there should be a discernible relationship, as to method, among their studies.

The first three, by Drs. Keane, Tarica, and Fleming, are based upon patiently constructed indexes-with-commentary on the imagery in the novels of the writers studied. Dr. Tolton's emerges from an equally patient inspection of André Gide's use of abstract nouns. Dr. Gilbert's doctoral subject involved the tracing of recurrent thematic patterns in so-called family novels and *romans-fleuve*. Each had time to let his completed work ripen in the dark before engaging in the re-inspection that resulted in his contribution to the present collection. In other words, the work for the doctorate was conceived as the construction of an *instrument de travail*, to be exploited subsequently. The original theses remain available, of course, in the Harvard Archives.

My own part in the enterprise has consisted of writing these prefatory pages and of assuming responsibility for editing. I should like it also to testify to the enduring pleasure of an academic association. It goes without saying that the contributors are absolved of all obligation to concur in the following observations regarding the nature and significance of their work.

That the closeness of relationship between the monographs should need pointing out may be attributed to the relatively undeveloped state of image study and the contiguous field of thematics at the present time. We have of course progressed since the day when Caroline Spurgeon attempted to reconstruct Shakespeare's biography on the assumption that poetic imagery regularly refers to the experiential content of the poet's own life; we are persuaded

1

that the psychology of image-making is by no means so simple. And we have been disillusioned by those studies of imagery that produce such statistics as that a given writer refers three and one-eighth times less often to one variety of flower than to another. As the late Leo Spitzer warned us years ago in a memorable footnote to *Linguistics and Literary History*, mere compilation affords no significant answers.

Spitzer believed that only if a study took as its point of departure a special perception of the nature of the imagery would what one wrote about it be likely to be worth the bother. But unfortunately what he proposed as a working method was nothing more specific than the combination of learning, faith, and intuition that so few of us can muster, and the patient contemplation of a text until the kind of scholarly epiphany, that he called "hearing the déclic," takes place. In ordinary mortals the functioning of intuition is only too likely to degenerate into sheer arbitrariness.

More recently, Professor Stephen Ullmann, in *The Image in the Modern French Novel*, has insisted firmly that a proper study of a novelist's imagery must take account of all the subject's novels. He does not propose that there can be any substitute for the literary flair and tact that lead to Spitzer's flash of recognition, and these are blessedly present in his own work. But the implication is strong not only that compilation, at least as a preliminary step, is perfectly in order, but also that, faithfully and industriously carried out, it is an obligatory preface to any further operation.

What, after all, is wrong with adopting the most cautious, least self-confident approach one can? Admittedly, no special genius is required to collect all the images, catalogue them, and classify them according to an elementary analysis based on the principles proposed by, say, Professor I. A. Richards. Or on the insights of Gaston Bachelard. If the moment of intuition must still come, why had it best not be when the student has before him all the assembled material, in the light of familiarity with all the contexts, and guided by a knowledge of the entire work that the construction of the index can hardly fail to afford?

Three of the present contributions are products of this general procedure. Dr. Keane, reviewing her materials, recognized an oneiric quality pervading all the novels of Bernanos. Dr. Fleming observed in Nathalie Sarraute's prose a prevalence of "tropistic" imagery such as to suggest that this novelist's familiar theory of fiction rationalizes an instinctive manner of apprehending the external world. And Dr. Tarica's scrutiny of the imagery in Malraux's novels led to the perception of a tendency to turn away from a perhaps painful reality into irony, a habit that cannot but have a connection with what Malraux himself has called *le farfelu*. In each case, methodical scholarship has led to the identification of a habit of a writer's imagination, the significance of which is clear in the light of what the writer has said, in other contexts, of his own work.

Perhaps curiously, a most convenient way of establishing the methodological relationship between these three studies and the other two lies in considering a danger inherent in the nature of the first three: they tend to divert attention from the novels as individual works of art and to focus it on them as materials for the study of the creative mind. The latter subject is, of course, hardly to be despised; we can surely use anything we can learn about the psychology of creation; and indeed such studies may be an exit from the dilemma revealed by Marcel Proust in *Contre Sainte-Beuve* — that the private personality that produces the great book is not identical with the public one accessible to biographical study. But if such knowledge were our unique aim we would be placed in the somewhat irrational posture of preferring the creator to the thing he has created. Salvation lies in our ability to remind ourselves that images are some part of the material of which the novel is constructed. Their nature is thematic.

The meaning of "theme" in the present context is the one most recently formulated by Professor Eugene Falk in *Types of Thematic Structure*: a theme is an idea — thus an abstraction — that recurs in a piece of fiction. It is represented in the fiction itself by all the concrete utterances, each a linguistic fact, that refer to it and bring it to the reader's mind. In Falk's vocabulary, these individual linguistic facts, of whatever sort, are "motifs," and the "motifs" can be said to "carry" the themes. Thus, in *Thérèse Desqueyroux*, Mauriac's references to walls, bars, grilles, cages, enclosed places, caged animals, and so forth, are motifs attached to the theme of captivity which Mauriac's introductory apostrophe identifies as the presiding one in the book.

Professor Falk's explanation of how themes interrelate with each other is amply elaborated in his own study and need not be repeated here. What concerns us at present is the kinship between imagery, on one hand, and theme and motif on the other. For following the line of analysis suggested by Professor I. A. Richards, an image (most explicitly metaphor) contains both motif and theme.

3

The analogical image, we remember, consists of a tenor (whatever is compared or equated), a vehicle (whatever the tenor is compared with) and the ground (the quality which makes comparison or equation possible). Thus in Mauriac's opening equation of Thérèse with a caged beast, the ground is that both are seen to be in a state of captivity; using Falk's vocabulary, captivity is thus the theme of the particular image as well as, we know from observation, the major theme of the book. At the same time, each later mention of caged animals or of cages is established as a motif, since it recalls the theme to the reader's mind.

The usefulness of these concepts became apparent during the construction of the image-indexes on which three of the present monographs are based. Each of the contributors came upon the same problem, what to do with an utterance (or linguistic fact) that brought an image to mind even when it occurred in a passage with no other structural element of the image to identify it. We were still at the point of believing that frequency of occurrence was an index of the importance of an image. If, for example, the sound of distant auto-horns has made a character feel his separation from the rest of the race, should one count each mention of horns as a recurrence of the image? Eventually, following Falk's suggestion, we recast the problem in terms of thematic study and decided that each mention was, structurally, a motif. By re-evoking the image, it evokes, of necessity, the "ground" which fixes the place of the image in the thematic structure, in addition to occupying a place of its own as well.

Because analogical imagery participates in the nature both of theme and of motif, an index of images may easily become an index of themes. All that is needed is the inclusion of "grounds" in the index. Theoretically the repertory may not be complete, since it is imaginable that themes may occur in any novel without being attached to an image, and in writers who tend to eschew imagery are almost certain to do so. But for writers since the beginning of the Nineteenth Century the chances are that the index will furnish at least a useful guide to the themes and in the case of writers like Bernanos (to take him as an example) whose imagery proliferates, the usefulness becomes paramount.

Bernanos has always offered a fertile field for studies involving the tracing of a single theme throughout his fictions, and most especially so to students who share his religious preoccupations. Theses on such topics as the theme of Agony and the theme of

4

Expiation already abound and increase in number yearly. Inevitably such studies turn rapidly to concrete instances (*les Expiations, les Agonies*) and thus eventually have to deal with clusters of supporting motifs. But the purpose of this research is, just as inevitably, to investigate the subjects of Expiation and Agony in themselves, and the study that results cannot but belong to the expanding activity, almost epidemic at this writing, of the theology of literature. One would not deny the legitimacy of such studies, but the likelihood of their authors' selecting certain themes for scrutiny, while neglecting others which may not appeal to their special tastes, is rather obvious.

Thus the theme of mediocrity, although admittedly prominent in Bernanos' writing, receives little attention. This despite the fact that most of Bernanos' political writing would be unintelligible without it, and the presence of characters in his novels like Father Sabiroux in *Sous le soleil de Satan*, incomprehensible. Doubtless the reason for the neglect is not unrelated to the fact that mediocrity, in Bernanos, regularly carries political overtones, while his politics, unlike his religion, is not particularly palatable to many of his followers.

This reasoning would seem far less cogent, however, in respect to other themes which carry much less political resonance, and yet remain neglected even though their presence may be responsible for much of Bernanos' harsh poetry. For example, the theme of human endurance. I quote the following passage at length because it is lifted from *La Grande Peur des bien-pensants*, which is likely to be unfamiliar except to certain specialists:

> Vieux amis des hauteurs battues par le vent, compagnons des nuits furieuses, troupe solide, troupe inflexible, magnifique machoire resserrée trois ans, pouce à pouce, sur la gorge allemande, et qui reçutes un jour, en pleine face, le jet brulant de l'artère et tout le sang du cœur ennemi, — ô garçons! . . . le onze novembre nous bûmes le dernier quart de vin de nos vignes, le onze novembre nous rompîmes le dernier pain cuit pour nous.
>
> On peut faire de son mieux sa page d'histoire, mais celui qui l'a faite n'est généralement pas celui qui la raconte. Les marchands de livres gardent l'avantage un siècle ou deux. Puis l'événement remonte lentement de l'oubli, surgit majestueusement des profondeurs qui le reçurent jadis, dans la conscience de la race. La race qui l'avait pieusement, saintement recouvert le découvre de nouveau. De nouveau nous serons pesés dans les mains fraternelles, jugés par un

regard vivant! Futures petites mains qui tournerez les feuillets, regards qui chercherez de page en page nos charges naïves, nos clairons, nos tambours, qu'importe ce que nous fîmes ou ne fîmes pas, bien avant que vous fussiez nés, dans cette plaine que vous voyez peinte sur le livre en ocre et en noir, avec les pompons blancs des explosions, les chevaux qui galopent, et ces engins bizarres! Le livre d'images ne vous mentira pas: nous sûmes faire face. (P. 28.)

One immediately thinks of the passage, so famous it need not be quoted, at the end of the introduction to *Les Grands Cimetières sous la lune*: "Compagnons inconnus, vieux frères [. . .] Troupe fourbue, troupe harassée [. . .] regards [. . .] ô regards qui ne se sont jamais rendus" (p. 12). How different the contexts: a book about Drumont and his times, a book about the civil war in Spain. And yet how many of the same thematic materials: age, common experience, unfavorable weather as a metaphor for the harshness of the experience, the look in the eyes, the metaphor expressing inexorable determination, the final appeal to the judgment of chilhood, and the supreme value attributed to the ability to endure, *faire face*. In both passages the writer also sees himself, literally in the first case and metaphorically in the second, as one of a band of soldiers.

There is objective evidence in both passages of the importance these particular materials had for Bernanos. He uses the same rhetorical strategies that turn up in his writing, fictional and nonfictional, whenever emotion heightens his style: prosopopoeia, the augmentative repetition of an identical noun followed by a different adjective or complement, parallel grammatical structures, chiasmus to double the stress on an important word.

The endurance theme these devices are associated with would appear to have been an important focus of Bernanos' emotions in 1932 and in 1936, and since in the later of the two passages he invokes Donissan, Cénabre, Chantal, Mouchette, and the curé d'Ambricourt, the possibility that endurance is a major theme from 1926 down to the end of his career as novelist invites investigation. For this we need an instrument.

When she was preparing her index, Dr. Keane had decided that the abstract "grounds" of the images were not her immediate concern, but one can still put her work into service (for which it was not intended) by the somewhat rough and ready method of scanning her index-headings for "vehicles" that may have the idea of endurance among their attributes. (This is, of course, an infallible way of missing an unexpected metaphor of the kind Richard Sayce calls "wide-angled," but this defect is palliated by the fact that unexpected metaphors are relatively rare in Bernanos.) One category, "athlete," seems promising, and indeed there turn out to be a half-dozen figures listed that involve reference to an old athlete, or wrestler, engaged or about to engage in violent struggle. All occur in *Sous le soleil de Satan* and are applied to Donissan — and the date, 1924, holds up.

But this particular image disappears in subsequent novels, and the theme of endurance does not occur in the stories of Cénabre and Chevance, and given the nature of the stories one understands why it should not: the good die young, Cénabre does not endure so much as persist, and Chevance is too fragile. From the evidence of the index, endurance is not part of the thematic structures of *L'Imposture* and *La Joie*.

Yet Cénabre is mentioned by name among the "troupe fourbue" of the *Grands Cimetières* of 1936, and so too, more surprisingly, is Chantal, the young heroine of *La Joie*. In a passage of *Monsieur Ouine*, perhaps written early in the history of that novel's tortured composition but certainly after 1932, old Devandomme feels that he has nothing left to hope except to "durer comme un arbre" (the figure appears twice), and the theme appears again in a passage that has been closely dated.

Il n'avait jamais été ici qu'un passant, et la vieille église le repoussait sans colère comme le rejetait ce village dont il pouvait apercevoir les toits, car église et village n'en faisaient qu'un. Aussi longtemps que l'antique citadelle dresserait ici sa tour, aussi longtemps que le clocher lancerait dans l'espace son cri d'appel, elle serait du parti de la paroisse, elle serait du parti des gens d'en face. Ils pourraient bien la profaner, l'abattre, elle leur appartiendrait jusqu'au bout, jusqu'à la dernière pierre elle ne les renierait pas. Oui, couchée dans l'herbe, elle offrirait aux traîtres, aux parjures, ses beaux flancs éventrés— leurs petits viendraient jouer dans les ruines. Faute de mieux la vieille Mère les protégerait de la pluie et du soleil. (P. 1514.)

This is what runs through the mind of the curé de Fenouille as he returns to his vicarage realizing that everything he touches goes wrong but that the church he serves remains eternal — a supernatural entity, indeed, but one endowed, *in extremis*, with a human virtue Bernanos clearly cherishes.

At this point in his manuscript Bernanos put aside *Monsieur*

Ouine to begin his *Journal d'un curé de campagne*. We can only speculate about his reasons, but I wonder whether it would not be profitable to re-read the *Journal* with the theme of endurance in mind. The country priest figures conspicuously in the "troupe fourbue" of the *Grands Cimetières*; and what, humanly speaking is this man if not another of those desperately determined to endure? It is thus not implausible to take the *Journal* to be — among other things but not necessarily last among them — a magnificent hymn to human endurance?

The other two monographs that are primarily concerned with image study could be used to illustrate the same point: imagery and theme study are so closely interrelated that the identification and analysis of an image leads naturally to the thematic function. In the instances of the two primarily concerned with thematic material — Dr. Tolton's and Dr. Gilbert's — only the direction is reversed: identification of themes and thematic patterns reveals the structural importance of the themes, and of the motifs that support them, in the individual works.

Dr. Tolton's research took him directly to Gide's vocabulary and the question of how the meaning of such words as "ferveur," "soif," or "attente," had varied in the course of Gide's long literary life. The dissertation proper presents a catalogue of terms, with definitions and commentary, necessarily of a semantic nature. His monograph, on the other hand, originated in a perception regarding the rather special kind of abstraction Gide tended to prefer — one that despite its abstractness conveys an image.

Here, of course, our perspective on the relationship between imagery and theme becomes complex. "Soif," "faim," "ferveur," and the like are familiar themes in Gide's work, but they are hardly literal in the sense that captivity, in *Thérèse Desqueyroux*, means literal deprivation of liberty. Gide's abstractions must be recognized as metaphors for feelings which add up to his personal and special response to life. These feelings are too deep, and perhaps too incoherent and undifferentiated, for direct articulation. The abstractions Gide calls upon habitually to name them are no more explicit names than suggestions — and they suggest as metaphor suggests. In this circumstance it is not surprising — once the phenomenon has been pointed out — that Gide should have preferred the kind of abstraction that conveys an image: this kind is the less specific and the richer in suggestion. Gide's debt to the Symbolism of the 1890's is apparent here, and just as apparent is

8

the permanence of this debt that after *Paludes* Gide was not eager to acknowledge.

But whereas the construction of an image index leads to the eventual identification of themes and their interrelationships, in the present situation we have the themes in hand and are ready to work toward the motifs that are attached to, and "carry," them. Significant help in such research could be found in Stephen Ullmann's excellent chapter on Gide's imagery, although of course much patient work in compiling the occurrences of the characteristic motifs would still be necessary.

Dr. Gilbert's is the only study of the five that did not originate in a lengthy labor of compilation. It is clear from even cursory inspection that in the years between the opening of the century and World War II there flourished in several countries a kind of novel, generally occupied with the affairs of a family, in which there appeared a symbol of some sort that represented continuity and permanence amid the flux of discontinuity and change. Outside of France, *Buddenbrooks* and the *Forsyte Saga* are conspicuous examples; in France the type proliferated, as is hardly strange with regard to a literature which was relentlessly dedicated to putting the middle-class family as institution on trial. To students both the sociological and formal aspects of the phenomenon offer appealing possibilities.

Dr. Gilbert's dissertation presented a meticulous tracing of the thematic patterns that persistently recurred in such novels, in relation to the central symbol around which they were organized. In interpreting them he could hardly have failed to invoke recent writings which have stressed the presence of old myths in modern literature. In one sense, then, the present monograph looks outward into the broad field where anthropological interests join with the purely literary.

But at the same time the student is obligated also to look inward toward the center of the work of art — toward the patterns and the themes that constitute them, and beyond these to the attached motifs, i.e. the organization of linguistic facts. In his dissertation Dr. Gilbert recognized the linguistic implications of his study, but the normal prudential considerations regarding the length of the Ph.D. dictated that he should not exploit them then and there.

In brief, all five monographs address themselves to the study of the material of which novels are made, its nature and its organization; they might thus properly be classed as examples of *Stoff-*

9

geschichte or *Stoffwissenschaft*. They aim at avoiding arbitrariness, through the accumulation of objectively verifiable fact. Whether, once the facts are in, the individual scholar interprets them in a manner tending toward modern structuralism, or reveals himself as being more or less committed to a formalist attitude, would seem to be a matter of less than paramount importance. Their approach does not exclude from consideration the issues regularly raised by the more traditional analysts of fiction from Percy Lubbock to Wayne C. Booth. Their assumption is, rather, that there is profit in multiplying critical perspectives, and that in the house of literary scholarship there are many mansions.

W. M. FROHOCK

DREAM IMAGERY IN THE NOVELS OF BERNANOS

BY SUSAN M. KEANE

Few writers have been less willing than Bernanos to discourse with readers on their own terms. He does not speak his interlocutor's language, but his own; and he refuses to install familiar landmarks in his imaginative world. The very landscapes are strange and frightening: perspectives are unstable, roads are interminable, and buildings are endowed with a kind of sinister life. Human relationships are equally disconcerting; characters are isolated from one another by mysterious barriers, or communicate in signs that they understand better than we do. Conversation, which in another novelist might provide some echo of the common world, offers none here; Robert Kemp has remarked that in the novels "tout le monde parle Bernanos." [1] If the reader is to find any common ground with Bernanos, it is not in the exterior world of concrete, objective realities, but in the responses that the writer's imagination awakens in his own. He is forced into adapting his own subjectivity to a new angle of vision.

It is in the light of this problem that we ought to approach the question of imagery in Bernanos. It is possible to define an image generally as an analogical statement transmitting a sense impression; but in practice the use of material elements in figurative language presents as many variations as there are writers. Many authors draw a clear boundary between literal and analogical language; Bernanos is not one of them. For some writers, the concept of imagery implies vivid evocation of something palpable and concrete; Gautier, for example, could explain his artistic principles by saying, "Je suis un homme pour qui le monde extérieur existe." Bernanos is almost a polar opposite of Gautier. For him, the exterior world seems to serve chiefly as a stimulus to the imagination. The reader is far more conscious of a subject than of objects. Thus, whereas it is fairly simple for an attentive reader to visualize Gautier's statue or still-life, it is frequently difficult to envision precisely what Bernanos is describing, because he is far less interested in

11

the object itself than in its effect upon the consciousness. A great many of his images are concerned with the experience of sensation rather than its causes:

> Cela vous vient comme une idée . . . comme un vertige . . . de se laisser tomber, glisser . . . d'aller jusqu'en bas — tout à fait — jusqu'au fond — où le mépris des imbéciles n'irait même pas vous chercher . . . (*SSS*, p. 97).[2]

> Je n'ai rien vu, rien entendu, je ne pensais même à rien. Cela m'a comme frappé dans le dos. (*J*, p. 715.)

Even when the vehicle of an image is easily seen to be water, or fire, or some other definable object, the reader is still conscious of strong feeling — and not merely perception — on the part of a subject:

> Ce qu'elle voyait se consumer au feu de la parole, c'était elle-même, ne dérobant rien à la flamme droite et aiguë, suivie jusqu'au dernier détour, à la dernière fibre de chair. (*SSS*, p. 200.)

> La Pensée que cette lutte va finir . . . n'est entrée en moi que peu à peu. C'était un mince filet d'eau limpide, et maintenant cela déborde de l'âme, me remplit de fraîcheur. (*JCC*, p. 1255.)

When the exterior world is perceived, it is with a sense of alienation; the subject's astigmatism distorts and estranges familiar things:

> Et soudain, pareil à ces paysages trop lumineux, trop vibrants, que submerge d'un coup le crépuscule, et qui réapparaissent lentement, méconnaissables, semblent remonter de l'abîme de la nuit, l'étroit univers familier dans lequel elle était née, où elle avait vécu, prenait un aspect nouveau. (*J*, pp. 562–563.)

> Le village m'apparaît bien différent de ce qu'il était en automne, on dirait que la limpidité de l'air lui enlève peu à peu toute pesanteur, et lorsque le soleil commence à décliner, on pourrait le croire suspendu dans le vide, il ne touche pas à la terre, il m'échappe, il s'envole. (*JCC*, p. 1208.)

> Mais il s'éloigna de son pas pesant, et aussitot Mouchette crut voir son image falote glisser avec une rapidité prodigieuse comme aspirée par le vide. (*NM*, p. 1344.)

In these images, the subject cannot really be said to be *observing* an analogy; in a sense, he is submitting to one. He is not consciously creating metaphors, any more than the dreamer creates the images that haunt his sleep. For the Bernanosian character, there is a close correspondence between mental image and metaphor; his imagination is less creative than receptive.

The images we have cited express the point of view of characters in the novels of Bernanos; but their essential passivity is similar to that which the writer observed in himself. "Cette image me hante" is a sentence found more than once in the polemical works.[3] A letter written to his fiancée during World War II shows that he sometimes felt himself to be a target for images, rather than a creator of them:

> C'est presque en vain que l'âme s'efforce de prendre conscience d'elle-même, au milieu de cette immobilité du néant; rien ne l'agite ici que les images décevantes et passionnées de son bonheur ancien, images mille fois pressées et flattées de tant de mains caressantes, pauvres images en exil et fanées comme les pages d'un livre trop de fois lu! (*BPLM*, p. 102.)

This tendency also affects his definition of his work as a writer. In a letter to the critic Claude-Edmonde Magny, he said: "Je suis un romancier, c'est-à-dire un homme qui vit ses rêves, ou les revit sans le savoir. Je n'ai donc pas d'intentions, au sens qu'on donne généralement à ce mot" (*OR*, p. 1857). The work of writing a novel was, for him, "un de ces longs voyages à travers les images et les rêves qui s'achèvent toujours prosaïquement chez l'éditeur" (*GSSL*, p. ii).

The writer's own testimony, then, would seem to indicate the existence of a strong involuntary element in the production of figurative language; for him, the relationship between mental image and metaphor seems to have been a fairly direct one. Gaëtan Picon lends support to this idea when he speaks of Bernanos' images as being "moins obtenues que reçues," and remarks that they do not make the reader aware of the artistic effort that may be involved in their creation.[4] He, too, considers that they are somewhat passive in nature. More direct evidence is provided by the fact that the images found in the novels of Bernanos are echoed in his polemical works and his letters: images of water and mud, animals and minerals, occur in *Les Grands Cimetières sous la lune* and *Les Enfants humiliés* as well as in *Sous le soleil de Satan* and *Monsieur Ouine*.[5] The sources of many of these images are traceable to Bernanos' childhood in Artois, and the writer attributes his involuntary use of certain themes to the tenacity of these early associations. In an eloquent passage in *Les Enfants humiliés*, he contrasts his own compulsions with the feelings of *déracinés* for their native country:

> Ils me font rigoler avec leur nostalgie de paysages français! Je n'ai pas revu ceux de ma jeunesse, je tiens à la Provence par un sentiment mille fois plus fort et plus jaloux. Il n'en est pas moins vrai qu'après trente ans d'absence — ou de ce que nous appelons par ce nom — les personnages de mes livres se retrouvent d'eux-mêmes aux lieux que j'ai cru quitter. Ici ou ailleurs, pourquoi aurais-je la nostalgie de ce que je possède malgré moi, que je ne puis trahir? Pourquoi évoque-rais-je avec mélancolie l'eau noire du chemin creux, la haie qui siffle sous l'averse, puisque je suis moi-même la haie et l'eau noire? (*EH*, pp. 37–38.)

The obsessive element which Bernanos recognizes in his own experience is extended in various ways into the lives of his characters. Like their creator, they tend to become overwhelmed by mental images at moments of strain. Donissan, the hero of *Sous le soleil de Satan*, experiences grave psychological distress just before his last battle; his pain and confusion are reflected in images (*SSS*, pp. 233–238). The apostate priest Cénabre, when he realizes that he has lost his faith and when he is about to regain it, passes through a somewhat similar state (*I*, p. 368; *J*, p. 715).

Frequently, the obsession of a character assumes the proportions of hallucination or vision. Donissan has a mysterious encounter with a horse-trader who may be the devil in disguise; the reader is never sure at what point reality leaves off and hallucination begins (*SSS*, pp. 167–184). Chevance, the reluctant witness of Cénabre's apostasy, wanders through the streets of Paris looking for him; it soon becomes apparent that the whole journey is the product of a dying man's delirium (*I*, pp. 505–524). Chantal de Clergerie, who has strangely fallen heir to Chevance's responsibility for Cénabre, has mystical visions involving both priests (*J*, pp. 678–679; 685–686). Monsieur Ouine, at the point of death, has a long conversation with Steeny, a young disciple; it later turns out that the boy was drunk at the time and probably imagined the whole encounter (*MO*, pp. 1540–1561). All of these episodes are characterized by long successions of images whose vehicles often change rapidly, as in dreams. If there is any logic in these passages, it is oneiric rather than rational: what Bernanos calls the "succession d'un cauchemar" (*I*, p. 426).

It is at first somewhat surprising that mystical images should be similar to those resulting from delirium or drunkenness. As a Catholic writer, and one of the less rationalistic members of his faith, Bernanos is a firm believer in the validity of mystical experience. At the same time, he recognizes that mysticism, like dreaming or delirium, is a state in which rational elements are no longer in control of the human consciousness. However inevitable or valuable such states may be, they are also somewhat dangerous. A man may be destroyed by his dreams; and the curé of Torcy, in the *Journal d'un curé de campagne*, points out that even mystics, absorbed in the presence of God, are not safe:

> Que veux-tu, mon petit, j'ai mes idées sur la harpe du jeune David. C'était un garçon de talent, sûr, mais toute sa musique ne l'a pas préservé du péché. Je sais bien que les pauvres écrivains bien-pensants qui fabriquent des Vies de saints pour l'exportation, s'imaginent qu'un bonhomme est à l'abri dans l'extase, qu'il s'y trouve au chaud et en sûreté comme dans le sein d'Abraham. En sûreté! (*JCC*, p. 1041.)

But these disturbing forms of experience never cease to exert a powerful fascination for Bernanos. It may be said that dreams provide the key to understanding this writer's figurative expression; but, if this statement is to be reliable, then the definition of *dream* must be a very broad one, embracing any condition in which the mind is prey to non-rational forces.

This close association between dream-image and metaphor has concrete results in the presence of certain metaphorical vehicles in the novels. The themes most frequently recurring [6] are: sensation; water in various forms; animals; light and darkness; sickness and death. Many metaphors are also concerned with children. Other vehicles, less notable for their frequency than for their occurrence at significant moments, are mirrors, roads, circles, obstacles, and stones. It has been remarked that these vehicles, which remain extraordinarily constant throughout the novels, have nothing particularly original about them. Indeed, the reader who is disconcerted by the strangeness of Bernanos' world may find that he at least recognizes the materials of which it is made.[7] These materials are the property of all human experience, and especially of that part of it which lies below the surface of consciousness. Even when the vehicles themselves are not particularly oneiric — some images are concerned with historical figures, for example — the perspective in which they are treated leaves little doubt as to the world to which they belong. In the following pages, we shall consider examples of some of these themes, and their role in the creation of a dream-like world.

In many cases the vehicles are definable only in terms of sensation rather than of objects. We have already noted Bernanos' general tendency to insist upon feelings rather than their sources. This tendency makes itself felt to varying degrees, however. It is difficult, for example, to refer to a sensation of sight and to ignore what is seen. To a lesser degree, a description of hearing also implies a description of what is heard, however vaguely. But in the case of touch (or pain, or vertigo), it is possible to be much more self-centered and oblivious to the outside world. It is not, perhaps, surprising that many images having to do with this kind of sensation are particularly appropriate for evoking states of dreaming or madness. It is worth noting as well that a similar perspective is characteristic of some mystical writing. Abbé Bremond, widely respected as an authority on the subject, says that "les plus hauts mystiques insistent plus longuement sur les ténèbres au sein desquels ils s'unissent à Dieu que sur une appréhension claire de celui qu'ils étreignent. Ils parlent beaucoup plus des touches divines que de celui qui les touche." He cites, as examples of images used by mystics, "un certain parfum," "une odeur de paradis," "un poids secret." He also speaks of the sense of being pushed by something, of being like a sponge in a vast ocean, of feeling the presence of a bird whose wings brush one's face.[8] The images mentioned here find precise echoes in those of Bernanos.[9] The implication here is not, of course, that Bernanos found his thematic repertory in a few pages of Bremond, but that these metaphors belong to a much more universal repertory of oneiric and mystical figures of speech. We can expect that images of sensation will be adaptable to a variety of contexts and carry many different implications.

The sensation of falling, which characterizes the dreaming or half-waking state, is typical of this category. It recurs frequently in the novels, and in a number of moral and spiritual situations. In *Nouvelle Histoire de Mouchette*, it is used to evoke a feeling of lassitude and hopelessness:

> Elle obéit à une loi aussi fixe, aussi implacable que celui qui régit la chute d'un corps, car un certain désespoir a son accélération propre. (*NM*, p. 1320–21.)

A similar image in *Sous le soleil de Satan* carries a more specific theological reference to despair:

16

Ce n'est plus ce cloître qu'il désire, mais quelque chose de plus secret que la solitude, l'évanouissement d'une chute éternelle, dans les ténèbres refermées. (*SSS*, p. 327.)

What is implied here is a fall into the spiritual abyss, away from God. The saints of Bernanos, whose strength is often combined with a kind of apparent weakness, also discover the abyss of light, the fall *into* God. The heroine of *La Joie* experiences this paradoxical sensation:

Elle croyait glisser lentement, puis glisser tout à fait dans le sommeil . . . Seulement elle tombait en Dieu. (*J*, p. 568.)

Dix fois, vingt fois peut-être, elle avait failli céder au vertige, rouler jusqu'au bord du gouffre de lumière, et n'avait sagement achevé son oraison qu'au prix d'un effort intolérable. Mais n'était-elle pas tombée à son insu? (*J*, p. 577.)

This image of falling into God was one which Bernanos may well have found in the works of Bremond.[10] It seems to have haunted him to the end of his career. It appears first in *La Joie*, and is given a favored place in *Dialogues des Carmélites*.[11] It is used ironically in *Un Mauvais Rêve* (p. 971) and *Monsieur Ouine*:

Je n'ai nullement songé à nier l'existence de mon âme, et aujourd'hui même je ne saurais la mettre en doute, mais j'ai perdu tout sentiment de la mienne, alors qu'il y a une heure seulement, je l'éprouvais ainsi qu'un vide, une attente, une aspiration intérieure. Sans doute a-t-elle achevé de m'engloutir? Je suis tombé en elle, jeune homme, de la manière dont les élus tombent en Dieu. (*MO*, p. 1560.)

The spiritual life is also described more conventionally in terms of an ascent toward God, but even in these cases there is an attempt to imbue the traditional metaphor with strong feeling:

Ainsi l'homme surnaturel est à l'aise si haut que l'amour le porte et sa vie spirituelle ne comporte aucun vertige. (*SSS*, p. 198.)

Oh! naturellement, rien n'est si facile que de grimper là-haut: Dieu vous y porte. Il s'agit seulement d'y tenir, et, le cas échéant, de savoir descendre. (*JCC*, p. 1041.)

It is notable that ascent, as well as descent, is usually a passive process in Bernanos' metaphors. The man who succeeds in scaling figurative heights through his own efforts is rare indeed; even the mountain-climber is not fully aware of what he is doing:

17

J'étais comme un homme qui, ayant grimpé d'un trait une pente vertigineuse, ouvre les yeux, s'arrête ébloui, hors d'état de monter ou de descendre. (*JCC*, p. 1161.)

Images of involuntary flight, or of extraordinary ease of movement, can also indicate that rational forces are not in control. Donissan, the unconscious prey of diabolical forces, is "alerte, dispos, léger, ainsi qu'après un bon sommeil dans la fraîcheur du matin" (*SSS*, p. 164). In *Monsieur Ouine*, the insane mayor of Fenouille muses in this fashion before a public speech:

Il parlera quand il voudra, il parlera presque à son insu, avec une facilité, une légèreté aérienne. Il parlera comme on vole. (*MO*, p. 1496.)

These images, which imply a kind of rejoicing in an illusion of power, are among the most sinister in Bernanos. Such a degree of ill-founded confidence means that the victim is, for the moment at least, totally deceived by his dreams. When reason succeeds in breaking through, a character is able to be somewhat skeptical about unexpected feelings of lightness and ease. Chantal de Clergerie, perhaps more than any other creature of Bernanos, is characterized by images of flying things: she is compared to a bird, an angel, a flower blown by the air (*J*, pp. 666; 543–544.) At the same time, she is seriously troubled by her own spiritual flights. Simone Alfieri, under a very different kind of compulsion, is astonished and disconcerted by the facility with which she manages to invent alibis for a projected crime (*MR*, p. 992).

Sensations of lightness do not always connote ease; they can be medical symptoms, as we see in the words of the dying Mme Dargent:

Mes pauvres os sont creux, légers comme des plumes — au-dedans et au-dehors il n'y a que du vide — oui! tout est vide et flottant, hors de cette affreuse tête de plomb. (*MD*, p. 6.)

Chevance, in the delirium which precedes his death, has the same symptom, as does the mother of the second Mouchette, (*I*, pp. 507–508; *NM*, p. 1314). Olivier Mainville, in *Un Mauvais Rêve*, experiences a lightness like that of a drugged man (*MR*, p. 977). The weightlessness of the dying Ouine has moral rather than medical connotations; recognizing that nothing is left of what was once his character, he says, "je n'ai plus de poids" (*MO*, p. 1560). Even here, however, he is still speaking with the voice of a patient describing symptoms. This perspective is perhaps significant for the interpretation of other metaphorical vehicles in Bernanos. A sick man, describing his condition, often creates images to do so; but he has very little interest in the beauty or inherent qualities of the vehicles he uses. He is concerned only with the accuracy with which they can describe the effect of a sensation upon his consciousness. Bernanos' characters are often sick men themselves; but even when they are not, this highly subjective angle of vision frequently prevails in their metaphors. Their choice of vehicles results more from inner compulsion than from objective appreciation. Aesthetic considerations are secondary.

Images of sound are a case in point. Although Bernanos occasionally evokes the chords of a symphony or the melodies produced at random by a pianist, he is more interested in the voices and music that exist within the mind, often despite efforts to the contrary. Terror, for example, is comparable to a loud cry:

> Je m'éveillais brusquement avec, dans l'oreille, un grand cri—mais est-ce encore ce mot-là qui convient? Evidemment non. (*JCC*, p. 1099.)

> C'est que je me suis crue morte, moi aussi, figurez-vous. C'est comme un cri, un très grand cri, mais que je n'entendais pas par les oreilles, vous comprenez? (*MO*, p. 1415.)

A more continuous kind of sensation is typified by a constant murmur or chant. The little invalid in *Monsieur Ouine* compares his chronic suffering to the murmur of voices:

> Souffrir, voyez-vous, cela s'apprend. C'est d'abord comme un petit murmure au fond de soi, jour et nuit. Jour et nuit, qu'on dorme ou qu'on veille, n'importe! Il arrive parfois que vous croyez ne plus l'entendre, mais il suffit de prêter l'oreille: la chose est toujours là qui parle, dans sa langue, une langue inconnue. (*MO*, p. 1384.)

In *Nouvelle Histoire de Mouchette*, there is a clear equivalence between music and obsession. The novel's heroine is unable to feel any order in the world surrounding her, and perceives events only through a confused rumble of sounds:

> La fuite de l'école, l'attente au bord du chemin, sa course errante à travers les taillis dans la grande colère du vent et le flagellement de la pluie, la rencontre de M. Arsène — cela n'arrive pas à faire une véritable histoire, cela n'a ni commencement ni fin, cela ressemblerait plutôt à une rumeur confuse qui remplit maintenant sa pauvre tête, une sorte de chant funèbre. (*NM*, p. 1301.)

19

It is when Mouchette is finally overcome by this obsessive murmur that she drowns herself. She is unable to maintain any kind of distance between herself and what she hears, or to organize it in any way; she is the passive victim of her sensations.

In Mouchette, as well as in other characters, Bernanos magnifies tendencies which he has perceived in himself. Obviously, he is able to organize his private world; otherwise, he would never have been an artist. But his choice of images does not seem to be particularly free. Like his characters, he has less interest in the vehicles as such than in their capacity to describe a given state of consciousness; and, indeed, certain vehicles seem themselves to form part of that state of consciousness.

One such compulsive theme is water. The water image is one that attracted Bernanos long before he thought of becoming a writer; we see it in letters he wrote as a schoolboy:

> Un rien m'agite et me fait rêver, mais ce mouvement-là dure trois jours, quatre jours, un mois, et l'eau s'apaise et redevient dormante, ainsi qu'avant, tant que je ne souffre point . . . (Lettres à l'abbé Lagrange, *OR*, p. 1734.)

> Prêchez-moi, grondez-moi, je tends l'oreille, je suis devant vous comme une terre sans eau — c'est David qui l'a dit le premier . . . (*Ibid.*, pp. 1735–1736.)

The young Bernanos is aware of the Biblical allusions called forth by his use of the water symbol; but it is perhaps significant that he never stops to analyze the symbol itself. The novelist Bernanos does not do so either. Unlike Claudel, for example, he has little or nothing to say about the multiple levels of meaning contained within the water symbol. Rather, he reaches out almost instinctively for whatever vehicle best expresses his angle of vision. And for him, as for other writers, water lends itself to the expression of many aspects of the dream world. Water metaphors can help to create the atmosphere of instability which is often typical of the oneiric perspective. They also lend themselves to descriptions of the soul and the subconscious. (Even the language of cliché tells us of the *depths* of the soul and the still waters that run deep.) The schoolboy letters of Bernanos reflect this equation between soul and water, and it appears in the novels as well.

The water metaphor is particularly adapted to the idea of impenetrable depth, and also to that of impurity — properties which, for Bernanos, are also attributable to the human soul. Cénabre, at the moment of yielding to temptation, is conscious of the "eaux dormantes et pourries de l'âme" (*I*, p. 355). The curé of Ambricourt discerns "une eau trouble, une boue," in the gaze of a parishioner (*JCC*, p. 1125). The father of Chantal de Clergerie takes this view of the soul:

> Chacun de nous a son secret, ses secrets, une multitude de secrets, qui achèvent de pourrir dans la conscience, s'y consument lentement, lentement . . . Toi-même, ma fille, oui, toi-même; si tu vis de longues années, tu sentiras peut-être, à l'heure de la mort, ce poids, ce clapotis de la vase sous l'eau profonde. (*J*, p. 592.)

It is evidently in contrast to images such as these that Bernanos means us to understand the description of the Virgin Mary by the curé of Torcy:

> Car enfin, elle était née sans péché, quelle solitude étonnante! Une source si pure, si limpide, si limpide et si pure, qu'elle ne pouvait même pas y voir refléter sa propre image, faite pour la seule joie du Père — ô solitude sacrée! (*JCC*, p. 1193.)

For Bernanos, sinfulness is less an aggregate of bad deeds than an innate state of being, something lurking in the depths of the soul. The Virgin was the only creature whose unconscious motives were pure; clear water, or a state of untroubled grace, is something generally denied to men.

In examples such as that we have just cited, it is quite possible to find doctrinal meanings in Bernanos' water images. But there are dangers in extending this procedure too far. The metaphors of Bernanos are not illustrations of intellectual perceptions, but analogies seized at a much more instinctive and ambiguous level. Water may be a symbol of grace; but water and mud may also signify, much more vaguely, "that-which-is-to-be-feared," or that which engulfs rationality and consciousness. They can frequently be equated with the broad concept of dreams which forms one of the bases for this essay.

The character who has yielded totally to his dreams is reduced to floating aimlessly about. The hallucinations of Mme Dargent involve drifting in lakes and oceans (*MD*, p. 7), and M. Ouine says of himself: "Comme ces gelées vivantes, au fond de la mer, je flotte et j'absorbe" (*MO*, p. 1368). Both of these characters have withdrawn into a solipsistic state and are incapable of reacting to any reality outside themselves. There are other cases in which the personality is not yet absorbed by irrational elements, but the possibility or danger is clearly present. A character in *Monsieur Ouine* compares herself, in a moment of terror, to a sinking ship: "je coulais à pic, comme un navire sabordé" (*MO*, p. 1416). Cénabre, on the verge of madness, evokes the same image:

> Tout tremblant encore de l'effroyable assaut, le regard exténué, la bouche amère, il reprenait possession, une à une, des idées et des images que la soudaine explosion de terreur avait éparpillées ainsi que des feuilles mortes: il essayait de raisonner avec ces pauvres débris sauvés du désastre, ainsi qu'un navire englouti à demi utilise ses derniers foyers. (*J*, p. 715.)

In a more spiritual context, Chantal de Clergerie sinks into mystical states, despite her own efforts to the contrary:

> Littéralement, elle crut entendre se refermer sur elle une eau profonde, et aussitôt, en effet, son corps défaillit sous un poids immense, accru sans cesse et dont l'irrésistible poussée chassait la vie hors de ses veines. (*J*, p. 681.)

The second Mouchette, whose drowning is physical rather than figurative, may also be said to have yielded to her obsessions; it is notable that several times during the hours before her death she unconsciously mimes the gestures of a drowning person:

> Mais aujourd'hui, d'un mouvement irréfléchi comme d'un noyé qui s'enfonce, elle a pris à pleins bras le paquet de chiffons fumant d'urine et de lait aigre . . . (*NM*, p. 1299; see also pp. 1329–1330.)

The same gestures are made by the first Mouchette, when the abbé Donissan forces her to recognize that her pride and sense of independence have been based upon illusions, that, instead of being a free spirit, she is a victim. This recognition produces a state of shock:

> Alors elle se dressa, battant l'air de ses mains, la tête jetée en arrière, puis d'une épaule à l'autre, absolument comme un noyé qui s'enfonce. (*SSS*, p. 207.)

This gesture, too, is a prelude to suicide.

The helplessness implicit in these images of drowning is also expressed by images of mud, with the difference that, whereas water may signify certain desirable qualities, it is almost impossible for mud to represent anything essentially good. It is used, quite naturally, as a symbol of humiliation or disgust. To become engulfed in it is to have given up on life. Those who are tired of life welcome it, as they would welcome even shame:

> Car le seul repos véritable qu'ait jamais connu, parmi des êtres qu'il déteste ou qu'il méprise, son cœur sauvage, c'est le dégoût. Incapable de justifier par des raisons la révolte de sa nature, son refus à peine conscient, elle se venge ainsi à sa manière de son incompréhensible solitude, comme à la limite de la fatigue, il arrive qu'elle se couche exprès à la place la plus boueuse de la route. (*NM*, p. 1338; see also *SSS*, p. 109; *JCC*, p. 1203.)

For the curé of Fenouille, the dead souls of his parishioners appear, almost palpably, as lakes of mud (*MO*, p. 1488). A similar metaphor occurs to the curé of Ambricourt, when he envisions the souls of the damned as "ce lac de boue toujours gluant sur quoi passe et repasse vainement l'immense marée de l'amour divin" (*JCC*, p. 1139). We have already noted images of the polluted waters of the soul, and of the "vase sous l'eau profonde"; the souls envisioned by the two curés are those who have yielded to such elements.[12]

Thus far, we have been considering water in its most drastic aspect, as the element that engulfs, and usually destroys. Sometimes, though, water represents an element in which a character can exist, and perhaps maintain a certain autonomy. His world is strange and distorted, and he himself is isolated. His perceptions are those of the dream world, transformed by water and mist, but they are still perceptions. The second Mouchette has the impression, at one point, of living in a kind of aquarium, disconcerting but not altogether unpleasant:

> . . . l'air lourd, visqueux, imprégné de cette buée grasse qui sort des tourbières, transmet la vibration aussi fidèlement qu'une eau profonde. (*NM*, p. 1278.)

The curé of Ambricourt, bewildered by an interview that is not going as he expected, focuses on the landscape and finds that it has assumed a watery unreality:

> Par la fenêtre ouverte, à travers les rideaux de linon, on voyait l'immense pelouse fermée par la muraille des pins, sous un ciel nocturne. C'était comme un étang d'eau croupissante. (*JCC*, p. 1146.)

Sometimes, as in cases of madness, the perspective is more thoroughly deformed. The insane grandmother in *La Joie* sees the world in this way:

> Puis le même brouillard qu'elle connaissait commença de recouvrir lentement les êtres et les choses, de moins en moins saisissables, pareils à leur propre reflet dans l'eau. (*J*, 656.)

The perception of this unstable kind of landscape is likely to result in an acute sense of alienation. The victims of this astigmatism are the prisoners of their own subjectivity; human presences, in this sort of environment, are extremely difficult to grasp. In *L'Imposture*, for example, a bewildered and desperate character sees his interlocutor in this way:

> A présent la tête énorme semblait flotter de l'une à l'autre épaule, telle une épave sur une eau morte. (*I*, p. 437.)

It is notable that Bernanos, who almost never describes faces clearly, evokes a number of images of faces seen through glass or water:

> Celle qu'il avait tant de fois caressée dans ses livres, et dont il croyait avoir épuisé la douceur, la mort — d'ailleurs partout visible sous sa froide ironie comme un visage sous une eau claire et profonde — cent fois rêvée, savourée, il ne la reconnut pas. (*SSS*, p. 282.)

> La grace divine (depuis des mois, il n'en sentait même pas l'absence) se montrait encore une fois: c'était comme la face d'un cadavre au fond des eaux, c'était comme un cri plaintif dans la brume. (*I*, p. 348.)

The image of the face seen through water expresses loneliness and incommunication: distances between persons cannot be breached, no matter how near the other may appear to be. When the face perceived is one's own, the combination of recognition and strangeness is apt to produce fear, or at least anxiety. Madame Dargent is terrified when she finds her own reflection in a hallucinatory pool (*MD*, p. 7). The heroine of *Un Mauvais Rêve*, about to commit a crime, is startled when she comes by accident upon her image in a mirror:

> La glace usée ne laissait paraître qu'une sorte de nappe diffuse, rayée d'ombre, où elle croyait voir monter et descendre sa face livide, ainsi que du fond d'une eau trouble. (*MR*, p. 1017.)

A fear mixed with fascination is felt by the curé of Ambricourt, when he cautiously approaches the task of writing a spiritual journal; and he, too, is haunted by a face that he half recognizes:

> Mon regard semblait glisser à la surface d'une autre conscience jusqu'alors inconnue de moi, d'un miroir troublé où j'ai craint tout

à coup de voir surgir un visage — quel visage; le mien peut-être?
. . . un visage retrouvé, oublié.
Il faudrait parler de soi avec une rigueur inflexible (*JCC*, p. 1036.)

The curé, a compulsive but somewhat reluctant author, is the only
one of Bernanos' writer-characters to be presented in a favorable
light. His imaginative processes are evidently similar to his creator's: Bernanos has the same troubled fascination with his own
image, and the same experience of a kind of involuntary creation
of characters. If we are to believe the testimony of the polemical
works, the use of water or mirrors to reflect faces is not a carefully
conceived technique, in order to make solid realities more vague.
On the contrary; it expresses the way in which Bernanos sees, or
rather feels, the presence of his characters. They were never solid
realities in the first place; they were the companions of his dreams.
A striking indication of his attitude toward them is provided by the
famous passage in *Les Grands Cimetières sous la lune* where he
addresses them directly: "Compagnons inconnus, vieux frères
. . ." In the following lines, he evokes the way in which his half-
formed creations haunted his imagination, even when he was a child:

> L'aube venait bien avant que fussent rentrés dans le silence de l'âme,
> dans ses profondes repaires, les personnages fabuleux encore à peine
> formés, embryons sans membres, Mouchette et Donissan, Cénabre,
> Chantal, et vous, vous seul de mes créatures dont j'ai parfois cru dis-
> cerner le visage mais à qui je n'ai pas osé donner de nom — cher
> curé d'un Ambricourt imaginaire. Etiez-vous alors mes maîtres?
> Aujourd'hui même, l'êtes-vous? (*GCSL*, p. iv.)

When Bernanos speaks about discerning the face of the curé of
Ambricourt, his angle of vision recalls the image of the face seen
through water. The sense of a vague, haunting presence is here,
and so is the unstable perspective. This time, though, the water-
mirror motif is absent, and the oneiric element is mentioned quite
specifically. This is true in other instances in Bernanos' works.
Olivier Mainville, in *Un Mauvais Rêve*, sees other people only
through the distorted lens of his own dreams:

> "Tu dégueules?" lui cria en passant un marmot à face blême, minu-
> scule, pareil à un jouet de cauchemar. (*MR*, p. 974.)

In *Monsieur Ouine*, the old peasant Devandomme is alienated from
his acquaintances by his private obsessions and tragedies; he, too,
envisions others in a nightmarish way:

Millediû! les vitres de l'estaminet sont toutes noires de dos d'homme et quand il passe ils se tournent tous à la fois, blêmes à travers la fumée des pipes, blêmes comme ces visages qu'on voit en rêve. (*MO*, p. 1482.)

These examples would seem to reinforce our assumption that vehicles, in and of themselves, are of secondary importance for Bernanos. Water is an important elsement in what Bachelard would call the "material imagination" of Bernanos, but it is far from being the only important theme that suits his purpose. Other vehicles are of considerable help in creating the oneiric atmosphere that is characteristic of this writer's world. Light is one such vehicle; and, indeed, light and water are sometimes confused in a single impression. The Bernanosian saint often sinks into a "gouffre de lumière" that contains properties of both elements. A minor character in *Sous le soleil de Satan* envisions the spiritual life in this way:

Je crois que le chrétien de bonne volonté se maintient de lui-même dans la lumière d'en haut, comme un homme dont le volume et le poids sont dans une proportion si constante et si adroitement calculée qu'il surnage dans l'eau s'il veut bien seulement y demeurer en repros. (*SSS*, p. 124.)

Light, like water, is often a force that requires passive submission; instead of being an aid to the senses, it can bombard them. Mme Dargent feels that her thoughts are being made clearer by a "lumière crue, aveuglante, implacable" (*MD*, p. 6). The brilliance of the summer sun, in *La Joie*, is notable above all for its cruelty:

Et c'était bien, en effet, à la morsure, à des milliards et des milliards de petites morsures assidues, à un énorme grignotement que faisait penser la pluie raide tombée d'un ciel morne, l'averse des dards chauffés à blanc, l'innombrable succion de l'astre. (*J*, p. 649.)

Even in cases where light is an aid, rather than a hindrance, to seeing, there is little discernment of color and line. Bernanos recognizes his own tendency to visualize things in terms of light and shade; in one letter, he speaks of the creatures of his imagination who "passent sur l'écran" in what seems to be a cinematographic fashion (*OR*, p. 1847). Scenes such as that which opens *Sous le soleil de Satan* tend to reduce a landscape to the play of light and shade:

Voici l'heure du soir qu'aima P.-J. Toulet. Voici l'horizon qui se défait — un grand nuage d'ivoire au couchant et, du zénith au sol, le

26

ciel crépusculaire, la solitude immense, déjà glacée — plein d'un silence liquide . . . Voici l'heure du poète qui distillait la vie dans son cœur, pour en extraire l'essence secrète, embaumée, empoisonnée.

Déjà la troupe humaine remue dans l'ombre, aux mille bras, aux mille bouches; déjà le boulevard déferle et resplendit . . . Et lui, accoudé à la table de marbre, regardait monter la nuit, comme un lis. (*SSS*, p. 59.)

Here, the medium of light serves a function similar to that of water, by endowing what is seen with the vagueness and instability of the dream world.

Like the water symbol, the theme of light is apt to call forth theological interpretations. Echoing a long religious tradition, Bernanos tends to associate fire and light with the presence of God, and darkness and cold with the presence of evil. The theological implications of these themes are particularly important in *Sous le soleil de Satan*, where the light-symbol is sometimes used ironically, and in *L'Imposture* and *La Joie*, originally planned as one novel under the title *Les Ténèbres*. But, although Bernanos is following a tradition of religious symbolism here, he is also capable of communicating a strong individual bias. The conventional pattern co-exists with personal, affective connotations, as in this example from Monsieur Ouine:

Qui n'a pas vu la route à l'aube, entre ses deux rangées d'arbres, toute fraîche, toute vivante, ne sait pas ce que c'est que l'espérance. (*MO*, p. 1409.)

The same association between morning and hope is present in a letter to a friend:

La chasse nous a menés très loin, bien plus loin que nous ne pensions aller, le soir tombe, et il s'agit de faire face aux ténèbres, et aux bêtes de l'ombre. Il faut que nous formions le camp, il faut que nous tenions jusqu'au matin. O mort si douce, ô seul matin! (*BPLM*, p. 120.)

The choice of symbols here would seem to be due to personal inclination or instinct rather than adherence to tradition.

Conventional symbolism is also a fairly minor factor in Bernanos' animal metaphors. Albert Béguin was much impressed by what he called the "bestiary" of Bernanos,[13] and, indeed, this category is the most numerous of any found in the novels. It is somewhat misleading, however, to use the term "bestiary," with its implication of neat rational equivalences. Memory, rather than reason, accounts for their choice. A great number of the images have to do with the domestic animals, minor pests, and small game to be found in many country regions of France, and certainly in that part of Artois where Bernanos spent much of his childhood. The animals belong to the landscape that he never saw in later life, but which had nonetheless become part of him. Like the metaphors of water and light, animal images in Bernanos can be located first and foremost in the country of the mind.

Sometimes landscape and animals are united in the same metaphor, so that the countryside becomes something endowed with sentient life. In *Sous le soleil de Satan,* trees blown by the wind grumble like bears (*SSS,* p. 83). In *Un Mauvais Rêve,* the city of Paris is seen by Olivier Mainville as "une bête familière," noisy and seemingly harmless, but unexpectedly voracious (*MR,* p. 897). In a slightly less sinister evocation, Steeny, M. Ouine's young disciple, sees the road stretching before him as "une bête dorée" (*MO,* p. 1414). The curé of Ambricourt, looking over the village which constitutes his parish, feels that his gaze is being returned:

> On dirait qu'elle me tourne le dos et m'observe de biais, les yeux mi-clos, à la manière des chats. (*JCC,* p. 1061.)

Here, animal life is used in the same way as some of the water and light images: to express a perspective in which objects are not stable or predictable. The practice of "animalization" of the inanimate may perhaps be seen as a variation upon the traditional rhetorical device of personification. It tends, however, to be more disturbing than personification, perhaps because the procedure has become less frozen by tradition, perhaps because the irrational is intrinsically more frightening than that which can think. This fear may well have some connection with the fact that animals frequently serve as a concrete symbol of what is sub-human in every person. Sometimes a kind of animal presence is detected in the soul: witness the letter in which Bernanos speaks of doing battle with the "bêtes de l'ombre." Cénabre is vaguely aware of "toutes ces choses aveugles et rampantes au fond de sa conscience" (*I,* p. 446). Simone Alfieri, on the point of taking a drug, is afraid of "ce premier accès d'euphorie qui réveille au fond de l'être on ne sait quelle petite bête sournoise, capricieuse, experte à toutes les trahisons" (*MR,* p. 988).

More often, though, this sub-human aspect is made apparent through the use of animals in characterization. The historian

Clergerie has a "tête de rat" (*J*, p. 535), and it is obvious that the metaphor has moral as well as physical connotations. The same image is applied to the choirboy in *Un Crime* (*C*, p. 815) and to the unfrocked priest in the *Journal d'un curé de campagne* (*JCC*, p. 1243). A sweet but fundamentally destructive disposition is compared to the nibbling of a small rodent (*MO*, pp. 1352–1353). M. Ouine, who is physically and morally the least attractive of Bernanos' characters, evokes comparison with creatures that are barely alive:

> Mon âme n'est qu'un outre plein de vent. Et voilà maintenant, jeune homme, qu'elle m'aspire à mon tour, je me sens fondre et disparaître dans cette gueule vorace. (*MO*, p. 1552.)

These images are chiefly notable because they arouse a fairly strong degree of revulsion; other images used in characterization, however, emphasize the wretchedness of the person concerned. Those who are oppressed by others are compared to hunted animals, or beasts led to the slaughter; those who are caught in impossible situations, are compared to trapped animals. There is still an element of the grotesque in some of these images, as in this description of Jambe-de-laine:

> Elle . . . se jeta en avant, comme pour rattraper son équilibre. Philippe pensa à un gigantesque oiseau blessé qui marche sur les ailes. (*MO*, p. 1357.)

But there is only pathos in the comparison of the murdered Chantal de Clergerie to "un oiseau mort," (*J*, p. 722) or in this complaint of the curé of Ambricourt:

> Mon Dieu, j'ai présumé de mes forces. Vous m'avez jeté au désespoir comme on jette à l'eau une petite bête à peine née, aveugle. (*JCC*, p. 1144.)

Occasionally, animal imagery is used to evoke more positive qualities. Chantal, who seems to attract "flying" images, is compared to a lark (*J*, p. 659) and to a gray pheasant (*J*, p. 666). The curé of Ambricourt is praised for his faithful, dog-like eyes (*JCC*, p. 1092). But aside from such exceptions — and they are relatively few in comparison with the total number of animal images — the "bestiary" serves above all to point out what is less than human in the characters of the novels. These images are not notable for the ideas they express, but for their emotional impact: the reader is above all conscious of the feelings of pity, fear, or revulsion that many animals arouse. The juxtaposition of human and animal elements reminds us of the metamorphoses that occur in dreams and in folklore: transformations that are horrifying, because they involve a change from a higher to a lower level of life.

If animal images can be used to emphasize what is sub-human in a character, plant images may represent a soul that has hardened into a kind of immobility. Old Devandomme, in *Monsieur Ouine*, is likened to a tree (*MO*, p. 1462). Chantal de Clergerie has a vision of Cénabre in which the apostate priest is seen as the dead Judas,

> fruit noir d'un arbre noir, à l'entrée du honteux royaume de l'ombre, sentinelle exacte, incorruptible, que la miséricorde assiège en vain, qui ne laissera passer aucun pardon, pour que l'enfer consomme en sureté sa paix horrible. (*J*, p. 685.)

In these examples, the plant represents something which, if it does not lack life, at least lacks feeling; as the second example shows us, Bernanos considers that this is a state bordering upon damnation.

The extreme degree of metamorphosis is that which transforms feeling into stone: Medusa is more terrifying than Circe. It is true that Bernanos seems to have felt somewhat ambivalent about images of stone and firmness. He sympathizes with old Devandomme's efforts to "demeurer ferme à travers ce qui bouge" (*MO*, p. 1461); and in his attitude, we can discern some vestige of that of the young schoolboy who had an overwhelming dread of softness.[14] Nevertheless, it remains true that images of hardness and stone are usually endowed with fairly sinister overtones. Donissan, reflecting on a moment of hardness, says, "Je me damnais . . . je me sentais durcir comme une pierre" (*SSS*, p. 236). Bernanos said of his second novel, "*L'Imposture* est un visage de pierre, mais qui pleure de vraies larmes" (*BPLM*, p. 173). The same might be said of the novel's protagonist. Cénabre, as he becomes more closed in upon himself, also becomes rigid and immobile: his tears are like water piercing through stone (*I*, p. 376), and his features seem carved out of stone (*J*, p. 692). Steeny is frightened when he feels his own features take on a kind of immobility (*MO*, p. 1451–1452).[15] Even Ouine himself, who usually attracts images of softness, prides himself on the diamond-like constancy of his faith in himself (*MO*, p. 1470). For the curé of Ambricourt, the souls in hell are "ces pierres embrasées qui furent des hommes" (*JCC*, p. 1157). To be fixed and immobile, once and for all, is to have no escape from one-self. This total withdrawal from life is not without some analogy with that which we described with respect to water images despite the fact that water and stone are dissimilar vehicles. The rock-like Ouine is also the creature who has become immersed in his own dreams.

Immobility can also be characteristic of things exterior to a sub-ject: obstacles that loom up in one's path, causing fear, or frustra-tion, or both. The immobile, frightening shadow of a priest is seen twice in the novels, and under very different circumstances: Simone Alfieri, stumbling away from the scene of her crime, encounters the young curé she met earlier in the day; Chantal de Clergerie, emerg-ing from a vision involving the abbé Cénabre, sees him standing motionless before her (*MR*, p. 1005; *J*, p. 687). The immovable obstacle can also be something really inanimate, like a wall. The young poacher in *Monsieur Ouine*, forced into a sitation whose only issue is suicide, feels that his way is blocked by "un sentiment simple et terrible dont il ignore le nom, un mur nu, lisse comme verre" (*MO*, p. 1478). The second Mouchette is frustrated by forces she does not understand; her wretchedness is "aussi infranchissable que les murs d'une prison" (*NM*, p. 1302). In the *Journal d'un curé de campagne*, hell is "la porte à jamais close," the one situation from which there is no exit (*JCC*, p. 1047, also p. 1255). In some cases, the constraint upon liberty surrounds the individual even more closely, and becomes a part of him. Mme Dargent, looking back upon the silent humiliation of her life, says, "J'étais scellée vive, dans un béton inexorable" (*MD*, p. 80). The oneiric quality of these obstacles is made explicit in this image from *L'Imposture*:

> Dans quel rêve, dans quel cauchemar frénétique s'agite-t-on ainsi pour voir se rétrécir autour de soi l'espace libre, se fermer toutes les issues? (*I*, p. 345.)

If the wall evokes the isolation of the individual, and his im-prisonment in his own dreams, a breach in the wall must represent a degree of awakening or of liberty. The consequences of this breach are not always pleasant: however harmful the wall of isolation may be, it can represent a kind of security to the individual. When a break in his defenses is made, catastrophe may follow. Thus, despair enters the mind of the second Mouchette through a kind of breach (*NM*, p. 1343). In *L'Imposture*, the wall symbolizes the self-decep-tion with which the abbé Cénabre has been surrounding himself

31

for some time; when he is finally forced to see the meaning, or lack of meaning, of his spiritual life, the wall is broken:

> Par la brèche mystérieuse, le passé tout entier avait glissé comme une eau, et il ne demeurait, sous le regard inaltérable de la conscience, que des gestes plus vains que des songes . . . (*I*, p. 334.)

For Bernanos, however, even such disastrous consequences seem preferable to a totally isolated mode of existence. In most cases, walls exist to be broken. For Chantal de Clergerie, a breach is an opening upon the world of the divine (*J*, p. 681). Cénabre is finally redeemed by the destruction of the wall surrounding his personality (*J*, p. 719). In the *Journal d'un curé de campagne*, this description is given of the moment in which the wall of solitude surrounding a human being for many years is at last broken:

> Il me semblait qu'une main mystérieuse venait d'ouvrir une brèche dans on ne sait quelle muraille invisible, et la paix rentrait de toutes parts . . . (*JCC*, p. 1162.)

Toward the end of the novel, the curé of Ambricourt says to a rebellious young parishioner:

> Jetez-vous donc en avant tant que vous voudrez, il faudra que la muraille cède un jour, et toutes les brèches ouvrent sur le ciel. (*JCC*, p. 1226.)

The element of frustration which is basic to wall images is also apparent in images of circles. The words *cercle enchanté*, which are relatively frequent in Bernanos, are used to indicate a situation in which the spirit is trapped in some way. In *L'Imposture*, a man commits a social error, and cuts himself off from the society in which he lives; he is said to have broken "le cercle enchanté des convenances" (*I*, p. 403). Such disparate characters as Cénabre, Chantal, and Simone Alfieri make attempts to break through the enchanted circle (*I*, p. 464; *J*, 572; *MR*, p. 999). In some cases, a narrowing circle denotes an increasingly desperate situation. The image is applied to Chevance when he realizes that he is about to die (*I*, p. 523), and to M. Ouine, when he has refused salvation for the last time:

> Il savait seulement que là-haut, derrière les tilleuls et les ifs, avait été sa dernière chance. Elle n'était plus. Le cercle enchanté, rétréci chaque jour, ne se laisserait plus rompre. (*MO*, p. 1470.)

The exasperation of circular journeys is also evoked in the novels. The first Mouchette, for example, cannot bear the thought of a way of life which would bring her nothing new:

A quoi bon s'engager une fois dans votre chemin, qui ne mène nulle part? Que voulez-vous que je fasse d'un univers rond comme une pelote? (*SSS*, p. 70.)

In *La Joie*, it is said to be better to attack one's problems directly than to circle around them (*J*, pp. 611–612). The characters in the novels sometimes literally travel in circles. The most notable example is in the long passage in which the abbé Donissan, seeking to make a simple journey from one parish to another, is led around in circles by a mysterious force that turns out to be diabolical (*SSS*, p. 162ff).

The frustrating journey is a commonplace in the dream world, and it does not need to be circular in order to be futile. Sometimes, the infinity of the road ahead is itself a problem. Olivier Mainville, in *Un Mauvais Rêve*, is haunted by visions of a limitless road which will allow him to escape the problems of his life:

Tandis que nous poursuivions cette conversation, je croyais voir distinctement, par-dessus l'épaule de Philippe, une longue route droite, éclatante, infinie, entre deux rangées d'arbres énormes, d'un vert pâle aux reflets d'argent, dont j'entendais frémir les cimes. (*MR*, p. 951.)

But the end of this road remains undefined. The last time the reader sees him, Oliver is running away with no more purpose than a small child.

For Olivier, the road represents a concrete temptation, and his flight is a real one. For other characters, the road stands for a more figurative kind of journey. Cénabre, when he acknowledges his apostasy to himself, sets out on a "route terrible à suivre, inconnue," and is forced to continue on a "route implacable" (*I*, pp. 327, 349). Steeny, in *Monsieur Ouine*, sees the road as a symbol of liberty: "La belle route! la chère route! Vertigineuse amie, promesse immense!" (*MO*, p. 1406). The curé of Fenouille finds that the one image that consoles him when he is discouraged is that of a beggar, pursued along the road by dogs (*MO*, p. 1515). Even when there is no compulsion to flight, however, Bernanos' characters are fond of roads. Chantal de Clergerie imagines how Christ himself must have loved, in his native countryside, "les routes grises, dorées par

33

l'averse" (*J*, p. 864). The curé of Ambricourt, when he learns that he is about to die, realizes how much he will miss familiar roads (*JCC*, pp. 1421–1422).

This love of roads was obviously shared by the writer himself. In the preface to *Les Grands Cimetières sous la lune*, he apostrophizes the "chemins du pays d'Artois, à l'extrême automne, fauves et odorantes comme des bêtes, sentiers pourrissants sous la pluie de novembre . . ." (*GCSL*, p. iv). The compulsion to some kinds of flight was doubtless also part of his make-up. Life, to him, was a journey; and the most superficial acquaintance with his biography will show that this was literally, as well as metaphorically true.[16] But the writer's strong attraction to roads is, in a sense, self-defeating; there is no clear consciousness of goals to be achieved; the "promesse immense" is constantly held out, but we are not made aware of the moment at which it is kept. The paths of dream-journeys lie within the individual consciousness, and rarely lead anywhere in particular. Bernanos extends this property to the actual and figurative journeys of real life; for him, most purely human goals are relatively worthless, overshadowed by dreams and illusions. The only real journey's end is death.

The theme of death is an extremely frequent one in the novels; it is hard to think of any other writer who includes so many deathbed scenes in a relatively short body of work. The macabre aspects of death are not neglected; even as a child, Bernanos was haunted by visions of "le petit trou noir où je serai un jour, en tête à tête avec mille choses désagréables" (*OR*, p. 1733). This obsession extends to his characters. The mayor of Fenouille, in *Monsieur Ouine*, is overcome by a self-disgust which, he thinks, must be analogous to that which a cadavre feels for itself (*MO*, p. 1518). A delinquent child tells the curé of Ambricourt that, when she has misbehaved, she punishes herself by pretending that she is dead (*JCC*, p. 1207). But, if death is given a nightmarish immediacy in some passages, it is idealized in others. It constitutes the one opportunity for escape from obsessive dreams, into the "lumière sans rêves" (*EH*, p. 257). "O mort si fraiche, ô seul matin" is a refrain that occurs more than once in Bernanos' writings.[17] And, in the prologue to *Les Grands Cimetières sous la lune*, the idea of death is combined with those of homecoming at journey's end, and childhood recovered:

Certes, ma vie est déjà pleine de morts. Mais le plus mort des morts est le petit garçon que je fus. Et pourtant, l'heure venue, c'est lui qui

34

reprendra sa place à la tête de ma vie, rassemblera mes pauvres an-
nées jusqu'à la dernière, et comme un jeune chef ses vétérans, ralliant
la troupe en désordre entrera le premier dans la Maison du Père.
(*GCSL*, p. v.)

It is perhaps too easy to accuse Bernanos of proposing escapist
goals here; the objects of hope, in this passage, are that part of the
past which is least recoverable and that moment of the future which
is least controllable by man. The ordinary objectives of adult human life in the real world are totally disregarded. But this is precisely because Bernanos has a somewhat ambiguous attitude toward
what most people call the "real world." We have noticed, in the
novels, a degree of confusion between literal and oneiric events; a
similar confusion exists at moments when Bernanos treats historical
reality. One might almost say that he manages to give an oneiric
structure to contemporary history.

Albert Sonnenfeld, in a recent study, attributes the dream-like
view of history to a number of twentieth-century Catholic writers.
He thinks that they are under a kind of compulsion to interpret the
modern world in accordance with their childhood dreams of glory:

> "Perhaps it is only in childhood that books have any deep influence
> on our lives," Greene wrote. Is it childhood reading which explains
> the recurrence of castles, knights and monastic priests in so many
> Catholic novels? Of one thing I am sure. The modern Catholic
> novelist, like the German Romantics, the former faced with two world
> wars and the consequent despoliation of traditional social and religious
> values, the latter confronted by the French Revolution and Napoleonic
> wars, longs for a simple, orderly world, for the world of childhood and
> of childhood fantasies.[18]

To dismiss Bernanos' polemical writings as childhood fantasies is to
accord them less than their full value; nonetheless, Sonnenfeld is
probably right when he characterizes some of the writer's philosophical opponents as his "hostile phantoms." [19] Admirers of Bernanos have not underestimated his capacity to lend a mythical dimension to contemporary history. The writer recognizes this tendency himself when he describes the Battle of Britain in the *Lettre
aux Anglais*: "Votre victoire est un rêve d'enfant, réalisé par des
hommes" (*LAA*, p. 10). And the childlike perspective is deliber-
ately assumed in *Nous autres français*, where he bitterly accuses the
ruling classes in the language of a reluctant schoolboy: "Vous avez
mis les peuples au collège" (*NAF*, pp. 153, 164–167). Even in the

case of visible contemporary events, it is impossible to dissociate dreams from reality.

The fact that the dream-world is inescapable, and yet dangerous, is responsible for a great deal of the tension that exists in Bernanos' novels. Struggles between human beings have little importance for his characters; their chief adversaries are their obsessions. Donissan's antagonist is the inner light that may be either celestial or infernal; Cénabre's, the impulse to pride that threatens to paralyze or petrify his soul; Ouine's, the unreal world in which he has consented to exist. The characters in *Un Mauvais Rêve* are driven into isolation by their separate dreams. Even the dream-states of mysticism are feared and resisted; hence the wariness of Chantal, confronted with a mystical experience whose nature she does not recognize. The curé of Ambricourt, communicating with his parishioners, deals not with their actions but with their ruling obsessions: "Nous juger sur ce que nous appelons nos actes est peut-être aussi vain que de nous juger sur nos rêves" (*JCC*, p. 1100).

The conflict between dreams and rational forces is apparent in those of Bernanos' characters who, like their creator, are writers in spite of themselves. To a certain degree, their work consists in transmuting mental images into metaphors, and it is evident that the process is by no means an easy one. The curé of Ambricourt is bemused by a mental image in which his parish is personified, and has its own face and expression. He tries to use the metaphor in a sermon:

> J'ai eu l'idée d'utiliser ce passage, en l'arrangeant un peu, pour mon instruction du dimanche. Le *regard de la paroisse* a fait sourire et je me suis arrêté une seconde au beau milieu de la phrase avec l'impression, très nette hélas! de jouer la comédie. Dieu sait pourtant que j'étais sincère! Mais il y a toujours dans les images qui ont trop ému notre cœur quelque chose de trouble. (*JCC*, p. 1052.)

The curé of Fenouille, preaching the funeral sermon of a murdered child, is less prudent; he allows himself to be carried away by his own images, and his lack of restraint precipitates disaster:

> Son humble regard pâlissait tandis que ses bras, avec une lenteur solennelle, se levaient à son insu, comme d'un nageur épuisé qui ne se défend plus, coule à pic. Trop simple d'esprit, trop peu poète pour avoir mesuré la puissance des images et leur péril, celle qu'il venait d'évoquer s'emparait de lui avec une force irrésistible. Il voyait, il

touchait presque ces montagnes d'excréments, ces lacs de boue. (*MO*, p. 1488.)

For the two curés, a metaphor is less to be sought out than to be restrained. A strong effort is required if the forces of imagination are to be controlled and dominated; and it is evident that Bernanos feels that this kind of effort is required of any real artist. A passage in *La France contre les robots* makes this idea clear:

> Un véritable romancier qui commence un livre part à la conquête de l'inconnu, il ne domine son œuvre qu'à la dernière page, elle lui résiste jusqu'au bout comme le taureau estoqué qui se couche aux pieds du matador, tout ruisselant de sang et d'écume.
>
> Rien n'est plus facile que de se persuader soi-même qu'on est vivant, très vivant, il suffit de gesticuler beaucoup, de parler d'échanger des idées comme on échange des sous, une idée appelant l'autre, comme les images, dans le déroulement des songes. Hélas! dès qu'on s'examine un peu on trouve très aisément en soi ces sources d'énergie corrompue, stérile. Un artiste les connaît mieux qu'un autre car tout le travail de création est précisément de les refouler, de les dominer, de faire taire coûte que coûte ce ronron monotone. (*FCR*, pp. 136, 142.)

For Bernanos, if not for every writer, the artist's work consists in measuring himself against his obsessions. The dream world is an adversary that must be dominated; images are like wild animals that must be tamed:

> Je travaille dans la nuit la plus opaque, je me bats avec les images et les mots d'une bataille extraordinaire; chaque page écrite me coûte un monde. (*BPLM*, p. 101.)

Paradoxically, it is perhaps because these efforts of Bernanos do not altogether succeed that his works have interested many readers. The dreams of his creatures do not always remain this side of incoherence; and, as we are made aware of a character's struggle with dreams or hallucinations, we are always conscious of the artist's struggle to dominate his own imagination. There is little sense of triumphant order, either in the events of the novels or in the style of the novelist. We are far more aware of tensions than of resolutions. If Bernanos attracts us, it is not because he communicates a sense of serenity but because he invites — or requires — us to share in his exertions.

37

IRONIC FIGURES IN MALRAUX'S NOVELS

BY RALPH TARICA

The novels of André Malraux are the records of men committed to changing the face of the world. From one novel to the next the reader becomes the witness of heroes who boldly pit their will and lucidity against a hostile reality in an intensely dramatic struggle. But from one novel to the next that reality remains an overriding constant. We need only to look at the events with which Malraux constructs his novels to understand this; he inevitably places them in the context of an extreme situation: imprisonment, besiegement, the battlefield, the spectacle of the death of others, the awareness of the imminent possibility of one's own death. Man's will to transform is forever countered by a radically inhuman universe that baffles his comprehension and frustrates his hopes, forever eluding a satisfactory consummation of the action engaged against it. There are occasional victories over local circumstances, but the sheer repetition of similar predicaments through six novels suffices to inform us that a definitive victory is out of the question. The predicament is never overcome; and the quality of experience that prevails through one confrontation after the other is one of anxiety.

This quality is communicated directly to the reader. For while it is true that the novels contain substantive passages of discourse and reflection which propound ideas and work upon our intelligence, what they focus upon most intensely is less the *idea* of a predicament as certain *feelings* born of the confrontation of the characters and their extreme situation. Indeed, it is that constantly shifting movement of anguished reaction, from expectation to frustation to ever renewed expectations, reported elliptically and nervously, that perhaps most readily identifies the author's style. It is equally characteristic that the anxiety escapes close definition as to the nature of its origins — psychological, physical or metaphysical — remaining, rather, a composite experience offered with little mediation to the affective intelligence of the reader: vague, profound, and as inextricably complex as life itself.

38

The structure of Malraux's world is tragic; for between man's desire to impose himself and the shape of the reality that opposes him there is an eternal hiatus. This essay is devoted to one of the most frequent devices employed by Malraux to focus upon that hiatus, the figures that communicate a sense of irony, in an effort to demonstrate that the predisposition in Malraux's characters to reflexes of anxiety is significantly related to the functioning of an impressive number of images in the novels which transform reality into illusion; that the sense of incongruity communicated by such images has to do with some essential mystery lying just beyond man's grasp; and that the intimations of this mystery are structured closely into the experience of confrontation itself in such a way as to call the conditions of that confrontation into doubt.

Perception and anxiety

There is a characteristic manner in which Malraux's characters confront reality that tells us a great deal about their predisposition to the anxiety reflex. What the characters perceive is often an ill-defined shape, a metonymic reduction to a shadow, profile, silhouette, spot or some other visual aura projected by a person or thing. There are, of course, practical reasons why details may be blurred for the observing eye. The narrator of *Les Conquérants*, for example, is not accustomed to the dazzling light of the Indochina sun, and so we read: "Fatigué par la réverbération du soleil sur la poussière de la rue et sur les murs, je me retourne un instant. Tout est brouillé. Taches de couleurs des affiches de propagande collées au mur, ombre de Garine qui marche de long en large . . ." Then, like a lens brought back into focus, the narrator's eyes make sense out of a moment of hectic activity — Garine has begun to distribute weapons to the people, so that the potential for action suggested in the posters crystallizes into reality: "Mes yeux, rapidement, s'accoutument à l'ombre. Ces affiches, en ce moment, prennent vie . . ." (*LC*, p. 87.) [1]

A good many episodes, in all the novels, take place in darkened areas or at night so that the perceived object is naturally obscured. Katow's men approach a boat: "La vedette avançait toujours: le roulis était assez fort pour que la silhouette basse et trouble du vapeur semblât se balancer lentement sur le fleuve; à peine éclairée elle ne se distinguait que par une masse plus sombre sur le ciel ouvert" (*CH*, p. 232). Vincent Berger sees two soldiers in his

39

trench: "Deux silhouettes passèrent confondues devant une faible auréole" (*NA*, p. 201). In other cases, the object may be too far to be seen distinctly. Darras sees Moorish troops from his plane: "il ne voyait que des taches kaki fuyant la route sous les points blancs des turbans" (*LE*, p. 518); soldiers: "Les silhouettes vertes et les casques recouverts de toile de la 132e convergeaient vers un grand pré creux" (*NA*, p. 209).

But practical reasons do not suffice to justify the greater number of Malraux's visual blurs — nor even some of those just cited, and others like them. Recourse to this sort of expression (not, for example, "il ne voyait que des Maures fuyant la route" but "il ne voyait que des taches kaki . . .") suggests several important tendencies which recur regularly in Malraux's creative imagination. One of these is a kind of visual composition which owes something to painterly or cinematic techniques; another is the dramatization of the terrain of confrontation; while still another is the dramatization of the act of perceiving itself. It is this latter tendency that will interest us here.

The metonymic blur obviously conveys a visual confusion to the reader; and this is not at all a poor descriptive technique but a rather good one for obliging the reader to sense with the character. Frequently, before a character fully recognizes an object or another character, his nervous apparatus informs him, and us, of an emerging presence. Claude Vannec in the jungle: "Sur le sol, une ombre dépassa ses pieds, s'approcha de la sienne en silence. Il se retourna; le boy qui venait derrière lui s'arrêta" (*VR*, p. 132). Kyo observes the attack upon an armored train: "Très inquiet, Kyo regardait confusément le trottoir, qui brillait sous le soleil provisoire. Une grande ombre s'y allongea. Il leva la tête: Katow" (*CH*, p. 271). Garcia works in his office: "Une mince silhouette voûtée montait seule au milieu de l'escalier immense: Guernico venait chercher de l'aide" (*LE*, p. 690). In such cases as these the colon resembles the focusing mechanism of a lens: it separates visual blur from visual resolution, creates mystery and dispels it.

In a number of instances, before the character arrives at a visual resolution, he formulates an incorrect appraisal. When Hemmelrich, for example, receives Tchen and his two friends, the reaction of confusion informs us of his particular anxiety: "de courtes ombres sur le trottoir, montrèrent que trois corps étaient là. La police? . . . Hemmelrich se leva [. . .] Avant que sa main eût atteint sa poche, il avait reconnu Tchen; il la lui tendit au lieu de tirer son revolver"

(*CH*, p. 310). After an extremely arduous climb up a mountain, Magnin and his group finally come across the lost crewmen they have been searching for. Here, Magnin's incorrect appraisal loads the scene heavily with epic heroism before settling into a picture of reality: "A l'angle du chemin comme le pommier tout à l'heure, attendait un petit guerrier sarrasin, noir sur le ciel, avec le raccourci des statues à haut piédestal: le cheval était un mulet, et le Sarrasin était Pujol, en serre-tête" (*LE*, p. 828).

In all these cases, the lapse between sensory perception and recognition not only expresses a character's anxious feeling of expectation, but marks a dramatic suspense for the reader as well — a suspense which Malraux occasionally prolongs to some length. Just as Tchen has consummated his first murder, for example, Malraux steeps character and reader both in tensely sustained terror: "sur le drap une tache sombre commença à s'étendre, grandit comme un être vivant. Et à côté d'elle, grandissant comme elle, parut l'ombre de deux oreilles pointues [. . .] il était paralysé, incapable de se retourner. Il sursauta: un miaulement. A demi délivré, il osa regarder. C'était un chat de gouttière qui entrait par la fenêtre sur ses pattes silencieuses, les yeux fixés sur lui" (*CH*, p. 184).

Malraux does not restrict perceptual confusions to the visual, but plays them out among the whole sensing and intellectual apparatus. Indeed, this kind of "double-take," as Geoffrey Hartman has aptly called it,[2] is a dominant recurring device in all the novels. Hartman cites as an unusually fine instance the temporal confusion in the mind of Hernandez as he watches his fellow prisoners, lined up by threes, being shot by the Fascists:

> Ils font un saut périlleux en arrière. Le peloton tire, mais ils sont déjà dans la fosse. Comment peuvent-ils espérer s'en échapper? Les prisonniers rient nerveusement.
>
> Ils n'auront pas à s'en échapper. Les prisonniers ont vu le saut d'abord, mais le peloton a tiré avant. Les nerfs. (*LE*, p. 650.)

At this point we are dealing with a kind of rhetorical figure, prolepsis, in which Hartman detects "a *metaphysical haste* which characterizes man in the face of the world" (p. 64), hence one of several structural devices meant to call into doubt, at varyingly frequent intervals, the notion of an absolute victory. Actually, this kind of figure works very much like many of Malraux's analogical images; it expresses the same kind of "as though" situation, but elaborates it explicitly rather than elliptically, in this case allowing Malraux to apply its effect not only subjectively to Hernandez but objectively to the entire group of witnessing prisoners. The narrating voice reports, through the senses of one character, the perception of an immediate phenomenon which registers upon the mind as a shocking infraction against logic; the cause is correct (the firing squad shoots), but the effect is wrong (the victims are already in the ditch), and it is wrong because the perceiver has failed to take into account a qualifying cause (in this case, a simple law of physics: it takes our ears longer to seize signals than our eyes). The reason for the failure is cited explicitly in the text: "les nerfs" over-reacting because of the extremeness of the context — the mind is simply not equipped to accept the full meaning of the event. Hernandez' confusion thus reveals nervous anxiety, and sets up a dramatic suspense between perception and resolution; but beyond that, it also serves as an ironic correcting device — an unheroic death at the hands of contemptuous enemies is not at all the fate anticipated by a man who devotes himself to a heroic cause.

The episode in which a character's senses put the world in question as dramatically as any of Malraux's creation is that in which Tchen must kill his victim, in the opening pages of *La Condition humaine*. It is a scene composed in large part of interrogations and incorrect, ironic formulations, some of which involve explicit images while others express, in various degrees of "as though" formulations, the tricks of momentary illusion being played by the character's gnawing anxiety. Tchen is afraid his act will be witnessed: "Quatre ou cinq klaxons grincèrent à la fois. Découvert?" This particular anxiety — the fear of being discovered, of finding himself accused of losing his own humanness through the act of murder — frames still another, the consummation of the fatal contact. His imminent act is so momentous for him that he cannot believe it can leave his surroundings unaffected: "Il éleva légèrement le bras droit, stupéfait du silence qui continuait à l'entourer, comme si son geste eût dû déclencher quelque chute. Mais non, il ne se passait rien: c'était toujours à lui d'agir." His sight begins to send false messages to his brain: "Ce pied vivait comme un animal endormi. Terminait-il un corps? 'Est-ce que je deviens imbécile?'" Next, it is the turn of his tactile senses: "Tchen frissonna: un insecte courait sur sa peau. Non; c'était le sang de son bras qui coulait goutte à goutte." Then, his hearing plays the same kind of trick upon him: "Toucher ce corps immobile était aussi difficile que frapper un cadavre, peut-être pour les mêmes raisons. Comme appelé par cette idée de cadavre, un râle s'éleva. Tchen ne pouvait plus même reculer, jambes et bras devenus complètement mous. Mais le râle s'ordonna: l'homme ne râlait pas, il ronflait." After his act of murder, one spell of anxiety appears to be broken: "Il était absolument immobile; le sang qui continuait à couler de son bras gauche lui semblait celui de l'homme couché; sans que rien de nouveau fût survenu, il eut soudain la certitude que cet homme était mort." And as though in answer to the first question ("découvert?"), Malraux completes the initial frame by introducing a cat who has witnessed the act, as we saw in the passage cited earlier. (*CH*, pp. 181–184).

In short, while Malraux's devices relating perceptual confusion set up a strong dramatic tension, a good many of them serve two other closely related functions. One of these is the reporting of anxiety. The effect of prolepsis and "double-takes" in the novels is not to weaken the force of an ultimately correct assessment, but rather to fix our attention upon the jumpy state of a character's nerves. In so doing, they touch at the heart of one of the dominant psychological states in all Malraux's novels. From the point of view of style, Malraux's special manner of reporting anxiety can generally be accounted for by two complementary factors. One of these is the narrating voice, which does not limit itself simply to describing the contexts of confrontation, but goes considerably further to amplify them dramatically through the measured counterplay of a number of devices: elements in décor that combine to form dense and nervous atmospheres, intrusions upon action and thought by exterior presences which tend to take on symbolic meanings, and an abundance of images that direct the mind and senses to focus tensely upon the predicament. The other factor is the perceptual capacities of the characters. Malraux endows all of his major characters, and many of the minor ones as well, with a remarkably finely tuned sensing apparatus, capable not only of perceiving the immediate elements unveiled, one by one, by the narrating voice, and of crystallizing imagery through recollection of past experiences, but of reacting profoundly to the potential significance of *all* these through mind, body and nerves.

The second function performed by the figures of perceptual confusion, as we have seen, is an ironic one. Beneath the overt symptoms of nervousness, the "as though" illusion communicates a sense of disparity: a disparity between a character's expectations and the

43

actual outcome of events, or, more broadly, between a general human capacity to comprehend and the inflexible, obtuse nature of reality. Irony is an essential factor of Malraux's thought and style, calling into doubt, in the very midst of intense confrontation, the premises upon which that confrontation is founded. This should become even more apparent when we consider certain patterns of imagery recurrent in the novels: the similes and metaphors which create an objective effect of surprise, or dramatize a subjective feeling of shock, by reference to an incongruous vehicle. In the pages that follow I should like to examine what some of these images are and the insights they provide for understanding certain of the more important kinds of experiences communicated in Malraux's novels.

Images of incongruity

Malraux's novels contain such traditional correlatives for situations of unreality as ghosts, dreams, sleepwalking, madness, and the "lunar," of which a large number express the shock of estrangement from an observed reality. The image of the ghost generally comes across as a menacing sign of imminent ruin, plunging the observer into a nightmare world. In humiliating Ferral, for example, Valérie has in effect denied the existence of this strong-willed individualist, who now must suffer anguished doubts about his dream of personal dominion over others: "Lui seul existait dans un monde de fantômes, et c'était lui, précisément lui, qui était bafoué" (*CH*, p. 339). In several instances the image communicates a strange and frightening vision of destruction out of which lone persons or objects loom dramatically into focus to haunt the scene. As Kyo walks into the *Black Cat* night club in search of Clappique, the deafening music ceases abruptly and the dancers retreat to their places, with one exception: an aging man, once respectable and now degenerate, who continues to dance alone, attracting the eyes of the other clientele who are roughly in the same situation: "Négociants en instance de ruine, danseuses et prostituées, ceux qui se savaient menacés — presque tous — maintenaient leur regard sur ce fantôme, comme si, seul, il les eût retenus au bord du néant" (*CH*, p. 196).

These signs of destruction carry an obvious ironic impact; men would prefer not to come face to face with the truth of their essential fragility. The ghost image frequently communicates still another kind of irony: a situation is reversed, and an event that had seemed

44

definitive is annulled to permit a counter-action. A Fascist tank in
L'Espoir, for example, animated as a kind of stupid monster which
has not yet understood that the popular forces have secured anti-
tank weaponry, is struck and butts into a rock, "cabré comme un
fantôme de la Guerre" (*LE*, p. 738); this monster-tank has been
brought down by an underestimated power, and so the illusion of
an easy victory held by the Fascists is halted. During the bombardment of Madrid, a new wave of fire reaches out to houses already
burned: "il les éclairait par derrière, fantomatiques et funèbres, et
demeurait longtemps à rôder derrière leurs lignes de ruines" (*LE*,
p. 757); yet underneath the ghostly vision of Madrid's destruction,
the journalist Shade will hear the rythmic voices of invisible people
chanting their determination not to give in. When the Germans
send out poison gas towards the Russian position, in *Les Noyers de
l'Altenburg*, the intervening valley is soon transformed into a yel-
low fog, above which rises, "seul, absurde et fantomatique," a tall
telegraph pole (*NA*, p. 203). Vincent Berger will undergo a severe
shock when he espies a soldier running spasmodically towards him
out of the devastation wrought by the gas: "A deux mètres l'appari-
tion leva son visage gris aux yeux sans blanc, ouvrit comme pour
hurler sa bouche d'épileptique" (*NA*, p. 231). This phantasm is
all that is left of a former human being, a sign of the imminent ruin
of Man himself, just as the lone telegraph pole preludes the destruction of the natural world; but the scene will shift from one of
phantasmagoric destruction to that of salvation, to become ar
allegory of man's urgent task to rescue Man from himself.

The image of the aging man on the dance floor, cited above,
works in a way that resembles a number of Malraux's analogies to
madness. Malraux conceives of the madman as a creature who lives
in the closed world of the self, apart from men. He cannot communicate with others, but he has the power to hold the observing
eye in a fatal fascination, attracting it to the precarious edge that
separates reality from dream, the outer world of action from the
prison world of the self.[3] The vertiginous feeling that one is caught
in the spell of dreamers or madmen thus appears frequently as a
signal that sets going a gnawing questioning of oneself. In *La
Condition humaine* the sense of alienation that weighs upon Kyo, as
a result of his failure to recognize his own voice on a phonograph
record, is painfully aggravated whenever he reflects upon the
peculiar madness of his comrade in arms, Tchen. The nature of
their relationship baffles Kyo's most intensely sustained hope, which

is to break through the barriers of the self in order to establish fraternal bonds. For even when they stand together, as when they join in the attack against the armored train of the enemy, they are none the less worlds apart: "Sous la fraternité des armes, à l'instant même où il regardait ce train blindé que peut-être ils attaqueraient ensemble, il sentait la rupture possible comme il eût senti la menace de la crise chez un ami épileptique ou fou, au moment de sa plus grande lucidité" (*CH*, p. 274).

Several of the examples in *La Voie royale* touch on a major theme in that novel — the test of the European mind to rise above the world of dream, and to resist falling into the primitive self symbolized by the jungle and its savages. Claude Vannec detests dreams, and scorns those men for whom "adventure" is nothing more than "la nourriture des rêves" (*VR*, p. 55). Yet he is very much afraid his own scheme to secure lost sculptures from the jungle is mad, until he communicates his plans to Perken: "Son dessein, tant qu'il l'avait supporté seul, l'avait retranché du monde, lié à un univers incommunicable comme celui de l'aveugle ou du fou" (*VR*, p. 57). The long catalogue of descriptions of jungle monstrosities that introduces us to the heart of the adventure culminates with an immense sense of frustration served, fittingly enough, by an analogy to madmen: "Quel acte humain, ici, avait un sens? Quelle volonté conservait sa force? Tout se ramifiait, s'amollissait, s'efforçait de s'accorder à ce monde ignoble et attirant à la fois comme le regard des idiots" (*VR*, p. 99–100).

The shock communicated by many of the images of dreams and madness thus relates to a menace of a very powerful sort: the possibility of losing one's grip on a determined outer action and of falling into the sterility of the self, and all that this entails of a breakdown in effective communication between men. When Vologuine tells Kyo of the official Party attitude towards the revolution in Shanghai, Kyo reacts as a man whose reason for living has suddenly been snatched away from him, and so we read: "Kyo sombrait, comme en rêve toujours plus bas" (*CH*, p. 279). The principal portion of *Le Temps du mépris* depicts the forcible imprisonment of an active man as a near catastrophic fall into the world of dreams and madness. In *L'Espoir*, Magnin is appalled to find his pilots bickering pettily among themselves, and feels as though he were witnessing the worst part of them, "une provisoire folie, un rêve dont ils dussent tôt ou tard s'éveiller, serre-tête sur le front, raidis sous leur combinaison de vol, dans la réalité de la mort" (*LE*, p.

683). Vincent Berger, too, has a low opinion of idle dreams, and admits no place for them in his own rather exotic mission in the Orient: "Il est peu d'actions que les rêves nourrissent au lieu de les pourrir" (*NA*, p. 64). But that mission will indeed become an idle dream, and he will not understand this until he encounters, in the wilds of Asia, a literal madman who beats him; and so, as though released from a hypnotic spell, he awakens from the world of dreams to return to the reality of Europe.

Another important pattern of dream-like imagery in the novels, to which can be joined a related group of analogies to the "lunar" and other-worldly, conveys a sense of weirdness in a situation or activity felt as unreal. In some instances the image expresses a reaction to an event almost too much to be hoped for. *Les Conquérants* ends with the gradual crescendo of a distant noise: "Ce n'est plus une rumeur, mais un bruit fait de secousses successives, très éloignées ou très assourdies, un bruit de rêve" (*LC*, p. 161); this turns out to be the long awaited arrival of the Red army. Similarly, Kassner cannot really believe he is being released from prison: "C'était l'autre planète, le monde inconnu, l'arrivée chez les ombres" (*TM*, p. 116); and outside the prison he finds a "ciel gris et bas de rêve" (*TM*, p. 119)

In other instances, the image contrasts a strange tranquillity against the frenetic movement of events. Rebecci, for example, has lived through the upheaval of the Chinese revolution "avec une tranquillité de somnambule" (*LC*, p. 23). As Kyo waits to cross over to Hankow to see Vologuine, and receive the news that will crush his hopes, he walks about a neighborhood of small shops: "les médecins aux crapauds-enseignes, les marchands d'herbes et de monstres, les écrivains publics, les jeteurs de sorts, les astrologues, les diseurs de bonne aventure continuaient leurs métiers lunaires dans la lumière trouble où disparaissaient les taches de sang" (*CH*, p. 277). Vologuine will himself strike Kyo as strangely apart from events when he announces his news: "une intensité fixe semblable à celui d'un somnambule donnait seule vie à ce visage figé" (*CH*, p. 279).

In *L'Espoir* this kind of image applies in a number of instances to planes on bombing missions, relegating them to a world strangely detached from the frenzied world of fighting. Jaime's plane is just about to fly over the Alcazar when we read: "L'avion qui tournait, comme une minuscule planète, perdu dans l'indifférente gravitation des mondes, attendait que passât sous lui Tolède, son Alcazar rebelle et ses assiégeants, entraînés dans le rythme absurde des choses terrestres [. . .] Il semblait que le paysage entier des nuages tournât avec une lenteur planétaire autour de l'appareil immobile" (*LE*, p. 555). The result of the mission: a successful bombing raid, but the appearance of enemy chasers; and we will learn some pages later that a number of the crew have been killed or wounded, and that Jaime has been blinded (*LE*, p. 569). After a successful raid over Talavera, Leclerc looks out at the wings of his plane and is startled to find that it has turned a phosphorescent blue: moonlight has transformed the plane into an eery décor, as though some force beyond man were transmuting the most forceful of actions into a hollow dream: "aucun geste humain n'était plus à la mesure des choses: bien loin de ce cadran de guerre seul éclairé jusqu'à des lieues, l'euphorie qui suit tout combat se perdait dans une sérénité géologique, dans l'accord de la lune et de ce métal pâle qui luisait comme les pierres brillent pour des millénaires sur les astres morts" (*LE*, p. 618).

At this point it might be interesting to turn back to the passage cited earlier, in which Kyo walks among small shops in Hankow, to pick up the next sentence: "Les ombres se perdaient sur le sol plus qu'elles ne s'y allongeaient, baignées d'une phosphorescence bleuâtre; le dernier éclat de ce soir unique qui se passait très loin, quelque part dans les mondes, et dont seul un reflet venait baigner la terre, luisait faiblement au fond d'une arche énorme" (*CH*, p. 277). The shadows, the ghastly blue phosphorescence, the reference to other worlds prolong the dream image set off by contact with exotic shopkeepers impervious to the outcome of the revolution; and, of course, it turns out that the kaleidoscope of events will render Kyo's revolutionary mission a matter of indifference to all except Kyo and his men. Malraux's dream image, then, has a very strong tendency to turn up a baffling predicament: the man who desires action is warned by dream and madness to keep on a straight course outward from the self, and yet at the very height of what seems successful action the dream image can exert a subtle, but extremely forceful braking effect by providing a glimpse into the absurdity of action.

Another important group of images has to do with circuses, fairs, carnivals and festivals — that is, what might together be thought of as a very special sphere of ritualized recreation. At times a visual resemblance between two kinds of activity is sufficient for setting up the analogy. During one of the battle scenes, for example, Tchen looks like a tightrope dancer as he walks along a window ledge, followed by the eyes of his men (*CH*, p. 250). In another battle scene, Siry has not actually seen the Moors attacking, but after the battle the woods are strewn with dead Moors "comme des papiers après une fête" (*LE*, p. 715). Fire sparks look like handfuls of incandescent confetti (*LE*, p. 721) and appear at the end of a fire "comme dans un feu d'artifice bien ordonné" (*LE*, p. 757). The rather large number of these images (about thirty-five) in itself suggests a field of experience, presumably one of childhood, that is strongly impressed upon the author's imagination.[4]

These images frequently inject a jarring note of incongruity into serious activity. The appearance and atmosphere of a crowd, in particular, often comes across as some kind of festivity that belies the purpose for its coming together. Kassner, in Prague, visits a political forum called to organize anti-Fascist sentiment, but the forum meets in an "atmosphère de championnat du monde, de kermesse et de menace" (*TM*, p. 154) and the speeches that ensue — mere human words — will pale before the subject matter of human cruelty and suffering. For Vincent Berger, the funeral meal that follows his father's death is felt as slightly absurd: "Les foies gras d'Alsace succédant aux écrevisses et aux truites de ce repas de funérailles, et l'alcool de framboise au Traminer, il s'en fallut de peu que la réunion ne finît en kermesse" (*NA*, p. 38–39). Despite the passing of the millenia, he concludes, man has yet to succeed in formulating an adequate response to the immediate reality of death.

L'Espoir is particularly rich in this kind of image. As they wait for their turn to fly, and perhaps run out of gas or be shot down, "les volontaires de l'aviation internationale, jubilants, chemises ouvertes par cette chaleur d'août espagnol, semblaient revenir de bastides et de baignades" (*LE*, p. 476). These images are usually associated with contexts of anxious waiting, but their impact, like those preceding, is frequently ironic in that they depict a situation that somehow reverses the anticipated one. During the burning of the Alcazar, after the fighting stops abruptly and a polite but cold meeting takes place between the combattants, the observing crowd grows thicker, "dont la marche eût pris l'aspect d'une promenade du dimanche si les yeux de tous ceux qui remontaient vers la place n'eussent été opiniâtrement fixés sur l'Alcazar" (*LE*, p. 597). The fierce hostility of the previous hours has suddenly been transformed into an unreal peace. A Fascist officer asks Hernandez to deliver a letter, and Hernandez gallantly accepts. When asked by one of his own officers what this gesture means, Hernandez reflects before answering — and we have another incongruous intrusion: "Sourcils froncés, l'air plutôt perplexe qu'ironique, il marchait à côté de l'officier, qui regardait le pavé où l'ombre des chapeaux mexicains jetait d'énormes confetti." And then Hernandez answers: "De la générosité" (*LE*, p. 598). Peace seems to have come, but the images insist on an illusion, and Hernandez is taken in by it.

There is another example where the images of a holiday and a circus coincide in the same context. Toledo is threatened by the Fascist army from without and by snipers from within, and the loss of control over the republican soldiers suddenly represents a real danger for Manuel: "la cohue était celle des gares aux grands jours de vacances [. . .] Ni la foule de Tolède jusqu'alors, ni celle de la procession du Corpus autrefois, ni celle des jours historiques de Madrid n'approchaient de celle-ci. Les miliciens portaient les chapeaux mexicains à bout de bras, verticalement, comme des cerceaux de cirque. Vingt mille hommes serrés dans la folie" (*LE*, p. 635–636). Again, the images paint an illusion; in reality, the whole structure of military discipline threatens to crumble before his eyes. Manuel manages to bring the troops under control, and they are evacuated from the city. Hernandez, with a kind of courage that smacks of proud indifference, prefers to remain with a few men to hold back the enemy invasion of Toledo. The Moors begin their infiltration (it is difficult not to recollect Roland's stand at Roncevaux); and suddenly Hernandez hears a distant noise which his senses question anxiously: "soudain, à contresens de la course des républicains, le vent apporta une musique de cuivres et de grosses caisses, celle des cirques, des foires et des armées." This strikes him as absurd; "Quels chevaux de bois tournent encore? se demande Hernandez. Il reconnut enfin l'hymne fasciste: la musique du Tercio jouait sur la place de Zocodover" (*LE*, p. 642). Hernandez' heroic stance has been futile; at the very moment he thinks he has held back the enemy, he will be captured by them, and subsequently executed.

A number of Malraux's images relating to the arts create an effect of incongruity by directing the imagination to the spectacular or fantastic. In *L'Espoir* the image of performing musicians appears several times to set up a sense of unreality in an observing character who cannot quite fathom the significance of the scene he is witnessing. After his plane crashes on a coastal Spanish road, Attignies, still suffering from his wounds and in a state of semi-shock, sets out to find aid for his men amidst the confusion of an enormous crowd fleeing a Fascist advance. He looks up at the road: "Au-dessus du remblai, les bustes inclinés avançaient toujours vers l'ouest, au pas et à la course. Devant nombre de bouches un poing tenait un objet confus, comme si tous eussent joué de quelques silencieux clairon: ils mangeaient. Une herbe courte et large, du céleri peut-être" (*LE*, p. 794–795). The series of hallucinatory visions continues until he reaches a telephone station, only to find that the lines have been cut. The image of violinists playing their instruments applies, in two or three instances, to wounded men wearing plaster casts on their arms; the picture is slightly grotesque, and the effect is that of suggesting a bitter irony. When Manuel, for example, begins singing the *Tantum Ergo* in hommage to Guernico, the men about join in the chorus: "Comme ses amis avaient retrouvé ce latin amicalement ironique, les blessés révolutionnaires, avec leurs bras courbés de plâtrés sur lesquels ils semblaient se préparer à jouer du violon, retrouvaient le latin de la mort" (*LE*, p. 697).

The image of a strange dance works in a similar manner: Malraux transforms the movements of men in a grim context into a surrealistic dream ballet. Fascist planes begin bombing a military hospital, and Ramos organizes the evacuation of the soldier inmates: "D'autres blessés, avec les bras des plâtrés, glissèrent comme un ballet lugubre, noirs d'abord en silhouette, puis leurs pyjamas clairs de plus en plus rouges, au fur et à mesure qu'ils traversaient la place dans la sombre lueur de l'incendie" (*LE*, p. 722).[5]

After poison gas has been propelled in the direction of the Russian trenches, in *Les Noyers de l'Altenburg*, the German troops move out to cross through the barbed wire protecting the Russian position. Vincent's binoculars frame the scene dramatically: "les taches humaines commencèrent à s'emberlificoter dans le réseau des fils, d'y gigoter comme des araignées dans une toile invisible, car mon père voyait seulement les poteaux. A l'opiniâtre progression que l'éloignement ralentissait comme il avait ralenti celle des gaz, succédait un long guignol sur place, une danse sinistre et qui ne finissait pas. Enfin, tous plongèrent dans la tranchée russe" (*NA*, p. 213). This long, suspenseful dance is "sinister" because it should be the one that culminates in the destruction of the Russians by the Germans. But Vincent has been hasty; he suddenly modifies his statement, in preface to the modification of the entire scene: "Non, certains restaient sur les barbelés." We do not need to be told why —

51

the soldiers have been taken aback by something horrendous they have seen. Instead of advancing they will retreat; instead of killing the Russians, they will attempt to rescue them.

Malraux's ironic transpositions from the realm of the real to that of the arts are most often grounded in allusions to the literary, the theatrical and the cinematic.[6] The effect, when applied to a character, is frequently that of comic grotesqueness. Rebecci, the Genoese "sleepwalker," is a believer in demons and magic, a day-dreamer whose visions turn most often to finer versions of the same cheap stuff he sells: mechanical toys and souvenir junk. Physically, he is a comic figure: "souvent, à l'heure de la sieste, on voyait déambuler sa silhouette blanche: casque plat, torse étroit, vastes pantalons que des pinces de cycliste transformaient en pantalon de Zouave, et les pieds en dehors de Charlot" (*LC*, p. 24). He has a "tête de Guignol"; "Garine l'avait surnommé Gnafron" (*LC*, p. 27). Clappique, in *La Condition humaine*, is a masterfully drawn creature of dreams. He is the very incarnation of incongruity: a moon-struck teller of extravagant tales, a "Polichinelle" disguised in a tuxedo, a "Fantomas" who will look into a mirror to see himself transformed into a "gargouille" and a "samouraï de carnaval." This sham buffoon, strangely, keeps turning up in some of the most important contexts of action, as though to contaminate with his own unreality the possibility of a real victory. Just as Malraux's incongruous image generally provokes a feeling of anxiety within the subjectivity of a character, the appearance of this incongrous figure intrudes an element of anxiety upon the movement of action and plot. Like the odd side of a coin, Malraux has made him insepar-able from the face side of action, in much the same way that he has characterized the dreamer, Rebecci, as the "accoucheur" of the terrorist Hong. Where the genuine heroes exteriorize myth, Rebecci and Clappique interiorize it, and the mere fact of their presence becomes a mocking sign exposing the element of madness and dream lying beneath the lucidity that leads to action.

Comic effects seem normal enough in the case of these two bizarre creatures; but they communicate a sense of incongruity in some of the characterizations of serious men, as well. Katow's extreme experiences in Russia, for example, have stamped his face with an expression of ironic naïveté. As Tchen addresses him, in a room dramatically framed by an overhead light, he sees "cette bonne tête de Pierrot russe — petits yeux rigoleurs et nez en l'air — que même cette lumière ne pouvait rendre dramatique"; but the narrating voice, as though to strip off the mask of irony momentarily in order to presage the final, consummately dramatic role that will be Katow's, reports through Tchen's mind: "lui, pourtant, savait ce qu'était la mort" (*CH*, p. 188).

In *L'Espoir*, Scali, "avec ses lunettes rondes, son pantalon trop long dont les jambes bouffaient, son air de comique américain dans un film d'aviation" (*LE*, p. 672), is not really a comic figure, but as an art historian and intellectual he does seem somewhat out of place in a wartime atmosphere; and indeed, he is one of the principal figures in the novel whose participation questions the meaning of war. Möllberg, in *Les Noyers de l'Altenburg*, is bald and thin and has pointed ears, so that he reminds Vincent of the "vampires des contes d'enfants" (*NA*, p. 107); he also looks like the statuette "monsters" of his own making that represent fantastic, semi-human creatures (*NA*, pp. 108, 129). Why Malraux should insist on this manner of resemblance several times is of some importance. This intellectual who has peered into the dark recesses of time and culture, who has brought back his gloomy analysis of the meaning of Man, has also lost sight of men themselves. He fashions grotesque figures and, ironically, looks like them himself, because, like Goya's sad monsters, he only has a dim memory of once having been human. All of these ironies, then, express paradoxes. Katow's naive look seems to conceal a great depth of hard experience, and yet his experience has prepared him to face life, and death, with greater simplicity. Scali's comic look seems to conceal a serious intellectual who has voluntarily involved himself in a war, but the reasons for war may sometimes baffle the intellectual. Möllberg's comically grotesque look seems to conceal a brilliant mind that has searched for an answer to the enigma of Man, but the enigma has only mocked him by proposing an answer which he accepts as *the* answer, and to which he has himself conformed.

Characterizations such as those of Katow and Scali have comic elements; but Rebecci and Clappique, as we have seen, are not only comic but grotesque, and they are not the only such figures in the novels. There are at least two others. Towards the end of *L'Espoir*, just before the image of an Indian décor done in *trompe-l'oeil* will insist, once again, that peace and victory are but an illusion (*LE*, pp. 856–857), an eccentric old man will suddenly appear from nowhere. Formerly with a circus in India, knowledgeable in antiquities, "avec le visage et le geste des acteurs de vocation, de ceux qui ne peuvent vivre que dans la fiction" (*LE*, p. 850), he has a number of familiar characteristics; and he will let us know that wars may come and wars may go, but the principal enemy of man is an inhuman force that would undo, in short order, the works of civilization if man were to let up in his efforts against that force. His particular form of "lunar" trade: he is a museum guide.

But there is another character, too, who shares more than one trait in common with Rebecci and Clappique, and that is Möllberg. Where the former is a dealer in art junk and the latter in art objects, Möllberg is a scholar in human artifacts — but also a fashioner of figurines. All three have had the dizzying experience of falling into the bottomless well of a distant culture — the first two in Asia, Möllberg in Africa. All three are "lunatic" — Rebecci plies a "lunar" trade, Clappique claims he will die "en allant cueillir la lune dans un étang" (*CH*, p. 197), and Möllberg's scholarly findings center about the fascination of primitive peoples with the moon. All have had visions of dreams and monsters, and in a very real sense have looked into the mirror of reality to see themselves reflected as grotesque creatures. And in all three, the lines of direct action and the unreality of dream, fiction and art seem to converge as though to prove definitively that those lines are never strictly parallel (although Kassner's experience in his prison cell leaves little to doubt here, in any case). The principal difference in these characters is that the former two come across as unsubstantial spirits whose presence has an insidious effect upon action, whereas, in Möllberg, the author has spelled out terms objective enough for the hero to grapple with directly (the idea of "grappling" may perhaps recall the sequence to which Malraux's last novel was to belong: *La Lutte avec l'Ange*).

Another pattern of imagery of the arts functions in a manner similar to one which we have by now seen several times: a figure intrudes incongruously to suggest an ironic situation. Tcheng-Daï's death in *Les Conquérants* is immediately seized upon by Garine as a chance to rally pro-revolutionary sentiment among the people. We know the English did not kill him, but the funeral does indeed turn into political propaganda, and the theatrical image suggests a sham décor. The narrator reports: " 'Mort à ces brigands d'Anglais,' puis-je lire au moment même où l'étrange symbole disparaît, caché par le coin de la rue comme par un portant de théâtre" (*LC*, p. 128). In an early, wildly undisciplined battle of *L'Espoir*, the anarchist Puig sends cars to crash through a military barricade and seize a canon emplacement: "dans un hurlement de trompes et de klaxons, deux Cadillac arrivaient avec les zigzags balayés des films de gangsters" (*LE*, p. 453). The drivers succeed, but die in the process; the reaction of le Négus: "C'est du boulot respectable, mais pas du boulot sérieux" (*LE*, p. 453). None the less, Puig tries the same tactic himself on another canon position: "Puig voyait les canonniers que leurs pare-balles ne protégeaient plus, grossir comme au cinéma. Une mitrailleuse fasciste tirait et grossissait" (*LE*, p. 454).

Allusions to the cinema can no doubt be accounted for, in part, by Malraux's strong interest in film techniques. In *L'Espoir* they also aid in establishing an aesthetic distance between reader and action, in such a way as to transpose chaotic activity into controlled, epic spectacle. During the bombing of Madrid, for example: "Un immeuble brûlait comme au cinéma, de haut en bas" (*LE*, p. 746); a portion of the battle for the Manzanares is witnessed for us by the novice soldier Siry, who at one point reports: "Nation après nation, les compagnies passent dans la brume qui semble maintenant de la fumée des explosions, courbées, fusils en avant. Comme au cinéma, et pourtant si différentes! Chacun de ces hommes est un des siens" (*LE*, p. 716). But it is very often the case that Malraux's cinema images take on the same connotations as those of the theater, and these usually suggest an ironic hollowness beneath supposedly solid activity. The message comes through quite clearly in a number of clichés of the comic-opera type. Garine wishes to make an efficient weapon out of his "bureau d'opéra-comique" (*LC*, p. 52), and will later recall his successful mission in China: "Dire que lorsque je suis arrivé ici, au temps de Lambert, Canton était une république de comédie!" (*LC*, p. 160). In *L'Espoir* the Spanish army suffers from a reputation of being an "armée d'opérette," and it is Manuel's goal to remold it into a serious enterprise: "Il n'y a pas d'armées d'opérettes, mon vieux Ramos, il y a seulement des opérettes sur l'armée. Ce qu'on appelle une armée d'opérette, c'est une armée de guerre civile" (*LE*, p. 506).

The meaning suggested by such images can be extended to cover more subtle situations, where the conditions of action itself are put into question by the ironic intrusion. Examples abound in *L'Espoir*. The opening days of the war in Spain appear as a beautiful spectacle of fraternal action, but that action, as le Négus informs Puig in the passage cited above, is simply not serious — the fighters have not yet learned the true cost of action. During a heated battle, for example: "Fusil au bras, des types apportaient des nouvelles, comme, à la buvette des studios, les acteurs viennent boire en costume, entre deux prises de vues"; by contrast, the barroom floor is covered with the prints of bloodied soles (*LE*, p. 464). The arms seized by the popular forces, in one romantic episode, include a jumble of modern rifles and "sabres de théâtre" (*LE*, p. 467). At one point during the early joyous days of victory, in Madrid, Lopez shouts facetiously: "En scène, là-dedans, gueulait-il: on tourne! Dans la pleine lumière des lampes électriques, Madrid, costumée de tous les déguisements de la révolution, était un immense studio nocturne" (*LE*, p. 468). Once the anti-Fascist forces become better organized, however, a more careful screening of prospective volunteers ensues: "les brigades étaient formées de combattants, non de figurants de cinéma" (*LE*, p. 665).

Garcia will explain Hernandez' gallant action in Toledo in these terms: "Vous savez bien qu'il y a pas mal de théâtre au début de toute révolution; en ce moment, ici, l'Espagne est une colonie mexicaine . . ." (*LE*, p. 607). There are indeed a number of allusions to things Mexican in *L'Espoir*: literal Mexican soldiers who look like Pancho Villa and such patently unreal décor as the sombreros cited earlier in connection with Hernandez' romantic gesture and Manuel's evacuation of his troops. One may or may not question the desirability of Lopez' dream to see a new revolutionary style born of the war in Spain, as was the case in Mexico (cf. *LE*, p. 472); but one may question — and the images aid us in doing so — whether one can win a difficult war in a play atmosphere.

Finally, one group of images is drawn from domestic life. They inject an ironic note of casualness into what otherwise seems quite serious. One of the effects Malraux achieves through them is an abrupt sense of finality. Katow, for example, awaiting death in the prison yard, wonders why the atmosphere seems nocturnal despite the presence of light: "Est-ce à cause des blessures, se demandait Katow, ou parce que nous sommes tous couchés, comme dans une gare?" The image of the train station then suddenly transforms his questioning into a certitude of the future: "C'est une gare. Nous en partirons pour nulle part, et voilà . . ." (*CH*, p. 400). Just before he is led off to a death by torture, he consoles himself by reflecting: "Allons! supposons que je sois mort dans un incendie" (*CH*, p. 411). The image here underscores a self-conscious, ironic heroism, but it is also of a general sort that recurs frequently in the novels, and the sense is usually the same: a tragic or spectacular way of dying is really like the most ordinary way — what is certain is the irreversible movement towards death itself. Möllberg employs a similar figure to strikingly dramatic effect when he describes the fatalism of primitive societies who would murder their rulers according to the movement of the heavenly bodies. The rulers understood perfectly well that they must die: "Ils ne l'ignoraient pas plus qu'un médecin urémique ou cancéreux n'ignore comment finissent l'urémie et le cancer: liés au ciel comme nous à nos microbes. Presque tous les dignitaires les suivaient dans la mort. Ils mouraient de la mort du Roi comme nous mourons d'une embolie" (*NA*, p. 132).

Among the more interesting examples of domestic images are those in which a wry sense of humor works its way into an essentially grim context. Kyo visits his military posts: " 'Je deviens le laitier qui fait sa tournée,' pensa Kyo" (*CH*, p. 234). The insurgents' battle planes are in a bad state: "l'ennemi, désormais, était bien moins l'armée fasciste que les moteurs de ces vieux avions, couverts de pièces comme de vieux pantalons" (*LE*, p. 615). The following passage contains, in addition to the cliché of a sieve and the surprise effect of a wash hanging up to dry, a good example of some of the strange art effects Malraux enjoys elaborating in *L'Espoir*, and the extra bit of jovial humor that comes from intimacy with statues: "Les miliciens tiraient, dans une atmosphère de chambre de chauffe, leur torse nu ocellé de taches de lumières de taches noires: les balles ennemies avaient fait une passoire de la partie supérieure du mur, en briques. Derrière Garcia, sur le bras allongé d'un apôtre, des bandes de mitrailleuse séchaient comme du linge. Il suspendit sa veste de cuir à l'index tendu" (*LE*, 539).

In such cases as these the images do not so much express an anxiety as exorcise it, reducing the mortal menace of combat to a human, comprehensible level. To this extent they may also be thought of as confirmations of innocence. Malraux's sentimental bias in favor of man comes through on many occasions, recalling to his reader the essential simplicity and vulnerability of man, as opposed to the complex, hostile reality he must confront. Images of domestic life, and especially those in which a childlike quality in man is made manifest, often underscore this attitude. When Tchen, for example, looks over the weapons possessed by his group of men, he notices that one man has nothing better than nails which he apparently plans to strew on the street to wound the hooves of horses: "Un adolescent examinait comme des graines, de gros clous à tête large qu'il tirait d'un sac" (*CH*, p. 244). The image colors the activity with a heavy bias in favor of the insurgents, who must temporarily forego the innocent, almost touching acts of ordinary life to take up arms against their oppressors.

Confrontations

The kinds of images Malraux employs to create effects of incongruity, as we have seen, are drawn from fairly wide and varied areas of experience and phenomena. But a second glance will suggest that a unitive thread runs through a goodly number of them. Some have to do with the mysterious realm beyond man's conscious life, others with spectacle and art, while still others with the ordinary circumstances of life and its normally innocent aspects. Together, they relate to what might be thought of as "pseudo" experiences — those of relatively insignificant importance, or else those wherein action is executed in a fantasy realm remote from man's genuine impositions upon reality. As such, they tend to function as shadow images for his important acts. If one may conceive of direct confrontation as a kind of exploration of man's relationship to the universe, the shadow image then represents a mirroring of that confrontation in another, muted register. For the split second of anxious shock, it estranges the character from the context of the real action in which he seems very solidly engaged, and calls into question the prior assessment of his relationship to the world.

Several patterns of confrontation are regularly served by the images that intrude an element of incongruity. A particularly significant one is the confrontation with death. In one of the analogies to domestic life the absurdity latent in incongruity comes to the surface and effectively dramatizes a profound sense of physical disgust and psychological dismay. This is the event that leads Garine to abandon the army in Europe: "Jusque là, les légionnaires, à l'occasion, avaient reçu de courts poignards, qui semblaient être encore des armes de guerre; ils reçurent ce jour-là des couteaux neufs, à manche de bois marron, à large lame, semblables, d'une façon ignoble et terrible, à des couteaux de cuisine . . ." (*LC*, p. 47). Kitchen knives, in their usual context of a domestic sphere, are inoffensive objects. But the simile sets up a clash that releases the mind from its habitual mode of thinking, to precipitate a new insight. One level of meaning might be this: a man may not find anything shocking about killing with a bayonet, but he is not normally prepared to kill with a kitchen knife; so that the domestic intrudes to accuse the military, to expose it, and thereby correct Garine's previous blindness to a truth lying beneath a ritual mask: the end of fighting is murder.

Another, more subjective meaning might also be read in Garine's shock: the discovery in himself, through the recollection of a familiar object, of one extreme and perverse form of potential human contact — the penetration of flesh. This reading might be further substantiated by reference to the one prolonged episode in Malraux's novels where a man discovers and consummates just such a contact: Tchen's murder of his sleeping victim. In this case Tchen stands before his victim holding a razor in his right hand, a dagger in the left: "Le rasoir était plus sûr, mais Tchen sentait qu'il ne pourrait jamais s'en servir; le poignard lui répugnait moins" (*CH*, p. 182). This impending contact between one man and another is further rendered grotesque by an analogy to the inoffensive contact of dancing: "Il tenait donc le poignard la lame en l'air, mais le sein gauche était le plus éloigné: à travers le filet de la moustiquaire, il eût dû frapper à longueur de bras d'un mouvement courbe comme celui du swing" (*CH*, p. 182–183).

Point-blank murder does not come easily for Malraux's man. In *L'Espoir*, le Négus is deeply impressed with the fact that a Fascist officer, with ample opportunity to aim his flame thrower against le Négus before being fired upon himself, does *not* do so. The episode in question comes across as a richly staged dream spectacle, with a setting that includes underground corridors, blue phosphorescent lighting, and a dance of maddened shadows projected upon the walls. Le Négus shoots; the Fascist "glissa enfin le long du Négus, avec un ralenti de cinéma, la tête dans le jet de flammes" (*LE*, p. 544). And it seems likely that Malraux has transformed this battle into the kind of unreal spectacle it is precisely to focus upon the disquieting lesson that le Négus will learn: "on ne peut sûrement pas se servir de la lance contre quelqu'un qui vous regarde. On n'ose pas . . . Quand même, on n'ose pas . . ." (*LE*, p. 545). Is this a kind of tribute being paid to the enemy? It is more to the point to think of it as a discovery of human qualities in the enemy — no matter which side a man may choose on the political spectrum, he still remains essentially a man.

The Fascist's act illustrates a dilemma. Where action must culminate in murder, it is disastrous to hesitate — hesitations leave one open to an invason of doubts that can only corrode action, and besides they give the adversary time to be the first to kill. But on the other hand, that very moment of hesitation is itself revelatory of an instinctively held value: human life. To veil that instinct seems to be one of the heaviest prices one must pay for acting effectively. Garine, in the passage cited earlier, encounters his fascination and balks at it; he is still profoundly vulnerable. Later in the novel he will have to kill one enemy agent in order to terrify another into revealing important information. Then he will not hesitate; he has learned his lesson all too well. Tchen must encounter his fascination at the very beginning of the action in which he is to play a role; he too hesitates momentarily, but, fatally, succumbs and goes on to become a dehumanized agent in the service of death.

The union of human beings through killing, like all other confrontations, can of course be viewed from two opposing sides. It is natural enough to expect a reaction of terror when the predicament is that of suddenly becoming aware that one is going to be killed. In these instances, too, we find Malraux resorting to incongrous imagery to express a sense of the grotesque. "Ils étaient là comme à l'intérieur d'une baraque foraine" (*VR*, p. 180) — this is what comes to Claude Vannec's mind as he realizes that his group, badly protected by their flimsy hut, are completely surrounded by savages who show every sign of wanting to do them in. A more subtle instance occurs in the execution scene of Hernandez, discussed above, where Malraux works out an entire process of coming to awareness through shock. The execution is represented in Hernandez' mind as a ritual to be eternally repeated: "A cette heure, sur la moitié de la terre d'Espagne, des adolescents pris dans la même hideuse comédie tirent dans le même matin éblouissant, et les mêmes paysans, avec les mêmes cheveux en avant, tombent ou sautent dans les fosses" (*LE*, p. 651). Since it is a Spaniard who reflects for us, the ritual is conceived of in terms of a traditional Spanish heroism, with allusions to such virtues as "noblesse de caractère," "courage" and "générosité"; yet, given the immediate context of the firing squad, the virtues seem totally out of place, and the images that come to Hernandez' mind transform the event into a horrible parody of life. His reaction to the bodies being shot into the ditch: "Sauf au cirque, Hernandez n'a jamais vu un homme sauter en arrière" (*LE*, p. 651). The vanquished, incredibly, seem to want to cooperate with the victors in this strange ritual:

"L'un ne sait plus s'il doit se placer de face ou de dos; on ne sait jamais quelle attitude avoir au départ du train . . . pense Hernandez hystériquement [. . .] Et les prisonniers semblent les aider, — s'efforcer de comprendre ce qu'on veut d'eux, s'y conformer. 'On dirait qu'ils vont à l'enterrement.'" And Hernandez adds with a certitude now beyond despair: "Ils vont au leur [. . .] Aura-t-on bientôt fini de disposer ces prisonniers comme pour une photo de mariage, devant les canons de fusils horizontaux? [. . .] Hernandez pense à Pradas, à la générosité. Les trois prisonniers sont enfin de face: la photo est décidément prête."

And now he understands, too late to rescue himself from the effects of the sense of fatalism that led him to be captured in the first place and, more profoundly, from the theatrical gallantry that he had tried to assimilate to war: "La générosité, c'est d'être vainqueur." (*LE*, pp. 651–652.)

There is another pattern of confrontation in which the incongruous image dramatizes a powerful shock of estrangement: the spectacle of the defeat of man. We are dealing here with one of the obsessive themes in Malraux, perhaps nowhere more concisely summarized than in *Les Noyers de l'Altenburg*, where the narrator recalls Pascal's well known image: "Qu'on s'imagine un grand nombre d'hommes dans les chaînes, et tous condamnés à mort, dont les uns étant chaque jour égorgés à la vue des autres, ceux qui restent voient leur propre condition dans celle de leurs semblables . . . C'est l'image de la condition des hommes" (*NA*, p. 289). This painful reality — and it is an ever present one — consistently offers the mind more than it can cope with, and drives it anxiously into the deep recesses of an unreal nightmare world. Such signs of ruin as the ghost image considered earlier are but one particularly recurrent, hence more visible means of communicating shock, but their sense carries over a general formulaic pattern to numerous episodes.

In the earlier novels, these episodes tend to be structured in such a way that a major protagonist, after standing as a dazed witness before the ruin of a human being whom he has loved or respected, will himself become a ruin to be witnessed by yet another character. The effectiveness of the estranging ghost formula is thus guaranteed: the foreboding of ruin will eventually be realized in fact. Garine, for example, is called to look upon the mutilated cadaver of his comrade Klein; later, the narrator of the novel will witness the rapid decline of Garine himself. Perken, searching for Grabot, will discover in a jungle hut, not the grandly mysterious figure he had expected to find, but a "puissante ruine"; at the end of the novel Claude Vannec will witness the disintegration of Perken. In the case of Grabot, the specific correlative for estrangement and futility is blindness; in the second case, the loss of feeling in Perken's hand. When, in *La Condition humaine*, May tells of her infidelity to Kyo, he reacts as though he were watching her die. The "ruin" in this case is not a literal body, but the disintegration of happiness, and the analogy that expresses it is that of a cloud disappearing into a grey sky (*CH*, p. 214). Malraux will later repeat this image when he has Gisors reflect over Kyo's death: "les nuages passaient au-dessus des pins sombres et se résorbaient peu à peu dans le ciel; et il lui sembla qu'un de leurs groupes, celui-là précisément, exprimait les hommes qu'il avait connus ou aimés, et qui étaient morts" (*CH*, p. 431). From *La Condition humaine* on, the principal characters tend to survive their predicaments, and the ghost formula of shock applies more broadly to men in general rather than to specified individuals.

Of these spectacles of man's defeat, Malraux's hospital scenes are particularly well served by images that depict an anxious dream reality. In *Les Conquérants*, Garine's developing illness necessitates a trip to the hospital, where the narrator visits him. The narrator's description of the scene contains elements that affect the meaning in both obvious and subtle ways:

> La moustiquaire est à demi relevée: Garine semble couché dans un lit à rideaux de tulle. Je m'assieds à son chevet. L'osier du fauteuil glisse sous mes mains moites. Mon corps fatigué se libère; dehors, les éternels moustiques bourdonnent . . . [. . .] L'odeur de la décomposition et celle des fleurs sucrées du jardin montent ensemble de la terre, entrent avec l'air tiède, traversées parfois par une autre: eau croupie, goudron et fer. Au loin, la grêle des mah-jonggs, des cris chinois, des klaxons, des pétards; lorsque arrive, comme d'une mare, le vent du fleuve et que nous nous taisons, nous entendons un violon monocorde: quelque théâtre ambulant, ou quelque artisan qui joue, dormant à demi dans sa boutique close de planches. Une lumière rousse, fumée, monte derrière les arbres; on dirait que là-bas s'achève quelque immense fête foraine: la ville. (*LC*, p. 113.)

The décor in this passage plays its usual important rôle in determining the total effect. There are, as is often the case in Malraux's scenes of foreboding, "les éternels moustiques." There is the same sort of dramatic separation from the world that we find at the beginning of *La Condition humaine*, creating the effect of a sacred place. There is even the same mosquito netting, a veiled sanctuary to which a man might come to probe a mystery. In the "sanctuary" hut of *La Voie royale*, Perken's interrogation of Grabot will elicit a one-word response: "Rien"; Tchen's questioning will end with an act of murder; here the accumulation of significant detail suffices to convey what the probe is about and what the answer is, without the need for explicit comment. The hypersensitive narrating voice registers for us the odors of decomposition and stagnation, and the sound of noises. Then the noises become music, leading us to imagine either the presence of a nearby theater or the kind of artisan who is usually depicted elsewhere as plying a "lunar" trade, and the passage concludes with the analogy to a fair — precisely the phenomena of that kind of shadow activity Malraux employs to expose the underside of serious action. The entire scene thus projects, in a coolly controlled manner, the anxiety of the narrator and a general sense of the vanity of action in the face of Garine's symbolic defeat.

In one particularly lengthy hospital episode, in *L'Espoir*, the incongruous images take over the development of a troubling theme: Manuel has just begun to understand that war, ironically, means doing the impossible, only so that bits of iron might penetrate human flesh (*LE*, p. 509). On his way to Barca's hospital room he must pass through an enormous ward with a high ceiling: "et ces personnages en pyjamas dont les corps noués glissaient sur leurs béquilles dans la paix inquiète de l'hôpital, ces ombres vêtues de pansements comme d'un costume de mi-carême, tout cela semblait un royaume éternel de la blessure, établi là hors du temps et du monde." He is relieved to be able to pass on into a normal hospital room, and leave behind the bandaged "ghosts" floating through this Inquisition dungeon. When he arrives in Barca's room, the conversation soon turns to the question of what prompts ordinary men to take sides, knowing the price that must be paid — and the images intrude again: "Dans l'aquarium, des béquillards glissaient à travers le cadre de la porte ouverte, les uns derrière les autres." Leaving Barca, Manuel must pass through the way he entered; and the spectacle of men who have become vestiges of action, question marks at the end of a heroic affirmation for justice, now explodes into a massive display of surrealistic transformations before Manuel's bewildered eyes:

> A travers la porte ouverte de la grande salle, avec leurs profils d'éclopés des Grandes Compagnies, les blessés dont le bras était

plâtré marchaient, leur bras saucissonné de linge tenu loin du corps par l'attelle, comme des violonistes, violon au cou. Ceux-là étaient les plus troublants de tous: le bras plâtré a l'apparence d'un geste, et tous ces violonistes fantômes, portant en avant leurs bras immobilisés et arrondis, avançaient comme des statues qu'on eût poussées, dans le silence d'aquarium renforcé par le bourdonnement clandestin des mouches. (*LE*, p. 514.)

Ironic figures dramatize still another kind of confrontation, a spectacle in which man's questioning of other men is carried to the extreme limits of an Inquisition. All of the novels contain at least one interrogation scene in which a character is forcibly obliged to give an account of himself to another; and all but one such scene is given an absurd cast through reference to incongruous imagery. The exception occurs in *La Voie royale*, where the dialogue between Claude Vannec and the director of the French Institute informs us explicitly of Claude's sense of frustration. This is the one novel in which the inquisitioner is the non-human universe; in all the others it is man himself. In *Les Conquérants* the scene has to do with a parody of conventional legal justice. Garine, brought to court for his aid in an abortion case, must stand trial: "Pendant toute la durée du procès, il eut l'impression d'un spectacle irréel; non d'un rêve, mais d'une comédie étrange, un peu ignoble et tout à fait lunaire. Seul, le théâtre peut donner, autant que la cour d'assises, une impression de convention" (*LC*, p. 45). This experience will both expose him to the intense humiliation Malraux associates with imprisonment and initiate in him the misanthropy that will endure, paradoxically, at the very moment he is heading a revolution ostensibly in the name of the people.

During König's interrogation of Kyo, the latter accepts the offer of a slice of bread: "Kyo resta debout (il n'y avait pas de siège) devant le bureau, mordant son pain comme un enfant. Après l'abjection de la prison, tout était pour lui d'une légèreté irréelle" (*CH*, p. 393). König begins his bluff: he stages a series of telephone calls which are supposed to frighten Kyo into revealing information. Kyo finally understands the trick: "Il pensait que l'appel était une pire mise en scène" (*CH*, p. 394). The fundamental characteristics of this sort of scene, then, are a focus on innocence, the fall into a dreamlike state, and a cheap theatrical staging on the part of inquisitioners who none the less take themselves very seriously. But it is no less interesting to note that the questioning *does* oblige the character to formulate an answer, satisfactory both to himself and to the adversary, as to why he is involved in his action. Given the extreme difficulty of the task — the accused character may have to lie to appease his judges, and in any case may not be entirely sure he can reconcile idea and action even for himself — the event becomes as a particularly painful experience in which a sense of futility is joined to that of humiliation.

Le Temps du mépris opens with an interrogation scene staged by Nazi inquisitioners. As Kassner awaits his turn he must witness the humiliating grilling of another Communist captive: "Kassner se sentait à la place du communiste, à la fois spectateur et acteur douloureux, et perdait sa lucidité" (*TM*, p. 21). The notion that he must himself conceal his identity, and is thus forced to play an odious role wherein he must become "inauthentic" in order to save his skin, fills him with intense uneasiness. Malraux even has Kassner go through the patently melodramatic act of swallowing a secret paper — and Kassner recalls with a heightened sense of the grotesque "l'odeur de carton des masques du carnaval" (*TM*, p. 26).

A similarly painful spectacle occurs in *Les Noyers de l'Altenburg*, where Vincent Berger is called in to record the interrogation of a captured Russian woman suspected of spying. There is a particularly well developed sense of the incongruous here. Again, images of innocent domesticity intrude to intimate the absurd: "On l'avait dépouillée de ses vêtements pour la fouiller et on lui avait donné une blouse noire comme les tabliers des écolières" (*NA*, p. 161); "Elle le regardait avec une intensité inquiète: c'était un géant au nez retroussé et aux petits yeux brillants, une assez sympathique bobine de Pinocchio. Frottant toujours ses mains contre son sarreau noir avec un geste de cuisinière devant ses maîtres" (*NA*, p. 163). She plays her womanly powers of seduction against the interrogator, Captain Wurtz; he informs her that she may very well be shot, and her shocked reaction ("On ne fusille pas les femmes!") reminds us of the effect of a domestic image cited earlier: one might accept the execution of men, but not of women. The determining factor for making her talk is the introduction into the room of a young boy — and the narrator suddenly wonders why it had never occurred to him that women spies might have children. The whole scene is, of course, a staged affair, and there are the usual allusions to the theatrical: "Son 'de grâce' avait quelque chose de théâtral, que marquait davantage encore l'accent russe. Chacun jouait un rôle, d'ailleurs" (*NA*, p. 162). The woman senses the presence of the boy: "comme si ce bruit eût atteint, non pas le personnage qu'elle s'efforçait d'être, mais le personnage terrifié qu'elle cachait, elle se retourna d'un coup" (*NA*, p. 165).

Vincent reacts to this ordeal with an overwhelming sense of shock and shame; his muscles tighten; he feels as though he cannot continue taking his notes. The end result: the woman will be executed, and Vincent will ask for, and receive permission to leave the secret service. But not before he receives a lesson from Wurtz: "De tels actes, dont vous avez peur, avait dit le capitaine, sauvent la vie de milliers de nos soldats" (*NA*, p. 167). Vincent reflects that his previous action had been of a political nature, "pas policière," and thereby voices one of the recurring stumbling-blocks we find in Malraux, the unresolved dilemma of the intellectual and moralist reflecting upon the nature of action, the *conquérant* who fears that the outcome of his action will endanger the justifications which led him to become active in the first place. Wurtz's estimate is, of course, correct, but by itself too simple. The feeling we get is that while "policing" may be a necessary activity, it must be carried out without letting oneself fall into the role of the policeman. This point is well illustrated in *Les Conquérants*. The official inquisitioner is Nicolaïeff, depicted as something of a sadist. But in an essential interrogation case, where thousands of lives are indeed at stake, Nicolaïeff's methods are shown to be not only odious but incompetent as well, and it is Garine's snap decision to shoot a man in cold blood that saves the situation (cf. *LC*, pp. 154–158).

In *L'Espoir* the tables are completely turned; it is an unmistakable "enemy," a captured Italian Fascist pilot, who must be interrogated by a thoroughly likeable protagonist, Scali, chosen for the task because he speaks Italian. Scali awaits the ordeal uneasily. Malraux disarms the scene to a considerable extent by applying irony to the interrogator himself. The prisoner is somewhat taken aback by this man: "Ce qui l'étonnait était peut-être Scali lui-même: cet air de comique américain, du moins à son visage à la bouche épaisse, mais aux traits réguliers malgré les lunettes d'écaille, qu'à ces jambes trop courtes pour son buste, qui le faisaient marcher comme Charlot" (*LE*, p. 549). Scali immediately separates himself from his role: "Un instant, dit Scali en italien. Je ne suis pas un policier. Je suis aviateur volontaire" (*LE*, p. 549). He does not understand a detail about Italian planes: "Que les policiers se débrouillent!" (*LE*, p. 550). Among the personal effects of the prisoner Scali finds a photographed detail of a fresco by Piero della

Francesca, and he reflects that, were it not for their political differences, this man might well have been his student. And so, when the Fascist shouts that he will be unjustly executed, Scali replies: "Vous ne serez pas fusillé du tout, dit-il, retrouvant soudain le ton du professeur qui tance son élève" (*LE*, p. 551).

The scene has no images of the theatrical; Scali consciously refuses to play the role of the interrogator, although subconsciously he comes close to being enticed by it: "Scali éprouvait avec violence la supériorité que donne sur celui qui ment la connaissance de son mensonge" (*LE*, p. 550). But as in the other interrogation scenes there are present the kinds of images that intrude ironically upon a serious confrontation, in this case calling into question the validity of the whole notion of who the enemy is supposed to be. And although there is no sense of shame here, we do find the expression of a shock at the end of the episode, this time applied to the interrogator as he identifies himself with the other and wonders how he would have been treated by the Fascists if *he* were the one being interrogated. Behind the prisoner, on a table, lies a great pile of assorted silver objects seized by the anti-Fascist forces; and buried beneath this "bric-à-brac tragique," these "trésors d'Aladin," a clock begins to strike.

> Ces pendules, — remontées pour combien de temps? — qui, au milieu de cet entretien, si loin de ceux qui les avaient possédées, sonnaient une heure quelconque, donnaient à Scali une telle impression d'indifférence et d'éternité; tout ce qu'il disait, tout ce qu'il pouvait dire lui sembla si vain qu'il n'eut plus envie que de se taire. Cet homme et lui avaient choisi. (*LE*, p. 553.)

Once again, a confrontation by interrogation is depicted as a painful ordeal of humiliation and futility, in which the images dramatize an intense feeling of unreality yet all the while oblige the character to justify his own action to himself.

Thus far we have considered the kinds of confrontations which work upon the state of a character's mind. There are numerous instances as well of situations in which a human *act* is directly affected. All of Malraux's novels convey the general notion of a struggle between a given reality and man's capacity to influence or alter that reality. At the level of immediate confrontation this notion is frequently communicated in terms of non-human phenomena which seem to become animated forces, impenetrable mysteries hostile to man's desire to impose himself.

In one such pattern, phenomena seem to actively refuse being influenced by men's action. The *Shan-Tung*, for example, a steamer bearing the arms that Katow's party must steal for their own cause, seems to play a deliberate game of evading the approach of the insurgents' boat: "Le courant, puissant à cette heure, la prenait par le travers; le vapeur très haut maintenant (ils étaient au pied) semblait partir à toute vitesse dans la nuit comme un vaisseau fantôme" (*CH*, p. 232). Here resistance lasts but a few moments before the men accomplish what they set out to do. But there are instances of prolonged resistance as well. In *L'Espoir*, Attignies, in a state of semi-shock as a result of his plane crash, will swim, walk and ride through several pages of frustrating obstacles before attaining his desired goal. These pages are filled with incongruous figures that intrude as though to hide victory behind a veil of deceptive illusions: men seem to be playing bugles when they are actually eating, peasants wear "Mexican" blankets, the passage through a tunnel becomes a fall into a strange dream world of floating in water, a visit to a farmhouse turns up the puzzling décor of "faïences mauresques et les fausses fresques romantiques à perroquets," and even a murder occurs from which the assassin returns "comme s'il fût sorti d'une coulisse, le sabre rouge à la main" (*LE*, pp. 795–800). And as though a crash landing were not a fate ironic enough for a pilot, the long awaited goal of action here is nothing more than safe arrival at a hospital, ultimately a defensive position where the men can recover from the insistent blows of misfortune. Once again we must witness a man contemplating with disbelief the defeat of man: "L'immobile lourdeur de l'électricité donnait à toute la salle un aspect irréel, dont la grande unité blanche eût été celle d'un rêve si les taches de sang et quelques corps n'eussent sauvagement imposé la présence de la vie [. . .] la salle s'emplissait de la fraternité des naufragés" (*LE*, p. 800).

In numerous instances the intrusion of an incongruous figure seems to question the tactics that men apply against a given reality. It is the image of the theatrical that most consistently serves this purpose, but there are others as well, helping to convey the two related attributes Malraux associates with a "romantic" attitude: a glamorous facade and a lack of discipline, both of them inadequate tools with which to confront the aggressive encroachment of reality. We have already seen a number of examples from *L'Espoir* which suggest strongly that a victory achieved through such a stance is a mere illusion. The most impressive instance is likely to be the episode in Toledo which terminates with the apparent victory of the anti-Fascist forces. What the journalist Shade senses for us sets up the two poles of contrast: on the one hand, an "irréalité mystérieuse," with recollections of an Indian décor including "les palais grenat envahis par les cocotiers," peacocks and monkeys that listen to the radio, and visions of a lunar landscape; on the other, the smells of burning and of rotting cadavers. The area around the Alcazar will turn into sheer décor, illuminated by theater projectors; an anarchist appears wearing a Mexican hat, the attendant crowds turn into Sunday strollers; and finally Hernandez will make his romantic gesture confirming a false peace. Shortly, Toledo will fall to the Fascists, and Hernandez will have fulfilled what Garcia calls his "Apocalypse personnelle": "ce qu'il y a de plus dangereux dans ces demi-chrétiens, c'est le goût de leur souffrance:ils sont prêts aux pires erreurs, pourvu qu'il les paient de leur vie" (*LE*, p. 609).

Hernandez thus shares at least one major trait with the terrorist heroes, Hong and Tchen, and with a number of minor personages who fall into the general category of "romantic" men. What they do can be called action, but it is badly conceived action, ineffective against the hard core of reality and ultimately destructive to the self. This helps explain why several of the major protagonists so strenuously reject the notion that they are identical with their legendary biographies — that is, in the sense that they are nothing more than the sum of their past romantic actions. Claude Vannec, for example, sees in Perken "cet homme indifférent au plaisir de jouer sa biographie, détaché du besoin d'admirer ses actes" (*VR*, p. 24). One of the implications is that an over-awareness of one's own legend is an enticement to the cultivation of the self, an invitation for playing one's own theatrical role, thus thwarting effective action. Perken compares his kind of action in Siam with that of his romantic predecessor thus: "J'ai tenté sérieusement ce que Mayrena a voulu tenter en se croyant sur la scène de vos théâtres. Etre roi est idiot; ce qui compte, c'est de faire un royaume. Je n'ai pas joué l'imbécile avec un sabre; à peine me suis-je servi de mon fusil" (*VR*, p. 86).

If the scenes of interrogation, considered above, seem so painful, it is in part due to the fact that Malraux's man resents having to give an account of himself in terms of his legend, as though that were all he were. When Walter Berger tells Vincent, plagued by men eager to read into his present his past actions, that man is

69

nothing but a miserable little pile of secrets, Vincent will retort angrily: "L'homme est ce qu'il fait!" (*NA*, p. 90) — "ce qu'il *fait*," and not "ce qu'il *a fait*." One can hardly say that Malraux's heroes are not "glamorous" — Malraux exploits all manner of dramatic ploys to make them eminently romantic before our very eyes. But there is a clear distinction to be made between the stylistic technique of dramatizing significant experiences, and a weakness in man that entices him to apply a fossilized image of himself against an ever-changing reality that must be confronted with fresh, well-disciplined tactics. The truly valid hero for Malraux can only be the eternal "conquérant," whose awareness of his own mythic aura is forever ironic.

But if romantic tactics are ineffective against reality, the anguishing fact remains that there is no proof whatsoever that serious tactics can secure a victory either, or at least not a victory in the sense of a satisfactory fulfillment of an entire program of action which can then be enjoyed by the victor. In the very midst of a serious enterprise, as we have seen in innumerable instances, the incongruous image can relate an anxious feeling of the futility of action, and actually forebode an eventual defeat. That is what happens, for example, when Jaime goes on his last bombing mission or when Kyo reaches Hankow to receive Vologuine's news. The unreal décor that dominates this latter episode, however, is a relatively minor clue compared to the overwhelming presence of Clappique. By the time Clappique comes out of the gambling room of the *Black Cat* night club, the fate of Kyo and the revolution have been determined, and the passage that follows merely recapitulates what is already well understood. Clappique steps out into the night air of Shanghai and we experience with him one of the novel's most prolonged transformations of reality into a dream décor; and as in the Toledo episode of *L'Espoir*, the two poles are again an eery lunar landscape and the overpowering odor of death transported by the wind (*CH*, p. 361–362).

Malraux seems to structure resistance into the very core of action as though to hold off single victories, and through a cumulative effect, within each novel and from one novel to the next, effectively puts into doubt whether a final victory is even possible. Geoffrey Hartman's assessment of the "obstacle-course" type of plot (*cf. p.* 63) seems to hold for all the novels, if we include under the general notion of "obstacles," in addition to that patent manipulation of plot by which hard-earned victories are swiftly followed by the appearance of fresh dragons, such varying devices as presages of doom, intimations of the absurdity of action, the transformations of real scenes into dream décor, the unexpected reversal of events — in short, all the effects achieved through the presence of incongruous imagery.

Conclusion

From the manner in which Malraux dramatizes perception we have seen how Malraux's characters are prone to undergo sharp pangs of anxiety when they confront certain of the "shapes" reality is wont to take. We have also seen how this anxiety is associated with the formulation of hasty, confused or illusory assessments of a situation. Paradoxically, these assessments are not at all "incorrect"; the products of a peculiar complicity between the narrating voice and the characters' senses, they guide the character to seize significant intimations beneath a surface reality.

At the subjective level, the sense of anxious surprise conveyed by the figures we have considered reflects a strain; when the intimations reality offers of its true nature become more than the human mind is prepared to assimilate properly, lucidity seems to collapse and the perceiving character falls into a dazed, dreamlike state. But unlike Gisors' opium dream, which closes a veil over an unwanted reality to promise a "sauvage harmonie" (*CH*, p. 431), these images intrude in such a way as to oblige the character to gaze directly upon a mystery whose existence was previously unsuspected by him, and the discovery of which sets up anxious feelings of incongruity. It is difficult to speak of a truly "objective" level in connection with these figures. They play a determining influence upon the course of action; and yet, for the most part, because they are structured so subtly within the very texture of action the reader is more likely to sense their meaning rather than deduce it clearly.

Malraux's strong sense of drama can be called upon to explain, at least in part, why the outcome of a desired action is so often suspended, frustrated or even definitively prevented; victory is naturally all the more impressive the more we see the heroes struggle to attain it. But it is the notion of victory itself, as we have seen, that suggests another reason beyond the dramatic. To understand this, it will be useful to consider for a moment the outlook of the narrating voice.

Regardless of the techniques of perspective in each of the novels, the narrating voice, even where it coincides with a first-person narrator, consistently guides the eye of the character, and the reader, to behold the same kinds of jolting predicaments. This narrating voice reveals a multi-faceted personality. It is the voice of someone who has understood that a man, having once experienced the intoxicating effects of direct action, can never relinquish his power to influence events. It is the voice of an intellectual who has understood that the cost for action frequently entails a price men do not want to pay, but which they may have to pay. It is the voice of a moralist who is repelled by certain prices which men, vulnerable beings among other vulnerable beings, cannot bring themselves to pay without sacrificing conscience.

It is also the voice of an artist who must organize his fictional experience in a satisfactory manner. The one constant in all the novels, the unswerving need to act, must be balanced against all the factors in conflict with it. Given this conflict, the likelihood of a definitive victory is no more visible than it is in those baroque tragicomedies whose endings are doors inviting outward onto still further action. The imagery we have considered points insistently to the author's view that lucidity is not hermetically impervious to an element of madness, or a sense of reality to a particle of dream; that there is no austere commitment to purpose without its fragment of comedy and human vulnerability; that there is no solidity that cannot be shaken by signs of ruin, and no solidarity uncontaminated by solitude; that there is no serious action that does not run into the ultimate danger of inviting the pose of the romantic or the role of the policeman; that there is no human consciousness oblivious to the eventuality of death. Given, in short, Malraux's notion of the human condition, there can be no such thing as a "definitive" victory; and the art of the novelist reflects faithfully, in the structuring of his fiction, what the activist, intellectual and moralist have understood to be true.

The vision of Malraux's characters comes remarkably close to being that of the innocent who repeatedly exposes himself to the anguishing dilemmas of life, who repeatedly encounters his own sense of bafflement. But does this not simply reflect a truth about the author himself and his notion of man? Six novels are sufficient evidence to indicate a fatal fascination for the predicaments against which the characters struggle, but also, surely, to disclose the eye of an innocent determined to affirm the essential nobility of man despite all. This nobility, implicit in the first three of the novels, becomes increasingly explicit in the latter three, as shock moves out of the realm of anxiety to express a profound sense of wonder about man, a wonder that is provoked precisely by man's ability to keep coming back to confront the universe with his questions. It is perhaps easy to forget that this sense of nobility is itself the product of a writer's dream about man, itself a myth, itself an illusion, given shape in a work of fiction; it is also easy to forget that the only victory that can be achieved in a work of fiction is an aesthetic one. The nobility of Malraux's man does not reside in his power to win victories on the battlefield, but in his capacity to lift the veil that conceals the absolute and behold its mysteries with an ever innocent eye. This is the spirit that infuses not only the action of the novels but also the creative impulse that led to their composition.

THE IMAGERY OF TROPISM IN THE NOVELS OF NATHALIE SARRAUTE

BY JOHN A. FLEMING

By using imagery suitable to the concept of tropism ("réaction automatique d'un être vivant attiré ou repoussé par une source d'énergie, réponse forcée et orientée par le facteur externe auquel il est spécifiquement sensible," Littré) and the movement of "conversation" and "sous-conversation," Mme Sarraute tries to reorganize and renew the novel. Even the most casual reader will be impressed by the fact that images are no mere decorative element in her work. Nor are they used simply for thematic or symbolic purposes. They have become a complex structural device which makes possible the elimination or diminution of traditional novelistic techniques in accordance with the general tenor of her critical writings.

The technical difficulties imposed by the content of her novels are formidable: to fix on paper what, by her own definition, cannot be fixed — a subterranean world of frenetic movement and pure emotion, psychological life at its most elementary level, at the very point of passing from virtual to real. Still by means of metaphor and analogy Nathalie Sarraute tries to suggest what cannot be stated precisely and to overcome, partially at least, the paradox she poses.

From a structural point of view further problems are created by her rejection of the traditional form of the novel and here too she seeks a solution in the use of imagery. The functions of plot, character, external description and the like are displaced by the analogical depiction of psychological states in formation. Form and content are thus inseparably linked through this single major technical device, and entirely dependent upon it. The basic psychological drives of man, Mme Sarraute seems to say, are similar to his basic physical drives and can therefore be presented through the extensive use of appropriate comparisons. Since the psychological organism responds to external stimuli in much the same way as the primitive biological organism, analogies which suggest tropistic movement will be central to her depiction of life. Preservation of the self, the need for food, attack and defense, these are the elementary physical drives; security-insecurity, solitude-contact, a need to communicate, these are the essential psychological impulses, to be concretized through a vast range of tropisms. As a result, Mme Sarraute's novels depict the oscillations of psychological existence through the imagery of tropism. The rhythms of conversation and sub-conversation imitate tropistic movement and give structural form to this concretization.

Mme Sarraute's first novel, *Tropismes*,[1] has an unusual and highly analogical form. The title of the book itself suggests her principal thematic materials in terms which continue to be used throughout succeeding works. The tropisms of which Nathalie Sarraute speaks metaphorically here are psychological movements at their most basic levels as they reveal themselves through the re-actions of her characters to the external stimuli of objects, people, and attitudes. "Il s'agit pour moi de saisir une matière psycho-logique qui n'est pas celle, immobile et comme figée dans le souvenir, que découpe, après coup, le scalpel de l'analyse, mais qui est en perpétuelle formation. Les mouvements intérieurs nombreux et rapides sont suivis comme par un appareil de prises de vues ciné-matographiques . . ."[2]

The twenty-four short sketches of this first "non-novel"[3] are tied together only by the concept of the tropism. In each brief scene anonymous *ils* and *elles* react to external stimuli of which the reader knows little or nothing. The stimulus itself is unimportant, or has disappeared, and we are left with the character's reaction to it, a re-action made concrete by means of analogy. This psychological cause-effect relationship is akin to tropistic movement. The basic psychological fact, like the basic biological fact, seems to be pre-servation of the self, a necessity which leads to conflict in the primal desire to survive.

While each sketch can be described as a "scene" (one depicts a grandfather and grandchild walking, another an old couple in a café, a third an English lady and her cook waiting for the moment to have afternoon tea), the physical circumstances remain minimal. The emphasis is always upon the emotional content of the scene, the continual fluctuations of commingling psychological movements which refuse to solidify and become fixed states. The banalities of a tearoom conversation, the most casual exchanges about literature, conceal emotional conflicts and insecurities which would seem to threaten the very existence of these anonymous beings.

Without the sustained use of metaphor and analogy the presentation of such a world of conflicts would be impossible, for there is no story, no identifiable physical "character" to precipitate narrative movement in *Tropismes*. Yet the intangible psychological impulses which are the matter of the novel must somehow be made concrete. The structural concept of the tropism which likens psychological response to biological response makes logical the extensive use of imagery which will suggest that likeness. The organization of tropistic imagery into conversation and sub-conversation in the later novels is a further development of this same idea. The movement from sub-conversation to conversation, and the variations upon this movement, will also be suggestive of the tropism. The frequent and highly metaphorical language of sub-conversation will be in marked contrast to the infrequent or banal images of conversation. An imagined quarrel between Martereau and his wife is depicted in exactly this way (*Martereau*, pp. 207–237); a conversation between Alain and Germaine Lemaire in *Le Planétarium* (pp. 294–310) appears in similar form; the conflicting opinions and emotions of the anonymous characters in *Les Fruits d'Or* (pp. 68–86) are also structured according to this concept.

The constant interaction between psychological movement and the *lieu commun* has another side to it as well. When the same scene is repeated as viewed by several of the characters (e.g. the confrontation between Aunt Berthe and her brother in *Le Planétarium*, pp. 250–281), their parallel psychological reactions touch only in the platitudes of conversation. These platitudes are the source of their inner agitation, but they are also symptomatic of man's inability to communicate in a meaningful way. Linguistic common denominators should lead to a coming together, yet the reactions of the characters are like so many parallel lines which lead them separate but similar ways. From an aesthetic point of view the coherence of a single scene described several times is preserved by these same platitudes. They are the narrative thread along which are strung the emotional tropisms of the changing voice.

The repetition of images within the mind of a single character has a somewhat different purpose, although such analogies may also be attached to conversation:

Cette rougeur, cette chaleur, ce sont les signes avant-coureurs, l'éclair qui précède le grondement du tonnerre, presque aussitôt, dans un fracas assourdissant, la foudre s'abat: *un homme de paille*: c'est cela.

Il reste cloué sur place, pétrifié, calciné: *un homme de paille*. Tout est clair: ce n'est plus la peine de chercher . . . Inutile, il n'y a rien à faire. . . . c'est là, ça brille comme les pépites d'or dans le sable, comme le diamant au milieu de sa gangue, dur et pur, impossible à rayer: *un homme de paille* . . .

Ils sont forts. Ils sont très forts. Ils ne font rien qu'à bon escient. On peut se fier à eux . . . *Un homme de paille* . . . ils ont découvert cela depuis longtemps, ils ont su dégager cela de tous les mélanges, de toutes les combinaisons les plus variées, un corps simple qui se combine à d'autres corps simples de cent façons différentes et forme cent corps composés, mais ils ont su l'isoler et ils lui ont donné un nom, ils ont étudié toutes ses propriétés . . . *un homme de paille* — c'est cela. Et je suis cela, moi, moi! *Son homme de paille.* Un nouvel éclair, le tonnerre, la foudre tombe, il brûle: *son homme de paille* . . . (*Martereau*, pp. 223–225.)

On the one hand sub-conversation threatens to destroy, at every moment, the form and seeming stability of conversation; on the other hand, perhaps ironically, the platitudes and banalities of social discourse at times penetrate the interior monologue and keep coming back as a spur to psychological distress. The interpenetration of the two word levels is complex and the continual shifting from one to the other is an essential aspect of our fluid, ever-changing nature. The nephew-narrator of *Martereau* imagines the effect of the phrase "homme de paille" upon Martereau who feels the narrator's uncle is taking advantage of his good will. It repeats itself over and over again in his mind, provoking at each moment of appearance a psychological reaction which takes the form of analogy. The worn out image of the "homme de paille" is the starting point for a series of reactions which are also conveyed by means of images.

Third person narration of action and event is displaced in this way by a new rhythm which coincides with the movement and progression of psychological impulses as they exist within the mind of the character. Characters remember or imagine something which has happened or is happening, and action appears in the form of reaction, concretized by means of analogy and metaphor. Like Beckett's tramps in *En attendant Godot* they seem to be marking time — nothing much actually occurs; life is a series of trivial concerns. The narrator of *Portrait* spends his time watching an old man and his daughter; the nephew in *Martereau* has little to occupy him physically and dwells upon his attempts to appreciate the true nature of Martereau; young Alain Guimiez of *Le Planétarium* is writing a thesis which seems to stretch on without end. The muscles of the body have atrophied, leaving the stage to the movements of the mind. Accordingly, words replace actions, since they are the logical carriers of our psychological movements. The psychological organism reaches out for the nourishment of social contact as the single-celled animal seeks its food in a physical sense.

Mme Sarraute uses three basic image patterns against this general background: recurrent images, the development of an initial image, and image sequences. Through their presence or absence the tropistic movements of the novels form and develop. When the narrator of *Portrait* imagines a money crisis between the old man and daughter there are fourteen images, some of them quite long, within the space of three and one half pages (pp. 183–187). The dramatic peaks of the novel coincide with these moments of emotional stress and are invariably expressed by such image concentrations.

The most important of the three patterns of analogy, because it is the most frequent, is that of the recurrent image. In fact, it can hardly be called a pattern since the recurrence of the major numerical groups is relatively even. In *Portrait*, for example, animal images are repeated throughout (about 73). Insect images are consistently present as well (about 55). With few exceptions these recurrent images are related to specific aspects of psychological life. They characterize situations often, as we have come to expect them to characterize people in the traditional novel. This new kind of characterization moves the novels from particularity to generality, from an intellectual differentiation of character and situation towards a more fluid and emotional apprehension of psychological life. The *struggle* of the old man and his daughter just mentioned is what is important, not the characters themselves, nor the external reason for the struggle — her request for six thousand francs. The confrontation of two characters with opposite desires will lead to images of attack or aggression which emphasize the impulse and emotion while weakening our awareness of the external situation which produces the emotion. This characterization of situations makes possible the elimination of the kind of coherent narrative in which events follow in logical order. Flashbacks in the form of a single happening seen by two or more characters have an imagistic cohesion if not a narrative sequential logic. The second half of *Martereau* presents a variety of interpretations of Martereau's actions after his purchase of the country house on behalf of the narrator's uncle. The narrator imagines Martereau's relationship with Mme Martereau, his uncle's attitude toward Martereau, his own attitude toward these three, the ambiguity of the motives and intentions of each. The purchase of the house and Martereau's subsequent actions become submerged in a flood of contradictory and vague speculations as to Martereau's real intent. Animal images, insect images, analogies of conflict, maintain a constant atmosphere of fear and pain in spite of the shifting point of view. At the same time this cohesion does not destroy the complexity and fluidity of the situation as seen from a variety of viewpoints, because it imposes no logical order upon it.

This sort of simultaneity is much more effective than that to be found in the works of Dos Passos for example, because our linear apprehension of the novel is less marked, while our appreciation of the complexity of the event remains less self-conscious. We slip from one point of view into another without much feeling of transition, and with little feeling of time. The reader is aware of a series of emotional confrontations, Martereau and his wife, the uncle and Martereau, the nephew and his uncle, depicted through the extensive use of affective analogies. There are no external intrusions into the nephew's enclosed imaginings. Dos Passos, on the contrary, tries to give an impression of simultaneity through the juxtaposition, often startling, of newspaper headlines perhaps, or newsreels, characters' reactions to these events, narration, and so forth. This technique is bound to seem more artificial because sequence is emphasized by the abrupt transitions from documentation to narration, the truncating effect of typographical changes and divisions. Mme Sarraute lessens our awareness of linear movement because the states of mind which she presents are tied together through the continuous use of certain images and lack obvious transitions.

In addition to the technique of repeating analogies of attack and defense, the natural world, and so forth throughout the novels, Mme Sarraute organizes many of these same images into other patterns which appear specifically at moments of psychological elaboration or emotional crisis. Like the rise and fall of biological activity which accompanies the relative state of physical equilibrium in lower forms of life, the density of analogical elements increases and decreases with the psychological tensions of her "characters."

The development of an initial comparison is one such pattern. Alain in *Le Planétarium* is engrossed in the contemplation of a

Renaissance statute of the Virgin in a shop window, unaware of the approach of an acquaintance who suddenly speaks to him.

> Alerte. Branle-bas. Pendant qu'il était là à parer Dieu sait quelles attaques imaginaires, à essayer d'éviter les embûches dressées par un adversaire inventé, l'ennemi, le vrai, le seul redoutable l'épiait . . . L'ennemi a fondu sur lui. (P. 284.)

In the following two pages there are eight further images of attack and enemy forces, separated by one short description and bits of conversation. These several pages are a good example of the way in which an image is often developed within the context of conversation and sub-conversation previously discussed. A dialogue takes place which is punctuated by the analogical presentation of the psychological movements which underlie the spoken words. The only portions of the novels which are relatively devoid of imagery are the passages of actual conversation, and even there images which have become clichés are fairly numerous.

Image sequences, the third pattern, are as frequent as are recurrent images. An initial experience evokes a series of analogies which describe and develop the nuances and changes inherent in the initial reaction of the character. When Alain and his father meet Germaine Lemaire in a bookstore, the encounter results in a sequence of comparisons which expresses Alain's feelings and those he imputes to his father. He is embarrassed by the necessity of making introductions:

> Et lui, honteux, affolé, lui, tiré et jeté là, devant eux, dans une pose ridicule, lui poussé sur la scène à coups de pieds . . . (P. 150.)
> Il est un insecte épinglé sur la plaque de liège, il est un cadavre étalé sur la table de dissection et son père, rajustant ses lunettes, se penche . . . (P. 151.)

Other images follow which develop such emotional aspects of the situation as Alain's confusion and shame. The changes in the sequence convey first of all the changing nature of the emotion, and secondly, the complexity and subtle variety of his embarrassment, but not in the analytical and often detached manner of the more traditional novel which uses imagery to clarify and develop a descriptive or narrative passage.

Balzac would have used these images to give the reader a better visual picture of the setting or the character, and this picture would have been used in turn to reveal the moral qualities of the person or the situation in question. Mme Sarraute uses images which are more affective and emotional than visual or explanatory, in an attempt to involve the reader as directly as possible. We react to the preceding passage emotionally rather than intellectually.

These final two patterns are themselves recurrent, creating through their presence and absence the quickening and slowing of psychological impulses. This distribution and arrangement displaces the narrative movement of the traditional novel through the creation of a new kind of psychological rhythm based upon tropistic reaction.

Since the concept of the tropism is basic to all the novels of Natalie Sarraute both thematically and as a structural metaphor, it is appropriate to find many images drawn from the natural world throughout her fiction. Reduced to its most essential condition, life for any organism consists of its struggle to survive, in a sometimes hostile environment, and the satisfaction of certain needs. The organism's tropistic reactions reflect the effect of external forces upon it, and the continually changing set of circumstances in which it exists. Mme Sarraute uses tropistic movement to suggest the psychological reactions of man; the basic unit of psychological life in her view corresponds to the basic unit of biological life — conflict. She proceeds from this assumption to draw upon the lower animal forms, instinctive and immediate in their reactions to external stimuli, for analogies which will convey this same condition as it exists within man, at the core of his emotional, or more widely, psychological existence.

"Animal" imagery is, therefore, frequent and varied, ranging from the most elemental and alien of life forms to the most common and everyday. Such images constitute the largest single group of analogies (139 in *Portrait d'un Inconnu* alone), and linked as they are to the concept of the tropism, occupy a central position in the novels. Even when they appear as little more than traditional comparisons their total numbers must be taken into account.

Animals, birds, crustaceans, insects, marine animals, and occasionally less well defined living creatures, all appear repeatedly throughout the novels in order to depict metaphorically or analogically the patterns of psychological attack and defense, and the concomitant emotional states of mind. They reveal the tropistic attitudes of the organism as it struggles to preserve its primitive and savage existence within a hostile environment. The narrator of

81

Martereau, for example, sensing a continual conflict between those around him and himself, expresses this feeling of conflict, as well as his own emotional reactions,through his particular use of imagery. Returning one day from the country he imagines his uncle's hostility toward his aunt and himself:

> Il va nous prendre haineusement par le cou, tourner nos têtes et nous forcer sadiquement à regarder — les poils de nos échines se hérissent de répulsion à cette seule pensée . . . (P. 118.)

The range of animals and the variety of situations in which they appear is extensive: dogs (*Tropismes*, p. 41), pigs (*Martereau*, p. 28), wolves (*Le Planétarium*, pp. 144–145), hyenas (*Portrait*, p. 32), cats (*Tropismes*, p. 69), bulls (*Portrait*, p. 67), mice (*Portrait*, p. 51), monkeys (*Le Planétarium*, p. 96), does (*Le Planétarium*, p. 267), a bear (*Le Planétarium*, pp. 304–305), a tiger (*Martereau*, p. 68), an elephant (*Martereau*, pp. 149–150), a mole (*Le Planétarium*, p. 45), foxes (*Portrait*, p. 66), horses (*Portrait*, p. 97), chickens (*Martereau*, p. 28), ducks (*Portrait*, p. 24), sparrows (*Martereau*, p. 28), magpies (*Martereau*, p. 27), doves (*Le Planétarium*, p. 87), ostriches (*Le Planétarium*, p. 38), vultures (*Le Planétarium*, p. 140), snakes (*Portrait*, p. 135), a toad (*Portrait*, p. 98), spiders (*Portrait*, p. 151), flies (*Martereau*, p. 257), lice (*Le Planétarium*, p. 125), a scorpion (*Les Fruits d'Or*, p. 44), bloodsuckers (*Martereau*, p. 27), ants (*Le Planétarium*, p. 305), dung-beetles (*Portrait*, p. 184), bees (*Martereau*, p. 148), crabs (*Martereau*, p. 289), and snails (*Portrait*, p. 39), to mention the most prominent, as well as a number of unspecified beasts (*Portrait*, p. 38), and the occasional monster (*Martereau*, p. 170).

The images themselves either mention the animal specifically, or simply express animal-like actions or characteristics (as for example in the use of such words as *flairer* and *dénicher* without actual mention of the animal). Most often these images are concerned with hunting or being hunted, being watched, trapped, attacked, and so forth. The parallel in *Martereau* between the pack of dogs in search of prey and the narrator's feeling of being spied upon is a simple illustration of the way in which images depict emotional and psychological states: "Comme ils tournent autour de vous avec précaution, comme ils flairent" (p. 8). The image suggests both the situation in which the character finds himself and the emotion inherent in it, the aggression of the hunters and the fear of the hunted.

Later in the novel when his aunt reproaches his uncle for certain things said to their friend Martereau, the narrator describes her remarks in animal terms: "Elle frétille toujours, l'échine basse, mais avance tout de même un peu plus . . ." (p. 131). A word or phrase is commonly used in this way to suggest an animal, without actually depicting or defining the animal itself. This technique serves to emphasize the emotion betrayed by an attitude, an action, a reaction, and to minimize pictorial detail which might tend to detract from the strength of the emotional portrayal. The animal attitude reveals the emotional state (real or imagined) of a human being. The suggestion is implicit that man's reactions upon an elemental level are the same as those of animals.

In the early novels many of the images are in the form of simple similes or substitutions such as this one, but later, in *Le Planétarium* and *Les Fruits d'Or*, the image usually takes the form of a longer analogy in which a situation is used to convey the emotional attitudes in question. This corresponds to the movement already noted, away from the external supports of plot, character, and setting. The actual structure of the images as simile, metaphor, or analogy, does not seem to be organized into a coherently significant pattern in relation to the other aspects of the novels, however.

Animal images are tied together not only by source and theme, but by language as well. Certain words recur constantly (*frétiller, flairer, l'échine basse*) thus creating an overall ambiance which is vital to the portrayal of psychological states in formation.

This atmosphere springs from the frequency of animal images, from the repetition within them of certain animal characteristics such as self-protection or aggression, and finally from their affective appeal to the reader's experience. The relatively narrow angle between tenor (psychological aggressiveness for example), and the vehicle (a pack of dogs in search of prey), makes possible an easy identification of the two terms of the comparison. The emotion involved is familiar and accessible to the reader.

More precise animal images are often less effective because their precision makes them less suggestive. Thus when Alain, upon his return from his first visit to Germaine Lemaire, describes himself as feeling "comme le renard poursuivi par les chasseurs" (p. 112), the image has little force partially because of its banality, but also because the specific naming of the animal seems to emphasize it rather than the emotion. Nevertheless simple animal similes of this kind, by their frequency, reinforce the other more unusual and un-expected comparisons from the world of nature.

More important are the images in which the emotion itself is "animalized" and the human intermediary element omitted. Hunting images and their opposite, images of being trapped or spied upon, are frequently illustrative of this characteristic. Perhaps the most vivid of these is the one in which the narrator of *Portrait d'un Inconnu* describes an encounter with the old man who is the object of his constant surveillance:

> Il sent vaguement avec son flair subtil quelque chose en moi, une petite bête apeurée tout au fond de moi qui tremble et se blottit. (Pp. 37–38.)

Occasionally animal images have a comic or satirical tone. Something as insignificant as the passing of a salad during a meal, or a careless "no thank you," can upset a huge emotional structure built around some casual remark such as "I like grated carrots." Alain in *Le Planétarium* has expressed his liking for grated carrots to his mother-in-law, but then refuses the salad she offers:

> Alain m'a dit qu'il aimait les carrottes râpées. Elle est à l'affût. Toujours prête à bondir. Elle a sauté là-dessus, elle tient cela entre ses dents serrées. Elle l'a accroché. Elle le tire . . . Le ravier en main, elle le fixe d'un œil luisant. (P. 121.)

Many of the animal images mention the eyes (*Martereau*, pp. 75–76, *Le Planétarium*, p. 140) or the sense of smell (*Portrait*, pp. 184–185, *Le Planétarium*, p. 206), both of which are essential to most animals in the search for food. The eyes in man perform a similar function in seeking out the emotions of others; they are the means by which psychological food is obtained. In much the same way the sense of smell in animals might be likened to man's intuition. We become aware of someone else's attitudes as a dog, perhaps because of a subtle chemical change, senses its master's moods. This explains, in part at least, the frequency of eye and odor metaphors and analogies, which are by no means limited to the animal images, but often occur independently.

A specialized sub-group of analogies concerns food and the alimentary requirements of the living organism even more specifically. Although the purely physical drive to survive is complicated in the human animal by impulses to psychological and social survival, the basic similarities between man and the lower forms of life are undeniable, and the retention of physical animal imagery to depict analogous psychological conditions is apt. Alimentary imagery plays a correspondingly important role. Images of this sort may operate to reveal either positive or negative psychological states — positive where the animal satisfies its needs or achieves some sort of balance, negative where it becomes the victim of some other animal or situation.

Words, phrases, conversations, provide nourishment for the psychological processes — as the narrator of *Martereau* puts it, "un os à ronger pour tromper notre faim, un hochet à mordiller pour calmer notre sourde irritation, notre démangeaison" (p. 74). At other times one character becomes food for another directly. The "vous" which the uncle directs at the narrator and his own family is like a spit upon which they are all impaled like suckling pigs (p. 28). The image of being bitten or gnawed upon is also used this way; the aggressions and defenses of the characters feed upon one another, upon words, innuendos, and gestures, for survival.

In addition to the images, already mentioned, which portray psychological conflict, the movement of attack and defense, being hunted or hunting, are those used to convey a feeling of being held in check or released, as with a pack of dogs. One can, in telling a story or anecdote, lead a number of listeners like a "meute de chiens en laisse" (*Le Planétarium*, p. 46). More usual is the image of the animal unleashed. When Alain speaks to Germaine Lemaire of her tyrannical power over her followers, the danger of his direct "attack" upon her arouses in him ambiguous emotions and desires:

> Tous ses chiens de garde lâchés flairent quelque chose. La tyrannie? la lâcheté? (P. 159.)

Once again an emotional state has been "animalized." When she counterattacks, accusing him of having practised a little psychology on her account, he reacts violently:

> La morsure le déchire, il fuit, hurlant de douleur, toute la meute est sur lui . . . — Non, maîtresse, non, pitié . . . daignez siffler vos chiens . . . (P. 160.)

In *Martereau* the narrator imagines Martereau's wife brutally calling him back from his youthful enthusiasms ("la fougue d'un jeune chien lâché dans la prairie . . ." p. 212) to the hard realities of life: death, sickness, and old age.

A further use of the animal image is to present this same psychological need in man through animal needs for shelter or protection. The nest image sometimes depicts this feeling, and corresponds to the shell of the crustacean so often employed in the same way, particularly in *Portrait d'un Inconnu*. In *Le Planétarium* the nest image is used by almost all of the characters (Alain, Gisèle, Aunt Berthe, Alain's father Pierre), a technique which tends to minimize the shifting point of view where the same external events are seen through several minds which place different interpretations upon what has happened. The traditional character who has his own mode of thought is thus weakened. He becomes a center of impression rather than a guiding intelligence, and although the reader is given a series of camera angles which conveys different impressions of external events and objects according to the position of the character, the common theme or emotion which underlies these various positions is maintained. Aunt Berthe has found just the right kind of velvet curtain for her apartment:

> et elle l'a rapporté ici, dans son petit nid, c'est à elle maintenant, cela lui appartient, elle s'y caresse, s'y blottit . . . (P. 8.)

Gisèle imagines the furnishing of her apartment, "la construction de leur nid" (p. 74), and later thinks of it again as a "petit nid" (p. 78). Her husband Alain also speaks of the efforts of his wife and his mother-in-law to build "un petit nid comfortable" (p. 85).

The image is a cliché to begin with, what Mme Sarraute thinks of as a worn out linguistic point of contact with others, but it is expressive too of one of the essential aspects of existence: the universal desire for security. Such an image has a double significance. It is related to the authentic, and yet takes the form of the inauthentic. This, in fact, is the nature of most conversation.

The basic element in all of these images dealing with being trapped, watched, restrained, unleashed, protected, and so forth, is conflict, and within the context of conflict, movement as the organism struggles for survival with some external power. The tropistic action of the psychological organism reflects a social context, as the similar action of the animal responds to a physical need or situation. Particular situations and animal characteristics are used, as well as simple animal comparisons, to concretize these psychological movements which they resemble so closely.

Bird images, although less frequent than animal images, are usually used in much the same way. There is, however, a more satirical tone to many of them, and some have a tendency to be more descriptive of situations and characters, perhaps because of this tone. Although a few specific birds (sparrows, doves, magpies, vultures) appear occasionally, bird images more often emphasize the actions or appearance of some vague bird which gathers bits for a nest (*Portrait*, p. 42), or spreads its feathers in the sun (*Le Planétarium*, p. 28). The bird so presented is frequently either a bird of prey, or one of the barnyard variety.

Bird imagery is used to describe women more often than men. Its ironic humorous undertone seems to be directed particularly against their "triviality of mind" and the forms this triviality takes. One of these is woman's acquisitive nature as seen by Mme Sarraute. When Gisèle proposes to Alain's father that he speak to Aunt Berthe about the apartment, she feels her own avid expression become fixed beneath his gaze:

> Une expression rusée, vorace apparaît, elle le sent, sur ses propres traits, dans ses yeux, elle a l'œil fixe d'un oiseau de proie, d'un petit vautour toutes ses serres tendues . . . (P. 140.)

One amusing exception to the usual bird-woman comparison likens a man who has been caught out in a conversational gaffe to an easily trapped ostrich:

> pareils à des autruches, la tête cachée dans leurs plumes et leur derrière pointant en l'air . . . (*Le Planétarium*, p. 237.)

Other bird images convey a feeling of naïveté, gullibility, or help-lessness; occasionally, as in the first example, they are used in the sense of 'bird of prey." It is the weakness, the frivolity, or the avidity of birds of which the reader is made aware, never the beauty. This leads to speculation as to the significance of the bird images in the overall structure of the novels. They seem more important in their satirical and social implications than as the concretization of form-less psychological states. This tendency is reinforced by their more externally descriptive nature which is often concerned with appear-ances rather than the subterranean world of psychological attitudes.

Some comment is also called for by the ironic affectionate dim-inutives which repeatedly accompany these images. Nest images mentioned earlier with reference to animals are frequent, as might be expected, in the bird analogies. The adjective "petit," which occurs so often in this context, is not used to describe physical size, but rather to give an impression of innocence, helplessness, fragility, and naïveté, to reinforce, in other words, the general affective content of the image. The danger from the outside world contrasts with this innocence. The image of the narrator, his aunt, and her daughter, who are like frightened sparrows before the uncle (*Martereau*, p. 28), is essentially the same image as the "tendres petits cochons de lait" on the same page. The affective quality of the adjective describes a particular emotional situation.

A further parallel could be drawn between certain crustacean or insect images and some of the nest images. In both cases the organism's need for shelter or security is likened to the same human need. A propos of old maids the narrator in *Portrait d'un Inconnu* describes the way in which they accumulate experience and assurance as a bird accumulates materials for a nest:

> elles avaient réussi à attraper par-ci par-là dans tout ce qu'elles trouvaient autour d'elles, des bribes, des brindilles qu'elles avaient amalgamées pour se construire un petit nid douillet à l'intérieur duquel elles se tenaient bien protégées, gardées de toutes parts, bien à l'abri. (P. 43.)

In this sense the nest image presents one of Mme Sarraute's major thematic preoccupations; the inauthenticity of the world of social convention and cliché which we construct in our search for security.

As with the animal images there is the concretization of a feeling which cannot be shown except through some situation or act which may stand for that feeling, but the bird images remain on the whole satirical or comic, and perhaps for that reason more descriptive. The world of subterranean conflict, after all, admits of little that is comic. Nor can satire exist at so primitive a level, and without a social context.

Insect and crustacean analogies also play an important part in the hierarchy of biological images. They are particularly suited to the concept of tropistic movement, representative as they are of very low forms of life engaged in an elemental struggle for survival. Disassociated from human emotions, mechanical often in their movements, alien in their form to most species of animal life, they arouse in the reader an immediate revulsion. For Mme Sarraute they have another purpose as well. They represent an entirely instinctive struggle for survival, automatic, non-emotional, uncolored by human emotions as might be a struggle between animals. Spiders, ants, dung-beetles, bees, lice, snails, crabs, and other unspecified creatures are all to be found in her fiction.

One of the more banal, yet still striking, of these insect images, because of the emotional context in which it appears, is that of the spider waiting in his web for the fly. It is used to describe the old man waiting at the table in his room for the arrival of his daughter or some of her supporters: "comme une grosse araignée immobile dans sa toile" (*Portrait*, p. 116). The image recurs in similar contexts, always to describe the mortal conflict imagined by the narrator to exist between father and daughter. Its second aspect, the universe which the old man has woven for himself presents a second psychological characteristic: the need to trap another, revulsion and at the same time, a desire for even negative contact. In another way it is like certain of the images which deal with crustaceans. The hard shell of the snail is not a trap however, but a defense against the world, a shelter from attack, the limits of a universe one constructs for self-preservation. In a sense the same may be said of the old man's "web." Both convey the opposition between the world of appearances which we construct, and reconstruct continually, in our search for security, and the continually changing and insecure nature of our psychological existence:

je vois la scène entre eux, comme ils s'affrontent, comme ils luttent, front contre front, engoncés dans leurs carapaces . . . (P. 48.)

Variations and repetitions of this image are numerous. They often occur in loose clusters with others of the same general nature. The entire page surrounding this last example is a complex insect-crustacean analogy describing the struggle between father and daughter as imagined by the narrator of *Portrait*.

The exoskeleton of the snail, or some other less well specified crustacean, represents the armor, the protective casing which man presents to the outer world. Like the snail he may be drawn from his shell for a moment, lulled into a false sense of security, but at the first sign of danger he retreats to do battle with his enemy from within.

This is not the only analogy employed to describe the protective or defensive attitudes of the human being. There is a similar use of the armor image in the description of the cocoon of an insect as an impermeable protection for the soft, defenseless larva which lies inside. In this case the materials for the cocoon are drawn from the outside world — a word, a gesture, anything which will satisfy or protect the organism:

C'était extraordinaire de voir comme elles savaient saisir dans tout ce qui passait à leur portée exactement ce qu'il fallait pour se tisser ce cocon . . . (*Portrait*, p. 43.)

This is, in fact, what we seek in "conversation" as opposed to "sub-conversation," the reassuring familiarity of cliché and convention, where the generality of readily recognized and accepted attitudes creates a momentary illusion of security. It is for this reason that the conversations of Mme Sarraute's novels are filled with cliché, the banality of overused words, and trite exhausted images. The tension created by the contrast between platitude and the emotional violence of the images which depict man's submerged psychological life is essential to the revelation of that life.

Few of the insect images are isolated. Most are repeated or developed in some way, extended into a further concretization of the basic attack-defense pattern of life. One of the best of these manages to suggest a whole way of life and an entire mentality in the space of a few lines. The narrator of *Portrait* describes, in a mixture of images, unoccupied old ladies who lurk behind doors, or in ballrooms, indulging their ritual thirst for information and security:

les goules tapissées de ventouses qui attendent derrière les portes, les catapultes, les poussahs, les vierges à l'ancienne mode, affalées sur les banquettes des salles de bals, les grand-mères aux lèvres pincées qui reboutonnent leurs gants avant de sonner, les larves qui agglutinent dans l'obscurité des salles de cinéma leurs cocons de cliché . . . (Pp. 47–48.)

This elaboration upon the simple insect image attempts to describe the instinctual responses of man whose psychological movements are no less a result of primitive drives than is the attack-defense of the spider or the leech.

The ghoul image which occurs above has its entomological counterpart in the bloodsucker or parasite also used to convey human attitudes of attack or defense. During a quarrel between father and daughter, as reported by the narrator, the old man feels his daughter to be a leech slowly draining him of his strength:

Ou peut-être lui semblait-il plutôt, quand il la sentait tout contre lui, tiède et molle et déjà avide — une petite bête insatiable et obstinée — qu'elle était comme une sangsue appliquée sur lui pour le vider, l'affaiblir. (*Portrait*, p. 174.)

The bloodsucker-vampire image is especially appropriate, bringing together as it does the vital fluid of life with the insect-parasite whose life is entirely dependent upon another. The question of "contact" is obviously important in such comparisons.

The insect and the crustacean, living things in constant struggle to survive, to supply their needs, are like the psychological process, caught in a perpetual search for equilibrium: the existence of both is regulated by this fundamental struggle in response to external stimuli.

Animal imagery is well suited to the portrayal of this pre-rational, non-analytic world, for animal analogies make no demands upon the reader's imagination in an intellectual way. Static, explanatory passages of psychological analysis are precisely what Mme Sarraute hopes to avoid in order to capture a more basic truth, the ill-defined amorphous attitudes and emotions in which her "characters" are forever enmeshed. The presence of a small number of images which are more descriptive in emphasis than analogical or metaphoric, only reinforces the principal functions of the animal, bird, insect, and crustacean images: to reveal psychological attitudes, movements, situations, and the relationships between the organism, its environment, and its needs.

In addition to this central group of analogies are many other important groupings which are less patently suggestive of the tropism, but which possess nevertheless one or several tropistic attributes. Military imagery and analogies of social aggression are illustrative of the conflict between every living thing and its environment. Medical images suggest the pain which inevitably accompanies life. Images of hardness, mass, smoothness on the one hand, fluidity, stickiness, vapors on the other, suggest a primitive, sensuous level of existence, and a kind of inescapable involvement in physical processes through their tactile qualities. Finally, analogies which personify, or otherwise make active, emotional states of fear and aggression, form a wide range of non-sensuous images which express the conflict of all living things with the external forces which influence and control their existence.

Mme Sarraute's prime concern is with the presentation of our psychological life at its most basic levels. The characteristics of this life are her thematic materials — the organism's instinct for survival, frequently in the face of a hostile environment, and the satisfaction of its needs. In this sense psychological existence, like biological existence, is a series of tropistic states and movements. Words, she believes, are the carriers of our aggressive impulses and the shield behind which we hide our sensitivities: they are our principal means of establishing, or trying to establish contact, but at the same time they lead to struggle and pain. The psychological conflicts of her anonymous characters, which are the conflicts of us all, move from sub-conversation to conversation and back again in a continuous tropistic response to external forces just as the single celled organism shrinks from the dangers which surround it or reaches out for the elements necessary to its survival. Mme Sarraute tries to give new meaning and continuity to the novel through the use of a wide range of analogical shapes suggestive of the protean quality of life, its fluid nature and infinite variety.

In *L'Ere du Soupçon* these techniques and intentions are clearly indicated in her discussion of the works of Proust, Kafka, Camus and Dostoievski. Seldom have theory and practice so closely coincided in the search for aesthetic renewal and the continuing discovery of man. The germ of the technique which will be central to Mme Sarraute's own fiction can be found for example in her analysis of Dostoievski's use of external gesticulations, grimaces and contortions as the manifestation of an inner life. But where Dostoievski uses physical description to reveal an inner psychological reality and agitation, Mme Sarraute will use motions and gestures which do not have an external descriptive significance to this same psychological end. The proper study of mankind is still man, but not man in the consecutive and necessarily frozen stances of description or psychological analysis. The analogical movements of her characters are, however, like the physical movements described by Dostoievski, revelatory of psychological activity:

> tous les gestes qu'ils font, tous leurs mouvements, ceux qu'elle essaie d'exécuter en ce moment, copiés sur ceux qu'on fait là-bas, à la surface, à la lumière, paraissent ici — dans ce monde obscur et clos de toutes parts où ils se tiennent enfermés tous deux, dans ce monde où ils tournent en rond sans fin — étrangement délestés, puérils et anodins, aussi différents de ceux que font les gens du dehors que le sont, des gestes de la vie courante, les bonds, les attaques, les fuites et les poursuites des figures de ballet. (*Portrait d'un Inconnu*, p. 201.)

Throughout *Portrait d'un Inconnu* the narrator, imagining conflict between an old man and his daughter, pictures their struggle in analogical terms because there are few, if any, physical manifestations of what is taking place. This tendency to minimal external description is one of the chief characteristics of her novels because

92

Natalie Sarraute feels that appearances conceal rather than reveal the truth of psychological existence. As she has said elsewhere, "these appearances which are composed of ready-made ideas, pre-fabricated images, commonplaces, clichés, 'trompe-l'oeil,' have always come between the writer and the unexplored reality, the existence of which he suspects and which he seeks to bring to light." [4] This comment would indicate a struggle between appearances and reality upon two levels. The first of these involves the creative process itself and the writer's difficulty in discovering and present-ing what he considers real. The second level concerns what "hap-pens" in the novel, the struggle between her characters and this same reality. Mme Sarraute continues in characteristic imagery to describe the way in which the world of external actions and ap-pearances conceals what is most real in our lives. This description indicates not only what her novels are about, but it suggests also the highly metaphorical form these novels will take:

> we have never ceased to secrete this slaver, composed of the pre-conceived ideas and picture book images used to weave the cocoon inside which we enclose our neighbour and the world in order to see them divested of their mobility and their formidable complexity, simplified to the extreme, mummified, subject to our will.

Mme Sarraute intends to channel the reader into an examination of psychological states by denying him all the usual indications which he seizes upon in spite of himself to construct *trompe-l'oeil*. The result is a continuing movement away from the externals of appearance and action toward the internal and intangible.

The almost maniac desire for contact which she senses behind the physical manifestations of turmoil described by Dostoievski is also one of her own major themes and to a large extent shapes her novels. Each of her characters is caught in a perpetual search for the security of reassuring contact with someone else. This, for example, is what the narrator of *Martereau* tries to establish in his conversa-tions with the eponymous hero: "quelque chose en Martereau me tire, m'aspire . . . plus près, se coller à lui plus près, caresses, chatouilles, agaceries, pinçons légers. . . ." (p. 289).

Dostoievski's heroes are what Mme Sarraute's characters will be in greater measure: supports for sometimes unexplored states of emotion which we find within ourselves. The conventional char-acter whose reality in the traditional novel was dependent upon lengthy descriptions of his appearance, surroundings, and biography, is replaced by an anonymous pronoun in Nathalie Sarraute's novels; she refuses to situate characters beyond this most elementary level. She rejects Balzac's technique of describing characters according to class, type, and profession, modeled upon the biological concept of classifying plants and animals according to genus and species, because she feels that the character who is a type, or represents a particular position in society, or particular characteristics, must disappear before the necessity of presenting psychological states which are basic and inevitable in all men. This is the realm of personality which is as yet unexplored.

In "Conversation et sous-conversation," Mme Sarraute outlines a complementary structural and thematic approach which is essential to the displacement of external situations, characters, and actions in her novels. This movement away from the literally descriptive, she feels, has far too long been held back by the conventions and the weight of authority of the traditional novel form, even though many modern authors have awakened in the reader a new awareness and curiosity in what hides behind dialogue and the interior monologue. The sensations, images, feelings, memories, impulses, and acts which combine, recombine, escape, reappear metamorphosed even as an uninterrupted flow of words continues within us are the raw materials of her work. And each novel is an attempt to come to grips with the problem of presenting these movements not when they have come to rest, fixed in the memory, but as they form and develop. It is her purpose to try to make the reader *relive* these subterranean actions, attacks, and retreats (*L'Ere du Soupçon*, p. 99). All such movements are in reaction to some external stimulus. Often it is provided by an imaginary partner sprung from our past experiences or dreams, although a real partner who constantly renews our stock of experiences is the essential ingredient of these dramas. He is the catalyst who precipitates tropistic reaction. He is both threat and prey, the antagonist whose unknowable reactions condition our own. The narrators of *Portrait* and *Martereau*, the anonymous protagonists of the other novels, describe just such conflicts.

Since external acts, movements, and narration, have long ago been classified and studied, since the most minuscule actions in comparison to our delicate interior movements seem gross and violent, Natalie Sarraute turns to words in the form of conversation and sub-conversation to plumb the depths of psychological existence, for she believes that words have all the qualities necessary for capturing subterranean emotional states. Under their banal appearance they are the daily arm used to commit innumerable little crimes. Nothing equals the speed with which they can reach the most secret and vulnerable places of another being, leaving him no time, means, or even desire to reply.

Her novels bear out her view that every conversational exchange contains two possibilities. Words can be either the external stimulus which leads to inner turmoil and pain, or the reassuring familiarity where we seek the security of established forms which may lead to contact and communication with other men. We fear words, and yet we use them to try to overcome our solitude. A constant conflict results between the established patterns of conversation and the underlying psychological reality which they conceal. Nathalie Sarraute's characters all sense the aggressions of others which hide behind the linguistic conventions of dialogue. The narrator of *Portrait* feels animosity every time he speaks to either the old man or the daughter whom he keeps under surveillance, yet their imagined hostility toward him never takes on definite external form:

> J'ai beau tendre l'oreille, je ne perçois plus dans les paroles que nous échangeons ces résonances qu'elles avaient autrefois, ces prolongements qui s'enfonçaient en nous si loin. Des paroles anodines, anonymes, enregistrées depuis longtemps. Elles font penser à de vieux disques. (P. 234.)

There is no observable rupture between the old man and his daughter, although such a conflict is the narrator's preoccupation throughout the novel. Nathalie Sarraute implies that one can only guess at man's formless states of mind which resolve themselves finally in habitual phrases and meaningless gestures.

In place of the traditional narrative, the "anti-novels" of Nathalie Sarraute rely upon the rhythm of these two levels of conversation which parallel each other. Sub-conversation is the world of the authentic, those half formed and highly charged emotional states which are reality, as opposed to the world of convention and ossified social forms represented by linguistic cliché. Each organism exists in a state of continual tension and fear upon the level of authenticity, the protoplasmic, viscous level of elemental emotions and impulses. This authenticity, by its very nature, drives us to the inauthentic realm of accepted ideas and polite formulae, where the individual seeks security in the generality of society. In this way sub-conversation underlies and conflicts with our expressions of social platitude, while at the same time dialogue becomes the external continuation of inner, subcutaneous movement. Speaking of Ivy Compton-Burnett's style (*L'Ere du Soupçon*, p. 123) Mme Sarraute presents what is, in fact, her own approach to conversation and sub-conversation:

> Les dictons, les citations, les métaphores, les expressions toutes faites ou pompeuses ou pédantes, les platitudes, les vulgarités, les maniérismes, les coq-à-l'âne qui parsèment habilement ces dialogues ne sont pas, comme dans les romans ordinaires des signes distinctifs que l'auteur épingle sur les caractères des personnages pour les rendre mieux reconnaissables, plus familiers, et plus "vivants": ils sont ici, on le sent, ce qu'ils sont dans la réalité: la résultante de mouvements montés des profondeurs, nombreux, emmêlés, que celui qui les perçoit au dehors embrasse en un éclair et qu'il n'a ni le temps ni le moyen de séparer et de nommer.

These are forces which exist in that fluctuating region between conversation and sub-conversation. Interior movements indicative of our true emotions and impulses threaten to reveal themselves in spite of the conventions of dialogue itself. Mme Sarraute feels that the reader given such conversations must mobilize all his instincts of defense, all his gifts of intuition, his memory, his faculty of reason and judgment to grapple with the threats which hide in soft phrases, the venom distilled from an expression of tenderness. He knows that clichés, platitudes and vulgarities are not, as in the traditional novel, revelatory of individualized characters, but the result of movements come from the depths of being, and common to all men. Furthermore Nathalie Sarraute wants the kind of dialogue which will reduce the distance between character and reader to a minimum so that the latter will have the illusion of re-performing, himself, the interior movements presented, with more lucidity, more order, more clarity and force than are possible in life, while at the same time preserving their indetermination, opacity and mystery (*L'Ere du Soupçon*, p. 118). Freed from the conventions and restraints of the traditional novel, dialogue through a change in rhythm and form will make it possible for the reader to recognize that action has passed from within to without. It is no accident then that Mme Sarraute's novels are more like poetry and drama than prose fiction in their use of imagery and dialogue, both more immediate in their appeal to the active participation of the reader.

Perhaps for the first time the novel assumes a shape which is in itself an expression of contemporary "reality." Nathalie Sarraute moves away from print into the realm of the oral and the imagistic, through conversation and sub-conversation. The printed word has a different value here than it has in the traditional novel. Its affective immediacy is more like the instant circuitry of radio and television. Narrative distance which orders and clarifies, which implies a time lag, is replaced by a continuous bombardment of verbal images. Because of the speed with which we apprehend them, no ordering perspective is possible. The multitudinous impressions which assail us in the act of living often remain unexplained or falsely interpreted, and so it is in these novels which transcend individuality of character and milieu to suggest the totality of psychological existence in the modern world.

Moving from plot, characters, and setting conditioned by the deterministic outlook of the nineteenth century toward anonymous characters who share nevertheless basic emotions and impulses, Mme Sarraute creates the atmosphere of a life in which each man has lost his individuality, his "story," and yet still retains the instincts of all organisms to individual survival. The reader is not expected to assimilate a gallery of characters who have an independent and individual existence. Quite the contrary. This would separate him from the experience which it is the novelist's intention to make him feel. The character exists not for himself, but to make it possible for the reader to recreate the psychological movement and moment in question. The imagery of tropism has filled the gap left by the displacement of physical details, and made possible the necessary concretization and generalization which accompany a new kind of psychic matter. The psychology of the idiosyncratic individual gives way to a psychology both collective and individual at the same time. Anonymous *ils* and *elles* experience threats to their individual existence which we readers assimilate directly, because they are our struggles too, yet we fill no mental museum with figures whose contours are well defined, and whose movements become mechanical. The imaginative form of this new psychology suggests its nature affectively as it depicts its substance analogically.

Faceless characters babble on as each organism attempts to find some stable point of reference in a hostile universe. But this stability in the end is false, or if not false, simply full of sound and fury signifying nothing much — imagistic clichés which have lost all significance. Through the empty preoccupations of her protagonists, and the triviality of their conversation, Mme Sarraute attacks our dependence upon the most insignificant aspects of physical existence. Paradoxically, what is most real and most vital may be attached to these trivia — our psychological life. As a result, images which depict the violence of psychological movement continually contradict the clichés and banalities of conversation. To give expression to this conflict is Mme Sarraute's major aim, for through the opposition between conversation and sub-conversation are revealed those undiscovered psychological tropisms she wants us to experience not second hand, but as living, forming movements.

IMAGE-CONVEYING ABSTRACTIONS IN THE WORKS OF ANDRÉ GIDE

BY C. D. E. TOLTON

Protean as André Gide undoubtedly was in both his private life and his published works, the themes which preoccupied him remain surprisingly constant. His works are readily recognizable for their insistence on the sincerity or authenticity of the individual in a world which is ironically full of counterfeit values and actions. They are obsessed with man's constant quest for happiness in a world where there seems to be little place for a person attracted by both spiritual fulfilment and sensual pleasure. They often stress the role of the artist who is constantly at grips with the task of transposing life into a disciplined and didactic yet palatable and permanent aesthetic form. At intervals they suggest a dichotomy between passionless love and loveless passion.

Gide's principal fictional and dramatic figures from *André Walter* (1891) to *Thésée* (1946) are all grappling with moral problems which often lead to an ironically inconclusive dénouement. Doubtless influenced by his own love of travel, he liked to set his characters on voyages which were sometimes literally trips from one identifiable place to another, sometimes figurative trips through the character's conscious past or present. During these voyages, Gide would often raise his characters to heights of glowing expectation, only to release them into depths of disappointment, disillusionment, or tragedy. Surely among all Gide's themes, that of unfulfilled expectation is his most ironical and recurrent.[1]

"Expectation" is an abstract noun. The other aforementioned themes can also be succinctly expressed by abstract nouns: sincerity, hypocrisy, happiness, and love. There are many, many others, such as selfishness and selflessness, freedom and constraint, joy and sorrow, truth and falsehood, anguish and ecstasy, pride and humility, and that phalanx of values which Professor Justin O'Brien so astutely observes at the core of the doctrine in *Les Nourritures terrestres*: restlessness (*inquiétude*), uprooting (*déracinement*), recep-

99

tiveness (*disponibilité*), and fervor (*ferveur*).² Yet while all of these themes are Gidean trademarks, the means which Gide uses to express them can be less simply summarized. For he does not limit himself in his choice of abstract diction. Moreover, he encrusts each of his abstractions with special meanings which are clear to only his more experienced readers.³ Gide himself suggested that abstract vocabulary allows for the extraction or the addition of certain new shades of meaning, certain ambiguities, which are less possible with concrete language.⁴ And at another time, he admitted to his own love of abstraction.⁵

In addition to Gide's declared interest in abstract diction, other factors invite us to examine his abstractions more closely. In the first place, Gide *did* use abstract vocabulary more often than his contemporaries.⁶ And in the second place, the very abstractions which one would expect to find expressing his major themes are sometimes not his most prevalent choices. *Renoncement* and *liberté*, for instance, appear even less often in Gide than in the works of his contemporaries. One wonders, then, precisely what vocabulary he substituted for the more obvious possibilities.

An examination of the frequency and expressiveness of Gide's abstract diction reveals a characteristic phenomenon; namely, that when he uses a particular abstraction less frequently than his contemporaries, he has probably opted for an abstract noun, adjective, or verb which conveys an image. Where one might expect to find *renoncement*, for instance, one finds instead *dénuement*. Where one might expect to find *liberté*, one finds *nudité*. Similarly, when we find Gide using an abstraction more frequently than his contemporaries, one can usually expect that this word is replacing a more conventional, less provocative one which he might otherwise be overworking. Such is the case with *soif* and *ivresse*, which Gide selects in many contexts where one could expect (instead of *soif*) *désir*, or (instead of *ivresse*) any one of the familiar *ferveur, exaltation, extase,* or *lyrisme*.⁷ Such words as *dénuement, nudité, soif,* and *ivresse*, which appear more frequently in Gide's writing than in that of his contemporaries, will be treated here as *mots-clefs*.⁸

Azur and *tiédeur* are two other image-conveying abstract *mots-clefs* which, while not replacing other abstractions, illustrate Gide's tendency to emphasize in his abstract language special meanings which contribute to the characteristic sensual flavor of his thought and style. In the light of the recurrence of all of these image-conveying abstractions, it is surprising to discover that the words *dé-*

racinement and *ardeur* are not Gidean *mots-clefs*. Their usage invites special attention.

The following examples of usage of each of these image-conveying abstractions are drawn principally from Gide's narrative, dramatic, and lyrical works.[9]

Dénuement and *Nudité*:

The root of the abstractions *dénuement* and *nudité* is the adjective *nu* meaning "bare". Gide's preoccupation with concepts of both barrenness and bareness can be seen in the relatively high frequency with which this whole family of words recurs, and in his exploitation of the potential symbolic significance of each one.

Occasionally he uses *dénuement* in the literal sense of "destitution" or "bareness" (of a room, etc.) [10] Gertrude's "dénuement" on her first appearance is depicted as clearly unenviable (*Symph.*, p. 15), as is that of Isabelle and her mother on their last (*Isa.*, pp. 278, 281), or of Anthime Armand-Dubois after his conversion (*Caves*, p. 311). In *Amyntas*, the word refers specifically to African landscape destitute of people — and hence conducive to profitable contemplation (*Biskra*, p. 279 and *Renoncement*, p. 268).

But Gide's experienced readers are more likely to be expecting a figurative, moral meaning in his use of *dénuement*. Justin O'Brien speaks of *dénuement* (or *dénûment*) in such a way that one might well link it with the four cardinal points which he sees within *Les Nourritures terrestres*.[11] And Gide himself insisted on at least two occasions that *Les Nourritures terrestres* was above all "l'apologie du dénuement." [12] His concept of *dénuement* may be defined as the liberation of the individual from all material and emotional ties so as to gain the maximum freedom in life. He best illustrates the idea with a simile in reference to himself, to the effect that to liberate himself completely, he even repudiated his personal opinions, his daily habits, his modesty, just as one throws off a tunic in order to be immersed in water, wind, or sunshine (*Journal*, l'été 1919, *O.C.* IX, 453). Furthermore, Gide's conscious disentanglement from the burden of property is a well-known biographical fact. It is not surprising that he gives as one of his motivating factors an "étrange soif de dénuement" (*Grain*, p. 443). With Gide's particular bias in mind, it is not too surprising either to find him remarking in quite different circumstances — in relation to Racine — that Phèdre's wish to rid herself of her "vains ornements" is likewise motivated by

101

a desire for "dénuement" (*Attendu*, p. 188). Similarly he relates the word *dénuement* to questions of literary style with the meaning of an unadornment or a simplicity not entirely unlike Roland Barthe's "degré zéro de l'écriture" (*Lettres*, p. 174, and *Journal*, le 22 août 1926).

Yet while Gide claims that the theme of "dénuement" is of major importance in *Les Nourritures terrestres*, the closest he comes to using the word itself in this text is one appearance of the adjective *dénuées* (p. 147). In this passage, the narrator is praising the virtues of a soul destitute of all encumbrances but love, hope, and expectation. Gide appears to have arrived at the concept of *dénuement* (here clearly a synonym for *renoncement*) falteringly, through resignation. He may not yet have been at home with it. By 1926, though, he had already conceived a good part of *Les Nouvelles Nourritures* and one wonders whether the remarks in his 1926 preface to *Les Nourritures terrestres* might not have been better applied to the later work, in which his increasingly humanitarian views were requiring a more complete relinquishment of former property and spiritual values.[13] His "dénuement" accomplished, the narrator now stands naked and erect on the virgin soil; all veils are removed, and before him lies nothing but brilliance and nakedness (p. 195).

Several of Gide's fictional characters are closely involved with his concept of *dénuement*. Both Ménalque and the narrator express the doctrine in *Les Nourritures terrestres*, and Michel applies it in the selling of his property in *L'Immoraliste*. The prodigal son felt closest to his father (who may be interpreted as a symbol of God) when destitute of all but spiritual considerations in the desert (*Prodique*, p. 9). When we first meet Lafcadio of *Les Caves du Vatican* we realize that his scorn of conventional values is perhaps unwittingly and ironically reflected in even the details of his living accommodations: "Le regard de Julius circula éloquemment à travers le dénûment de la pièce" (p. 165).

Gide, then, appears to have found *dénuement* a suitable substitute for *renoncement* — and even *misère* and *émancipation*, which are other abstractions he used less frequently than his contemporaries. He appears to have found it even more pleasing to replace *liberté* (*libre*) with the symbolical images contained in *nudité* (*nu*).

Gide has undeniably played a part in liberating this century's mentality from cobwebs of archaic prejudices. The aged Thésée's famous statement, often referred to as Gide's own final optimistic, self-satisfied word on the subject, is perhaps worth repeating: "Il m'est doux de penser qu'après moi, grâce à moi, les hommes se reconnaîtront plus heureux, meilleurs, et plus libres" (*Thésée*, p. 123). There are two steps in Gide's emancipation program: first, to liberate man from the bonds of convention in works like *Les Nourritures terrestres, Le Retour de l'enfant prodique, Corydon*, or *Si le grain ne meurt*; and secondly, while warning him against excesses as in *Saül, Le Roi Candaule*, or *L'Immoraliste*, to preach the constructive values of a controlled or chanelled freedom in works like the moralistic parts of the *Journal*, his African and Russian social messages, or *Thésée*.

It is in connection with his first step that Gide uses images of nakedness. It is, moreover, noteworthy that *nudité* more often expresses ecstatic freedom than smirking sexuality.[14] At an early age, Gide himself was disturbed by the unnecessary sense of shame clearly manifested in Van Eyck's naked figures of Adam and Eve, and by the unsophisticated reaction of young girls and businessmen alike on viewing the painting (*Journal*, août 1891, *O.C.* I, 480). In works like the African travel commentaries, nudity is an inevitable element in descriptions of the people. Gide presents his material neither smugly nor awkwardly. In later years, he will find it curious that so many people find the very notion of nakedness sexually arousing (*Journal*, le 17 mai 1936).

Gide's examples of nakedness span a whole range from total nudity to partial nudity to nudity of specific parts of the body. He refers to total nudity in two of his earliest paragraphs so far published: an imaginary hamadryad, who has been swimming, and the hero (who has not) are both nude in the *Fragment de la "Nouvelle Education sentimentale"* (*OC*. I, 3). Hereafter in his earliest works, we find with some regularity a number of passages expressing exaltation in the freedom one can feel when swimming naked or watching naked swimmers. As a young man, Gide enjoyed watching fishermen's children swimming and sunbathing nude (*Paysages*, p. 248). André Walter speaks of vagabonds who swim stark naked (*Cahiers*, p. 156). The chief characters of *Les Poésies d'André Walter* recall their nude swimming with special pleasure (p. 188). Swimmers and divers in *Le Voyage d'Urien* are consistently handsome, nude, and happy (pp. 302, 314, 316). Gide's passion for nude swimming leads him to an especially appropriate simile in *Amyntas*: he wonders if what he is looking for again at Fontaine-Chaude is not a sensation similar to what one feels when diving hot and naked into

cold water (*Renoncement*, p. 321). It is, though, not just for swimming that Lafcadio spends a period of his adolescence without
clothes. By the age of 15 he proves his total liberation by being
photographed completely nude (*Caves*, p. 160). But free as he is,
when Lafcadio imagines how much uglier some train passengers
would be undressed than they are dressed he seems to be observing
that some people are never meant to be released from their "crustacean" inhibitions (p. 367). Truly liberated people like Protos
and his friends, on the other hand, rarely remain dressed in the
same clothes for long.

Examples of total nudity involving sexuality are all the more
striking because of their infrequency. André Walter's tortuous mind
dreams of nude couples making love (*Cahiers*, p. 148); Luc watches
Rachel bathe nude under leafy branches (*Tent.*, p. 228); Bethsabé,
the supreme symbol of unwitting temptation, is nude in both *Les
Nourritures terrestres* (p. 133) and *Bethsabé* (p. 232). The nude
demon in *Saül* (p. 363), Moelibée who whisks Angèle off to Rome
(*Prom.*, p. 156), and the African shepherd who cunningly exposes
his nakedness to a passing train (*Renoncement*, p. 258) all leave a
sexual impression. Yet in all of these examples, the naked sexuality
can be related to the freedom from convention and inhibitions which
these characters are seeking or have acquired. The whole question
of Sara Keller's nude portrait in *Geneviève*, for instance, while illu-
strating Geneviève's lesbian tendencies, is more important as a pre-
text for contrasting the liberalism of the Kellers with the hide-
bound scruples of families like Geneviève's (*Ecole*, pp. 194, 198,
199, 202, 204).

Gide takes care in specifying the extent to which his characters
are nude. Partial nudity is sometimes more seductive than total
nudity, and just as much a symbol of emancipation. One morning
Luc finds Rachel almost nude, inhibitions drop, and their relationship is at last consummated (*Tent.*, p. 227). While in bourgeois
Paris, the narrator of *Les Nourritures terrestres* warmly remembers
African women who came to a well almost nude (p. 217). One of
the motivations for young Jonathan's saying that he would like to
be a goatherd, nude under a sheepskin, is his desire for freedom in
the open air (*Saül*, p. 319). In *Thésée* all the men and women who
meet the ship at Cnossos have nude torsos (pp. 25, 29). The
emancipated Ariane wears the sort of floating dress under which
one can sense that she is nude (p. 50), while the handsome Icare is
bare to the waist (p. 67). Surely Gide is trying to indicate to his

readers that the society at Cnossos is the least crustacean of all his creations.

As for the specific parts of the body which Gide depicts as naked, the image of bare feet recurs most often. It stands almost always for at least partial liberation. Rachel's group of dancing flower-gatherers in *La Tentative amoureuse* (p. 226), whirling dervishes and fishermen in *Le Voyage d'Urien* (pp. 299, 306), handsome young gleaners and the narrator in *Les Nourritures terrestres* (pp. 65, 76, 100, 127, 154, 213), an assortment of Italians and Arabs in *L'Immoraliste* and *Amyntas* (*L'Imm.*, pp. 39, 44, 159; *Mopsus*, pp. 6, 7; *Renoncement*, p. 277), and Lady Griffith in *Les Faux-monnayeurs* (p. 77), are fettered by neither fears nor footwear. Gide's personal pleasure in going barefoot in *Amyntas* symbolizes the joyous freedom expressed in much of this work (*Renoncement*, p. 305). Bardolotti's unconventionality is indicated by the bare feet which are ironically visible in his disguise as a priest (*Caves*, p. 293). Lafcadio had begun his life of liberation by going barefoot (p. 195). A glance at Geneviève de Baraglioul's bare feet at the end of the *sotie* alerts him to the possibility that she too is progressing in her emancipation (page 402). And reminiscent of the fact that Lafcadio's training had been gradual is Sophroniska's symbolic admonition to Boris that it is preferable to go barefoot for a while if one wants eventually to be able to lie down naked in the snow (*F.M.*, p. 279).

While bare feet symbolize a lack of inhibitions, women's bare arms serve as symbols of sexual lasciviousness. Jérôme feels that Alissa's mother's bare arms and shoulder indicate her sensuality (*Porte*, pp. 79, 83). The naïve Amédée Fleurissoire, having recently been surprised to find himself sharing a bed with a naked Carola Venitequa, is disturbed by the bare arms of a voluptuous serving-girl (*Caves*, p. 293). Thésée rather unnecessarily tells us that the infamous Pasiphaé had bare arms as well as unclad breasts (*Thésée*, p. 30).

By this time, the usefulness which Gide found in this family of words should be clear. *Dénuement* and *nudité* serve to express abstract concepts of renunciation and liberation in a more pictorial — and more forceful — way than would the word families of *renoncement* and *liberté*. At the same time, *nudité* in particular adds a subtle touch of sensuousness to his works. And after the lessons taught by the Gidean image of bare feet, a reader might well, like

Julius de Baraglioul, instinctively look at a stranger's footwear for an instant clue to his character.[15]

Soif:

In Gide's use of *dénuement* and *nudité* the sexual implications were subtler than the image of nakedness might have at first promised. In his use of *soif*, however, Gide exploits to the full this word's less obvious sensual images. Only rarely does he allow the word to retain its literal meaning of physical thirst without suggesting a figurative meaning of passion, lust, or desire for sexual satisfaction. By this indirect means, he succeeds in speaking of sexual desire in a relatively tasteful and even poetic way.

The full sensuous force which Gide felt in the word *soif* can best be found in *Les Nourritures terrestres*, where the theme of desire is of prime importance. In this work, *soif* is most clearly a synonym for *désir*, and the object of the desire is very often sexual satisfaction. Quenched thirst is sexual fulfilment, the orgasm itself. With these meanings in mind, one can establish a Gidean attitude towards sexual contentment. In a refrain with only insignificant variations, he is saying that satisfied passions have brought him immense joy.[16] Often even more pleasing than the orgasm, though, is the state of desire, the state of expectation. In Ménalque's explanation of his joy in long periods of unfulfilled desire, *source* can be interpreted as the potential source of satisfaction and *soif* as desire.[17] In teaching Nathanaël, the didactic narrator admits that he wants first to inflame the lad with a new desire and then to introduce him to means of gratification (p. 166). He teaches him of the never-ending temptations (*sources*) which, when yielded to, will bring satisfaction; there are, in fact, more than enough springs and fountains to quench his figurative thirst (p. 167). Since a life without desires can be empty, occasionally one must search for a thirst that needs to be quenched.[18] Extremely strong desires, sexual frustrations, are quickly brought to climax.[19] If the desire, the frustration, the temptation, should reach a peak of desperation, one will be led to use unusual, less desirable means of fulfilment. Fruits of the earth represent one succulent means of satisfying desires, and they may be interpreted as the sexual partners. Some varieties are, of course, less satisfying than others.[20] Often with inadequate sexual partners the fulfilment is incomplete; moreover, a scar or stain (here in the form of blotched lips or torn hands) is left as an unpleasant re-

minder.[21] The disastrous attempts to satisfy desperate desire with
overripe fruits (p. 213) may symbolize experiences with tired pro-
fessional lovers. Ironically, sometimes the more one drinks the
thirstier one becomes (p. 214). Sometimes too the satisfaction of
the thirst or desire brings a realization of the inadequacy of the
means of satisfaction (the sexual partner).[22] The narrator worries
lest the commandment of God will unfairly exact from him new
punishment on account of his persistent thirst for everything he finds
beautiful on earth (p. 165). But the problem of desire is more than
a personal one. It results in universal confusion.[23] With such importance allotted to desire in the world of the *Nourritures*, it is not
surprising that Gide has Hylas give the place of honor at his table
to "Soif" (p. 138).

In works immediately following *Les Nourritures terrestres*, Gide
continues to use *soif* as a symbolical image for *désir*. Saül, a figure of
passion, is, for instance, thirsty (*Saül*, p. 271). In the Second Act
scene with the demons, the cup which they offer to quench his thirst
represents temptation on a sexual level (p. 302), and the later
scene where Saül satisfies a demon's thirst illustrates the success
which the demons have had with him (p. 396). El Hadj's song to
the prince frankly equates thirst with desire.[24]

In the preface to *L'Immoraliste*, Gide again uses the image of un-
satisfying fruit consumed in a moment of desperate desire. He compares his book to enticing but bitter apples which burn rather than
quench thirst (p. 5). This time he uses a familiar image not to
suggest sexual desire, but to emphasize the misleading nature of the
book's first impression. Two other images of thirst are, however,
again sexual. Michel speaks glowingly of thirst-quenching lemons
at Ravello in one of his earliest sexually-oriented moments (p. 58).
About the same time, he seems almost redundant when he says that
on occasions when he lay down beside a tempting "source" he felt
full of both "soif" and "désirs" (p. 60).

The word *soif* is probably the most significant one in the brief
Bethsabé. In this work, Gide mingles sensual desires with spiritual
ones, showing how David failed to realize that the true object of his
desire (*soif*) was Urie's happiness and not Bethsabé's body (pp.
223, 228, 232). It is the sexual significance of insatiable thirst
which Gide exploits in *Amyntas*. The narrator hopes that a young
boy will offer him thirst-quenching grapes (*Mopsus*, p. 9), and is
prepared to search for the last pomegranate on the branch (*Renoncement*, p. 250). A thirsty landscape complements the nar-

rator's desires (*Mopsus*, p. 9 and *Renoncement*, p. 267). The prodigal son confesses to having loved his thirst when it was at its greatest, its least satisfied, in the arid desert (*Prodigue*, p. 9). In his conversation with his younger brother about the symbolic wild pomegranate (p. 26), the younger brother foresees a moment when his thirst will be strong enough to make him partake of this bitter fruit of the earth. The prodigal son warns him that the pomegranate will more likely encourage his desire than quench it. In *La Porte étroite* the thirst is ostensibly more spiritual than physical: Jérôme speaks of the thirst for religious fulfilment which he experienced on hearing the influential sermon (p. 91). Yet, while one can accept literally the spiritual implications of the thirst of this lethargic lover, Alissa's use of the word (pp. 159, 237) hints at her suppressed passion.

Later works of fiction use *soif* more sparingly, and not always with reference to sexuality. Isabelle's letter to her lover does express her desire in terms of thirst.[25] The still young Gertrude says as she lies dying: "J'ai soif . . . J'étouffe" (*Symph.*, p. 86). Armand of *Les Faux-monnayeurs* uses a thirst image to describe his precarious moral position. Like an Arab who needs only one drop of water to keep from dying of thirst, Armand is only one step away from total moral corruption (p. 411).

Only in *Les Nouvelles Nourritures*, among the later works, does *soif* regain the full expressiveness (if not the frequency) which it enjoyed in *Les Nourritures terrestres*. On the first page the narrator observes that it is his desire (*soif*) which his reader will eventually inherit — presumably by reading the book (p. 191). When the narrator asks the sun to bring thirst to his lips (p. 194), he indicates that as he has grown older his eagerness to feel sexual urges has not diminished. He confesses, though, that he now prefers thirst (desire) to quenched thirst (satisfaction) even more than in his youth (p. 248). Yet with the inconsistency which typifies this work, he elsewhere hopes that his reader will not suffer from similar unquenched thirst (p. 281).

The majority of examples of Gide's use of *soif* symbolically meaning sexual desire appear in works published between 1897 and 1909 (from *Les Nourritures terrestres* to *La Porte étroite*). How does one explain the partial disappearance of so distinctive a theme and stylistic trait after 1909? Perhaps his passions had been satisfied; or despite his claims to the contrary, perhaps the years had simply caused his urges to fade. At any rate, the theme of desire and the image of thirst had become a less essential part of his aesthetic baggage.[26]

Ivresse:

As in the case of *soif, ivresse* (*ivre, enivrer, ivrogne,* etc.) appears most often and most tellingly in Gide's early lyrical prose.[27] But while drunkenness (*ivresse*) would logically seem to be simply a step or two beyond quenched thirst (*soif étanchée*), surprisingly enough when Gide strays from the literal meaning of alcoholic inebriation, only rarely does he associate any sexual implications with the word. Instead, he exploits the less sensual of its figurative meanings of rapture, ecstacy, or intoxication of the senses. *Ivresse* thus becomes a most serviceable synonym for *ferveur, exaltation, extase,* or *lyrisme.*

Gide the moralist does not lose sight of the literal meaning of *ivresse.* In fact he sounds at times like a temperance preacher. In his *Réflexions sur quelques points de littérature et de morale,* Gide formally tackles the problem of alcoholism. He points out that rich and poor alike use alcohol as an unsatisfactory substitute for happiness (*O.C.* II, 416), an argument which also appears in *Les Nourritures terrestres* (p. 161). It is not surprising, therefore, to find that the happiness of Candaule's drunken banquet guests is only temporary (*Roi,* pp. 305, 314, 321, 333). Nor is it surprising to find that it is "Gygèse sobre" who emerges triumphant. Even after the loss of the simple happiness which he possessed at the beginning of the play, he refrains from any substitutes for happiness, and acquires a new (but no less tenuous) form of contentment as king. The unfortunate Saül does not fare even as well as Candaule's guests in his search for alcoholic bliss; for, ironically, his wine is too weak to be effective (*Saül,* p. 252). Gide is most specific in his value judgments about alcoholism in *L'Immoraliste.* The driver whom Michel beats is an "ivrogne" (p. 65). The drunken Pierre brings nothing but trouble (p. 123), and Ménalque argues that "ivresse" can be attained in ways other than drinking. Moreover, the kind of intoxication which Ménalque finds — in sobriety, as it happens — is a feeling of lucid exaltation as opposed to a withdrawal from life (p. 99). In *Amyntas* the drunken farm laborers at Cuverville are far from attractive (*Renoncement,* p. 267), and in *Les Caves du Vatican* a drunken Amédée Fleurissoire is even more comical than usual (p. 299). Edouard finds that intoxication brings out disturb-

109

ing vulgarity in Sarah and Armand (*F.M.*, p. 163), and it is drunkenness which triggers Olivier's jealousy of Bernard and Sarah at the literary banquet (p. 428), and motivates the subsequent shame which plays a part in his attempted suicide (p. 454). Intoxication through drugs rather than alcohol occurs in *Thésée* when Dédale promises Thésée that he will be overcome by narcotic perfumes in the labyrinth (p. 63). Dédale's advice may well be Gide's: that salvation lies in remaining lucidly master of oneself in the midst of even the greatest adversity.

But if alcoholic intoxication is to be avoided, figurative intoxication of the senses is to be sought out and cherished. In several contexts Gide explicitly indicates the analogy he sees between alcoholic and non-alcoholic intoxication. In *Le Voyage d'Urien* the excitement of a crowd watching dancers is compared to drunkenness,[28] and in *Les Nourritures terrestres* a perfumed garden intoxicates "autant que des liqueurs" (p. 198). Michel comments that while travelling south with a sick Marceline, the limitations imposed on his pleasure made him drunk with desire (*soif*) "comme d'autres sont ivres de vin" (*L'Imm.*, p. 150). The ecstatic narrator of *Amyntas* walks at night, "ivre sans avoir bu" (*Renoncement*, p. 318).

More often, though, Gide allows the reader to disengage by himself the metaphor implicit in *ivresse*. The ecstasy and frenzy which this word suggests have a variety of sources other than alcohol. André Walter reaches it through thoughts of Emmanuèle (*Cahiers*, p. 100), the sight of white paper (p. 69), stimulating books (p. 104), perfumes and imagined caresses (p. 106), music (p. 115), and a struggle towards religious tranquility (p. 132). Luc and Rachel find "ivresse" together while making love (*Tent.*, p. 228). This sensual source contrasts strikingly with the peace of mind which brings Luc solitary rapture at the end of the *traité* (p. 242). Urien reaches a state of ecstasy on viewing a silent city (*Urien*, p. 338).

It is the narrator of *Les Nourritures terrestres* who is the ultimate authority on the various non-alcoholic means of intoxicating the senses.[29] Nathanaël should become inebriated by every emotion he experiences (p. 83). And the narrator will show him how.[30] Among the possible and sometimes unique means are pride in not sinning simply (p. 62), sensuous, thought-provoking stories (pp. 138, 142), sleepless, thought-filled nights (p. 150), hunger in the morning and thirst in the evening (p. 152), evenings in the country (p. 153), love (pp. 181, 209), flower perfumes (p. 198), smoking (p. 200), and salt air (p. 211).

But this narrator is not the last of Gide's characters to comment on sources of figurative inebriation. In *Le Roi Candaule* Syphax speaks of a woman's beauty (p. 319). In *L'Immoraliste* Michel's listeners are intoxicated by the newness of the African climate (p. 11). Michel is drunk with fresh air (p. 86), and with night (p. 134), as is the narrator of *Amyntas*,[31] who is also intoxicated with the pleasure of walking in an orchard (p. 86) or simply being alive (p. 303). The impressionable young Jérôme apparently became intoxicated by a compound of love, pity, inspiration, self-denial, and virtue, on seeing Alissa in tears and prayer (*Porte*, p. 89); and it is his intoxication with his own headstrong discretion (p. 95) which is a motivating factor behind his passivity in their love relationship. The source of Alissa's intoxication is livelier: the pleasures of a morning walk in the fresh air and sunshine (p. 168). She is able to compare her sensation to an early morning joyfulness and a slight dizziness, again revealing both her acute sensitivity to physical sensations and her capacity for exactness of expression.

In later works, contexts involving figurative *ivresse* are sometimes ironical. Amédée Fleurissoire is intoxicated by the nobility of his mission (*Caves*, p. 309), and his wife is said also to have become ironically intoxicated by the attentions of her two ridiculously passionless suitors (p. 234). Vincent Molinier's triumphant ecstasy in *Les Faux-monnayeurs* will be ironically shortlived (p. 210), and in a moment of dramatic irony Œdipe does not realize that he is speaking of himself when he asks what has become of "cet enfant de l'ivresse" (*Œdipe*, p. 264).

Also in the later works, Gide sometimes links *ivresse* with literary inspiration. He points out that Ronsard owes much of his inspiration to a mythological, philosophical, even Christian "ivresse" (*Anth.*, p. 23). In *Thésée* Gide is satirizing the classical notion of poetic inspiration when he has Dédale say that the vapors rising from his chafing-dish create an "ivresse pleine de charme" (p. 62). This intoxication invites a mind to undertake the sort of vain activity which results in merely imaginative works — such as his own labyrinth.

In *Les Nouvelles Nourritures, ivresse* does not regain the importance it had in *Les Nourritures terrestres* even as much as did *soif*. It occurs only in reference to the dawn of creation,[32] and later, to the narrator's desire for increased religious fervor: "Seigneur! augmentez mon ivresse" (p. 216).

Both literal and figurative intoxication concerned Gide enough to use the word *ivresse* in both senses throughout his whole career. But while the frequency and importance of contexts where the word means literal alcoholic inebriation may remain fairly static, we can see a sort of evolution in his handling of the word in the figurative sense. Occurrences of *ivresse* as a substitute for *ferveur, exaltation, extase*, or *lyrisme* become less frequent after 1909, and the word is then more often exploited for ironical than for didactic purposes. But it is still the metaphor of non-alcoholic intoxication or ecstasy as it is so often found in *Les Cahiers d'André Walter, Les Nourritures terrestres, L'Immoraliste*, and *Amyntas*, which springs to mind as a key image on encountering the word *ivresse* in connection with Gide. This *mot-clef* and *mot-thème* was a very essential part of his linguistic apparatus for expressing the theme of fervor.

Azur:

Gide's use of *ivresse* is sometimes reminiscent of Baudelaire ("Il faut être toujours ivre"). His use of *azur (azuré)* at first reminds one of Mallarmé. *Azur* can mean literally a blue mineral substance, an ore of copper. Figuratively, the word means the blue color in general, and the blue of a bright cloudless sky in particular. Since the Seventeenth Century, writers have quite logically used *azur* in metonymical contexts to mean *ciel*. And Mallarmé chose to use the word metaphorically in the sense of the infinite, the boundless, through which man's aesthetic ambitions wish to soar. Gide too uses the word literally, metonymically, and metaphorically — but always drawing from it a special meaning of his own.

The closest Gide comes to the original literal meaning of *azur* is in contexts where the word denotes the color blue. But in his hands — particularly in his earliest works — the word takes on suggestions of mysticism associated with the infinite qualities of water and air. *Azur* is a part of Gide's poetic sketch of the Garden of Eden.[33] In the unreality of a mystical grotto, one becomes lost in an azure light (*Urien*, p. 313). On a pale, uncertainly moonlit beach, azure sands move like waves (p. 317). A mysterious city lies beneath the sea like an azure vision (p. 337). During an evening of phenomenal happenings, one of the most improbable is that the moon becomes azure (p. 345). At a soporific swimming pool, children's arms take on an azure color in the light (p. 305). An association between *azur* and eternity is suggested by a reference to "une mer azurée" also as a "mer éternelle" (p. 282).

The emphasis on *azur* in the descriptive detail of *Les Nourritures terrestres* is explained in a diary entry for 1934: Gide rejoices that everything is bathing him in splendid azure as at the time of his *Nourritures* (*Journal*, le 18 août 1934). In this work, *azur* is ubiquitous. In Rome, the air shines with diffused light as if the blueness of the sky were becoming liquid rain (*N.T.*, p. 97). At Syracuse, the fish as well as the fountains are azure (p. 166). In Algeria, the azure salt lagoons reflect the beautiful blue of the sky (p. 202). At Blidah the narrator notices azure leaves on eucalyptus trees (p. 105). In "La Ronde de la grenade" he speaks of pomegranate berries as blood in azure cups (p. 130), while in "La Ronde de mes soifs étanchées" he expresses a preference for waters which are coldly azure rather than tepidly transparent. In this work, azure is decidedly the color which Gide associated with perfect beauty and physical well-being.

In works published soon after *Les Nourritures terrestres*, literal, suggestive blueness appears most often in connection with African and Italian scenery. In *El Hadj*, the prophet marvels that after the heat of the day the sands retain a light which makes them appear "azurées" (p. 73). This is a forewarning of the deceptively paradisiacal image of "la plaine doucement azurée" on what seems to be the threshold of the Promised Land (p. 84). In *Amyntas*, the second sentence of the *Feuilles de route* describes a sky at San Miniato passing through phases of almost total blueness (p. 5). The narrator expresses disappointment in the Blue Grotto because its water is indigo rather than azure in color (p. 17), but azure fish in tepid water (as in *Les Nourritures terrestres*) contribute to the beauty of a scene at Syracuse (p. 20). There continues to be a lack of tangible reality in elements which are strongly azure, as in the case of distant sky-blue mountains which lose their blueness and gain reality as they are approached (*Renoncement*, p. 260).

In Gide's last works blueness is most often a symbol of hope. *Azur* is a part of blind Gertrude's imaginative description of field lilies in *La Symphonie pastorale*.[34] As Olivier's health returns in *Les Faux-monnayeurs*, the sun shines, a fresh breeze clears the last leaves from the trees, and everything appears limpid and azure (p. 455). In *Le Retour du Tchad* the blueness of the sky is almost tender (p. 21). In *Les Nouvelles Nourritures* the narrator's heart is happy when confronted by a seascape full of laughter, brilliance, and blueness (p. 193).

Gide is merely following poetic traditions when he uses *azur* to denote sky in synecdochic contexts. He does so often, as in *Les Nourritures terrestres* (pp. 69, 96, 100, 150), *El Hadj* (p. 79),

Amyntas (*Biskra*, p. 280), and the *Voyage au Congo* (p. 94). He is more original when he uses *azur* to refer to the sea, thus underlining the sea's color-tones and perpetual boundless qualities which are analogous to the sky's. Towards the beginning of *Le Voyage d'Urien*, for instance, rowers take pleasure in feeling liquid "azur" resist their oars (p. 289).

Examples of Gide's most interesting use of *azur*, however, occur when he adds a metaphorical level to the word's metonymical meaning. In these contexts, not only is Gide using the quality of blueness to denote the whole sky or sea, but he is also suggesting that this *azur* is a living entity endowed with certain capabilities. The African "azur" in *Amyntas* inspires a feeling of physical fitness (*Renoncement*, p. 286). It also has a mystical ability to absorb or dissolve not only clouds (*Mopsus*, p. 11, and *Renoncement*, p. 252), but also people (*Mopsus*, p. 7, and *Renoncement*, p. 339). Perfect azure's ability to absorb mists serves as a useful analogy to underline the ease with which Alissa's smile can dissolve fear and worry (*Porte*, p. 125). On the day when Bernard meets the angel, the Parisian "azur" is smiling at him (*F.M.*, p. 484).

In two works, Gide uses the metaphorical capabilities of *azur* to drive home a special moral message. In the framework letter of *L'Immoraliste*, the writer mentions that he is sitting beneath perfect "azur" (p. 10), a remark which immediately establishes the brilliance of the African sunshine as a pervading feature of many of the following pages. Symbolically, Michel awakens joyously sensitive to the "azur" on a day when he feels his health improve (p. 50). Stimulated by the climate with the exceptionally blue sky, his interest in physical fitness and beauty increases at the expense of moral and intellectual considerations; and finally, he sinks into a state of demoralizing inertia. In a sentence which should by no means be overlooked in an interpretation of *L'Immoraliste*, Michel puts much of the blame for his final condition on the African climate, its clear blue sky: "Rien ne décourage autant la pensée que cette persistance de l'azur" (p. 169). Gide, like Camus in *L'Etranger*, is saying that external circumstances such as climate can motivate man's action and that though man is ostensibly left with his guilt, he should not always be held totally responsible. As a further example, in *Thésée* it is once again the dazzling Mediterranean sky which treacherously attracts a restless Icare to flight.[35] Œdipe's blindness has blotted out the sky (p. 118). When he retires into his darkened world, he is glad that his thoughts ("ciel intérieur"),

114

no longer dimmed by the "firmament azuré," will alone govern his actions. He will have most ironically and completely escaped one source of his (and Michel's) dilemma.

The spread of implications in Gide's use of *azur* would seem to have passed far beyond the bounds of traditional metonymy and even of Mallarmé's aesthetic metaphor. In its most clearly denotative contexts, an azure color suggests a host of mystical or supernatural abstract concepts, such as the beautiful, the deceptive, the hopeful, the unknown, the infinite, the eternal, the divine, and the perfect. His synecdochic use of *azur* to signify the sea is a minor but resourceful stylistic device. And in connotative metaphorical contexts Gide the moralist uses what is literally his most ethereal image to warn his readers to be wary of influences beyond themselves. In its frequent occurrences the word *azur* thus contributes poetic imagery and a didactic message to the aesthetic and moral texture of Gide's writing.

Tiédeur:

The word *tiédeur* (*tiède*) follows a pattern of frequency very much like that of *azur*. Both words occur most often in *Le Voyage d'Urien*, *Les Nourritures terrestres*, and *Amyntas*. They even appear together on many of the same pages. *Tiédeur* means "tepidness," "tepidity," or "lukewarmness." The sensation (or image) which it conveys is one of touch. It may refer literally to temperature, such as that of air or water. In the figurative sense it can be applied to feelings with the very often pejorative meaning of indifference. It is, in this case, the opposite of *ferveur*. What renders the word unique in Gide is not only the relatively high frequency of its occurrences, but also the extraordinarily pleasant or seductive qualities which Gide insists on associating with it.

Thanks to his autobiographical works, there can be no doubt about the personal pleasure which Gide himself took in tepid temperatures. In the 1920's he rejoices in the mild air after a storm (*Congo*, p. 87). In 1930 he speaks ecstatically of a radiant sky and luke-warm air (*Journal*, le 26 avril 1930). In 1940 he mentions an exquisite "tiédeur" which seemed to invite one's whole being to joyful fulfilment (*Journal*, le 6 mai 1940). In the summer of 1948 glorious tepid days revive him after some cold ones (*Journal*, le 8 juin 1948).

Characters in Gide's earliest narrative and lyrical works enjoy the same simple physical pleasure. André Walter praises the tepid air of a beautiful night (*Cahiers*, p. 39). In *Les Poésies d'André Walter* the pleasure of mild weather is associated with earlier, happier days which the lovers recall (pp. 187, 188). It will be a tepid evening which will first tempt them to venture outside (p. 182). But ironically, once they are outside, it is a tepid wind which extinguishes their light (p. 183). The nature depicted in *La Tentative amoureuse* harmonizes with the emotions of the lovers. As spring advances, their love progresses and they enjoy the increasingly luke-warm air (p. 228). But in summer, when their love is lingering on its highest plateau, the tepidness which their hands have acquired will symbolically wilt the flowers (pleasures) which they have imprudently enjoyed (p. 232). The pleasure of mild breezes plays a part in luring Urien's sailors away from their books (*Urien*, p. 289), and during the voyage they enjoy swimming in luke-warm water (pp. 292, 299). The narrator of *Les Nourritures terrestres* has discovered the pleasures of bathing in tepid waters even before meeting Ménalque (p. 70). Mild air, moreover, will be one of the first and most constant pleasures which he will praise throughout the whole work (pp. 81, 145, 146, 178, 187, 193). The narrator appears to have an unusually keen sensitivity to temperatures. He admits to a preference for water and damp articles because they allow him to know their temperature (p. 154). When in contact with tepidness, every part of his body seems to increase its sensitivity. Even his feet are able to enjoy tepid mud. Luke-warm water which softens his skin contributes to his special enjoyment of a shave in Naples (p. 97). In a forest his nose can detect more tepid temperatures because these smell of the earth while cooler ones smell of old leaves (p. 150). And he spends one night awake beside an open train window enjoying a mild breeze which his eyelids have detected as being cooler than during the day (p. 102). The African climate is at its best in *Amyntas* when either air or water is luke-warm rather than hot (*Feuilles*, p. 27, and *Renoncement*, pp. 302, 306, 340). In a description of a canal traversing a fertile garden, the swelling tepid water, heavy with earth, subtly promises luxuriant growth. The sentence is constructed so that the word "tiède" forms a single emphatic breath group.[36] Tepidness is clearly Gide's favorite temperature.

In *Les Poésies d'André Walter* and *Le Voyage d'Urien*, an innocent physical pleasure derived from tepid temperatures proved tempting enough to serve as a motivating factor behind the actions of several characters. In many other contexts Gide more specifically associates tepidness with sexual seductiveness. André Walter (*Cahiers*, p. 144), and the narrator of *Les Nourritures terrestres* (p. 148) are affected by the touch of tepid breath. In *Le Voyage d'Urien* excessively tepid water results in a dangerous languor which draws the sailors' attention to slender children (pp. 304, 305). In this same passage they are breathing a luke-warm mist. When attempting to seduce the travellers, the queen has them bathe in tepid swimming pools (p. 311). Too tepid baths are an apparent factor leading to tropical illness which may symbolize sexual indulgence or even venereal disease (p. 318). Insidious destructive qualities of mildness are again emphasized when Urien blames the strangely diaphanous appearance of the first icebergs on the almost luke-warm sea (p. 339). El Hadj almost faints from emotion when he feels the prince's tepid hand on his forehead (*Hadj*, p. 83). In *Les Nourritures terrestres* the narrator sums up the sensual powers of *tiédeur* when he points out that tepid perfumed climates tend to relax one's moral rigidity (pp. 105, 145).

In Gide's subsequent works the seductive implications of *tiédeur* explain the actions of some of his principal characters. The mildness of an Italian spring with which Michel tempts Marceline to travel south will ironically arouse in him the uncontrollable sensual obsessions which will drive them on to Africa (*L'Imm.*, pp. 149, 150). Alissa's sensual instincts are suggested when she comments on a perfumed garden and tepid air in one of her most excited letters to Jérôme (*Porte*, p. 157). Soft tepidness in the air is one of the seductive details in the mysterious setting which intrigues Gérard Lacase in *Isabelle* (p. 189). And when Gérard dreams of Isabelle's embrace one night, her arms are tepid around his neck (p. 242). Gide is perhaps quietly laughing at his own obsession with *tiédeur* when he makes tepidness an unlikely attribute of Lafcadio's remarkable beaver hat (*Caves*, p. 340). The tepid air which the chaste Amédée Fleurissoire encounters at Genoa may be ironically forecasting his subsequent sexual encounter with Carola (p. 259).

The pastor's relatively frequent use of *tiédeur* in *La Symphonie pastorale* is a clue to his sexual temptations. In the far from detailed description of Gertrude's training, for example, he tells us that she learns to distinguish between hot, cold, and luke-warm (p. 25). On the same page he curiously chooses to compare her progress with the gradual triumph of the tepidity and persistence of spring over winter. At the end of the first notebook, Gertrude has expressed her love, and the pastor basks in the mild air of sunset (p. 56). Two nights after they have kissed, the pastor thinks of her, as, beside his open window, he listens to the immense silence of the heavens: "L'air est tiède . . . (p. 77).

The joys involved in tepidness frequently occur on the same page as the perfect beauty of azure in Gide's early lyrical works. Nowhere, however, are they more closely and more significantly juxtaposed than in *Les Faux-monnayeurs* when Bernard meets the angel in the Luxembourg Gardens. The scene is symbolically set for a struggle between the earthly, represented by the physically seductive tepidness of the air, and the spiritual, represented by the infinitely mysterious azure of the sky.[37] And tepidness, like azure, is one of the features of the first morning of the world in both *Perséphone* and *Les Nouvelles Nourritures* (*Pers.*, p. 311, and *N.N.*, p. 192). Significantly, the day's caress is so seductively tepid that it would cause even the most timid soul to abandon itself to love.

Tepid air retains its seductive power until the end of Gide's literary career. *Geneviève* is a *récit* almost totally free of descriptive detail; yet, Geneviève tells us explicitly that on the day of her last encounter with her mother, the air was almost pleasantly tepid (*Ecole*, p. 246). One may at least partially attribute Eveline's sentimental recollections to the encouragement of the weather. Ariane reveals her passion to Thésée on a mild spring night which palpitates in sympathy with her heart (*Thésée*, p. 49).

It is at first surprising to find that the author who preached the doctrine of fervor almost never chose to use *tiédeur* to convey the contrasting idea of indifference. But such usage would have detracted from the special significance which Gide exploited in this word. The recurring image of tepidness which ranges from meaning a source of simple pleasures to suggesting insidiously seductive power remains constantly literal and earthbound: the pleasures which tepid temperatures are able to provide are physical, and contrast strikingly with the more spiritual pleasures to be found in the Gidean image of azure. But just as the image of azure is an important part of the *lexique* which Gide uses for the indirect expression of some of his spiritual preoccupations, the image of tepidness is one of the devices which succeed in making his expression of the sensual so persistent yet inconspicuous.

Déracinement and Dépaysement:

The polemical writings of André Gide have been as responsible as Maurice Barrès' *Les Déracinés* for extending the usage of *déra-*

cinement in a figurative sense. Since the 1897 publication of the Barrès novel, the notion of uprooting — traditionally applied quite literally to plants and trees or by extension to the eradication of human faults — has been popularly connected with human beings who move from their native habitat. This particular meaning would be more literally expressed, of course, by *dépaysement*, another image-conveying abstraction. Barrès had used the disasters of a group of young men who had left Nancy for Paris to illustrate the dangers of uprooting. André Gide, on the other hand — particularly between 1897 and 1909 — took pains to oppose Barrès and encouraged young people to leave home in order to allow their individuality to develop. Only the weak or the guardians of the French frontier should remain ineradicably entrenched in their native soil.[38]

Since this theory became closely linked with Gide's public image, it seems strange that both the abstractions *déracinement* and *dépaysement* appear so seldom in Gide's narrative, dramatic, and lyrical writings. They appear not at all in *Les Nourritures terrestres* and *Le Retour de l'enfant prodigue,* where uprooting is a central issue. The fact of the matter is that once again Gide is too subtle and astute a writer to spell out his principal themes directly. In spite of the images conveyed by *déracinement* and *dépaysement*, Gide was no more likely to overwork these two words than he did *renoncement, liberté, désir,* or *ferveur.* Usually he simply allows the reader to assimilate by himself the lesson implied by his various uprooted or firmly rooted characters. Excesses of either sort seem to be inadvisable. It is true that the uprooting of Philoctète, Michel, the prodigal son, Lafcadio, and Œdipe develops potentially valuable aspects of their characters. But the various unpleasant possibilities which may result from uprooting are suggested by their misfortunes. One remembers especially Protos explaining to Lafcadio that uprooting is all that is needed to make a rascal out of a gentleman (*Caves*, p. 375). The narrator of *Les Faux-monnayeurs* states explicitly that Laura Douviers and Vincent Molinier make love at the sanitarium because their uprooting has liberated them from moral inhibitions, and invites the reader to believe that Vincent's later loss of will power may be the result of his feeling of "dépaysement" in the presence of the formidable Lady Griffith (*F.M.*, p. 211). The figures who remain rooted to their stagnant lives provide no worthier examples to follow: the narrator of *Paludes*, the prodigal son's older brother, Alissa, Isabelle (whose

119

name is similar enough to Alissa's to remind us of some unexpected similarities) and the various "crustaceans" of *Les Caves du Vatican* and *Les Faux-monnayeurs*. The answer to uprooting seems to lie in the examples set by Bernard and Thésée, who both derive a feeling of purpose during their uprooting and return home ready to apply it to their lives. Thésée even refers to the benefits of his uprooting explicitly in connection with his admiring astonishment at the culture of the Cnossos court (*Thésée*, p. 40).

It would appear, then, that by generally expressing one of his most characteristic themes indirectly through the device of characters' actions, Gide has suppressed what might have been the normal frequency of *déracinement* and *dépaysement*. Gide's tendency to avoid the most obvious means of expression has here superceded his preference for image-conveying abstractions.

Ardeur:

The word *ardeur* (*ardent*) never loses its fundamental etymological image of intense heat. In figurative contexts, where it means human passion, it suggests an even stronger feeling than do *ferveur* and *lyrisme*. And yet Gide chose to use this image-conveying word less frequently than did his contemporaries.

Ardeur appears most often in literal contexts and in its adjectival form *ardent*. Gide applies it to a variety of elements in nature such as clouds at sunset, stars, the desert, and the sun.[39] Moreover, through imaginative variations in standard syntax, he sometimes gives special poetic emphasis to the word.[40] But he did not choose to use the heat image so implicit in *ardeur* when dealing with sexual desire or acts. *Ardeur* serves, rather, to add a gentler sensual quality to Gide's descriptions in a way which is more reminiscent of his use of *tiédeur* than of *soif*. But unlike both *tiédeur* and *soif, ardeur* is neither a *mot-clef* nor a *mot-thème* in Gide's works.

One is at first tempted to attribute the relative infrequency of *ardeur* to limitations which Gide imposed on the word's figurative meaning. For passages in his autobiographical works reveal that at least after 1931 the word signified to him a contrived emotion which he consciously substituted for the more spontaneous "ferveur." [41] After adolescence, "ferveur" becomes very elusive, and a middle-aged person wishing to keep feeling young must nurture "ardeur" — even at the expense of "quiétude" (*Pages*, p. 28). In earlier narrative, dramatic, and lyrical works, however, it would seem that Gide had not yet arrived at his specialized definition: the "ardeur" of André Walter, Emmanuèle, and Gérard Lacase seems in no way contrived (*Cahiers*, pp. 60, 102, 109, 145, and *Isa.*, p. 247). *Les Faux-monnayeurs* is the first work where it is possible to see Gide's later definition; for the youthful ardor which the naïve Azaïs quite unnecessarily prescribes for Sarah and Armand is, to the elderly gentleman at least, a synthetic emotion (*F.M.*, p. 370). And the narrator's plea for "ardeur" (rather than "ferveur") in *Les Nouvelles Nourritures* is indicative of the special meaning which the older Gide imposed on the word (*N.N.*, p. 194).

But with so little evidence of a restricted meaning in works prior to 1931, one cannot attribute the infrequency of its occurrences to any personal semantic limitations imposed on the word by the author. Apart from its use in literal contexts, *ardeur* (*ardent*) was simply not a favored part of Gide's abstract diction.

It is always difficult to draw definitive conclusions about an author as changeable in his literary moods as is André Gide. The critic is always grasping at what he believes are "constants." One must especially guard against vast and unjustified generalizations about "stylistic dominants" when one is basing one's judgments on a limited number of examples drawn from a long and varied career. Here, though, we can at least say that the frequency and expressiveness of these image-conveying abstractions are indicative of the value which Gide found in this specialized kind of vocabulary. We have seen that in a wealth of descriptive, didactic, psychological, and ironical contexts these words' combination of imagery and abstraction seemed particularly suited to the fulfilment of his various aims.

In his use of *dénuement, nudité, soif,* and *ivresse*, Gide appears to have gone consistently and widely beyond these words' literal meaning. By exploiting the images they contain, he thus eased the work load on such comparatively imageless words as *renoncement, liberté, désir,* and *exaltation*. He has thereby also been successful in adding a most unobtrusive yet telling texture of sense impressions to the intangible moral concepts which he is expressing. The fact that he does not similarly exploit *ardeur* is perhaps just another example of Gidean inconsistency, or else the exception which proves the rule.

Gide's use of *azur* and *tiédeur* illustrates the subtle variety of implications which he could extract from image-conveying abstrac-

121

tions which appealed to him. Whether the means he uses are metonymy or metaphor, or whether the issues he is dealing with are spiritual or sensual, he is constantly drawing uniquely Gidean implications from the expressive potential of his favorite color and temperature. And finally, Gide doubtless found it ironical himself that while seldom using the word, he was one of those who brought an importance to *déracinement* which must have surprised even Maurice Barrès. Frequent and infrequent, literal and figurative, metaphorical and metonymical, sensual and spiritual, moralistic and ironical, Gide's image-conveying abstractions are all of these. But is this all we can conclude?

The word "classical" has become a commonplace in discussion of Gide's writings. Certainly, if we look at Gide's own definition of classicism, "l'art d'exprimer le plus en disant le moins" (*Billets,* p. 39), Gide was then undoubtedly a master of the art of classical writing. Moreover, his adaptations of classical myths, his blending of the *dulce* and the *utile*, and his interest in psychology rather than external description are more reminiscent of a seventeenth-century dramatist like Racine than of a post-Revolutionary novelist like Balzac. So is the high density of his abstract vocabulary. Yet when one looks at Gide's handling of his abstractions, one finds that he diverges from standard seventeenth-century procedure. We have seen that Racine's *ardeur*, for instance, does not figure largely in Gide's vocabulary. Neither does La Rochefoucauld's *amour-propre*. Furthermore, words like *dénuement, nudité, soif, ivresse,* and *azur*, which have usurped the importance of *ardeur* and *amour-propre*, have appeared in a quantity of metaphorical contexts which would have been highly unusual in seventeenth-century writers. While these writers readily perceived and made use of the metonymical potential of, for instance, *azur* (for ciel) and *ardeur* (for *passion*), they were generally reluctant to exploit implicit or submerged metaphor. Hence, while we must in general agree with Ramon Fernandez, who admired the reticence in Gide's style and claimed that the subtlest manifestation of it was his return to the "style abstrait" of seventeenth-century writers,[42] we must also keep in mind the liberties which Gide took with the metaphorical potential of his abstractions. For the highly metaphorical texture of Gide's abstract *lexique* prevents him from being placed squarely beside seventeenth-century writers.

Ultimately we must concede along with our other conclusions that, as far as his use of abstract diction is concerned, Gide cannot be classified as totally "classical." More than two centuries of general usage and a liberation of the French language had, of course, allowed for shifts in the relative importance of much abstract diction. But a much more important factor behind the unconventionality of this aspect of Gide's so-called classicism must surely be the individuality which he regularly brought to both his life and his art. Even in his use of abstract diction, it would appear, he succeeded in that sort of uniqueness for which Gide himself reserved the epithet "irremplaçable."

SYMBOLS OF CONTINUITY AND THE UNITY OF *LES THIBAULT*

BY JOHN GILBERT

The question of the unity of *Les Thibault* is a vexed one that has elicited divergent critical responses.* Claude-Edmonde Magny, in a persuasive chapter devoted to Martin du Gard, focuses on what she calls: "Le ciment des *Thibault*: sa lézarde." She proceeds to argue that, in spite of the density and compactness given to the narrative by the use of narrative nodes — "nœuds d'événements" — the vast novel remains irremediably split in two:

> Pourtant il est arrivé aux *Thibault* une chose extrêmement grave, pour un livre destiné à être aussi rigoureusement construit: c'est que l'auteur, par excès de scrupules, a mis trop longtemps à l'écrire, si bien que l'œuvre s'est trouvée scindée en deux parties, que leur esthétique et leur intérêt romanesque opposent plus encore que ne les différencient les dates de publication: un premier bloc qui irait jusqu'à *La Mort du Père*, paru en 1929 et comprenant les six premiers, et brefs, volumes; puis le massif, à la fois touffu, et homogène, que forment les trois tomes de *L'Eté 1914* et *L'Epilogue* publié peu après.[1]

Commenting later on Mme Magny's opinion, Thomas White Hall claims that the seeming disproportion that exists between the first six volumes and the later ones may be justified by the intrusion, in *L'Eté 1914*, of the events of the World War, an intrusion which entails an alteration in the dimensions of the novel. Although Hall's article remains somewhat inconclusive on this point, he seems to come out on the side of unity against Mme Magny's claim of rupture in composition.[2] Jacques Brenner also maintains that the unity of the work is not impaired by the sudden enlargement of the scope of the narrative, that the change of tone after *La Mort du Père* is ordained inevitably by the nature of the subject. The sudden entry of History with a capital H into the private history of the novel's heroes could not have been carried out, according to Brenner, without some very obvious upheaval. In short, he considers the course of the novel to have been disrupted but he does not tell us how the intervention of History does not result in incoherence.[3] More recently, Denis Boak, in his full length study of the novelist, tends to view *L'Eté 1914* and the broadening of scope it represents as a comparative failure.[4] But as was pointed out in a review of Boak's book, far from being settled once and for all, the issue remains very much alive: "Whatever one may feel on this crucial issue, it must be said that Boak weakens his case considerably by his far too casual dismissal of *L'Eté 1914* as propaganda: in view of the importance attached to the novel by previous critics, a more thorough examination of the problem was surely called for." [5]

On a satisfactory appraisal of this problem rests not only our assessment of Martin du Gard's success as a novelist in this his major endeavor but also of the place the novel occupies in the development of twentieth-century French fiction. The divergent views of the critics may only be reconciled if the sudden expansion of the second half of *Les Thibault* may be seen as aesthetically and structurally dependent on the first part, if, in fact, an intrinsic source of unity can be discovered which nullifies the seeming disproportion between the two halves, and which enables the narrative to shift from one register to another without rupture. For this to become apparent, some idea of the range of the novel must be gained from a comparison with works of a similar type.

Les Thibault has come to be considered representative of a kind of sub-genre of the French novel, namely, the *roman-fleuve*. Many of the novels falling under this classification hold little interest for the reader of today although for the critics *Les Thibault* still stands out as an exceptionally accomplished example of the genre and one which, in our view, shows that these novels were not mere aberrations or throwbacks to an earlier phase of the novel's development, but represent a grappling with new problems in fiction and a groping towards new themes and dimensions. Seen in this context, the question of the unity of *Les Thibault* sheds light on the technical elaboration of the genre as a whole and on an important period in the progress of the contemporary novel.

Along with such works as Duhamel's *Les Aventures de Salavin* and *La Chronique des Pasquier*, Jacques de Lacretelle's *Les Hauts Ponts*, Jacques Chardonne's *Les Destinées sentimentales*, *Les Thibault* shows a consistent set of features which account for the comparative isolation in which these novels find themselves. Length is the obvious criterion for classification but it is in their deeper preoccupations that these novels betray their common heritage as well as their kinship with works much shorter in length but of striking similarity of technique and purpose. Their distinguishing characteristic is a pervasive interest in the family, with the family represented as something continuous and endowed with its own life and permanence as opposed to the more or less ephemeral, certainly brief, lives of its members. At times, the established family itself takes on a certain symbolic quality and stands for the continuity which its members value, often defend, frequently rebel against. At others, the symbol for the family's continuity becomes objictified in a business concern, an estate, or a mere piece of woodland. In all cases — this also being characteristic of the fictional type — the members of the family identify themselves fundamentally by their relationship to the group; their essential meaning as individuals derives from the nature of their family ties.

Clearly novels of this type are not confined to French literature; *Buddenbrooks* and *The Forsyte Saga* come to mind as being equally representative, nor can shorter novels be discounted which follow much the same pattern, novels like Jean Schlumberger's *Saint-Saturnin*, Gide's *L'Immoraliste* and Mauriac's *Thérèse Desqueyroux,* where we find the same focus on the family. In all the novels, however, what E. M. Forster calls personal relations fall into recognizable patterns. Parents and children, sibling and sibling, child and property, parent and property, are combinations which appear to permit only a limited number of dispositions and attitudes. Such relations recurring from novel to novel also imply that similar problems of analysis confronted the novelists; they place similar demands on resources of technique.

A curious factor, in terms of French literary history at least, is that there was a spate of such novels written or begun around the critical period of the first World War. This time of upheaval and the unstable years that preceded the actual conflict may well have counted for much in the genesis of the fictional type. For all these novelists these were formative years and for all of them, with their uniformly middle-class backgrounds, they must have been experienced as years in which the values of the society into which they had been born and in whose ways they had been educated were called into question. Although, for the most part, their novels were completed between the wars, they record events leading up to 1914, with the war itself figuring, in two of them at least, as the consummation of a decline in society and civilization. Already in a

126

novel like Barrès's *Les Déracinés* the decline is measured in terms of the divorce between individual and group. The process of *déracinement* reflects a loss of national and regional identity among young people, as well as the decline of the family as a centre of loyalties. The 1890's and the decades that followed were pervaded, according to one historian, by "a sense of impending doom, of old practices and institutions no longer conforming to social realities," by a sense of the "demise of an old society." [6] The same historian suggests that through these years may be traced a search for new values necessitated by this sudden uncertainty. The tangible certainties of positivism and materialism are relinquished in favor of new excursions into the unconscious and the intuitive, and are replaced by a search for less recognizable goals. Martin du Gard's early novel, *Jean Barois*, mirrors just such a period of interrogation and demonstrates the failure of religion and the undermining of established institutions by an event like the Dreyfus case. The Affair, which proved to be the watershed of a whole era, almost coinciding as it did with the turn of the century, became the catalyst for the kind of revision of values that is reflected in the novels of the generation that followed. Those very institutions which the Dreyfus affair laid open to attack are the ones that are under scrutiny in the long novels of Martin du Gard and his fellow chroniclers: if the actual proceedings of the Affair appear only in *Jean Barois*, its spirit permeates *Les Thibault* as it does say *La Chronique des Pasquier*. That very continuity which is the central theme of these fictional sagas came under direct attack in the last years of the nineteenth century and largely due to such events as the Affair. As Barbara Tuchman makes clear in her portrait of the world before the war: 1890–1914, the Affair reflected the great schism between the forces of the past and those of the future and was as much a proof that the old values were under assault as the spread of socialism and the vehement outbursts of the Anarchists. [7]

This crisis of continuity underlies the structure of all the *romans-fleuve* listed above and is what distinguishes them from historical and social chronicles. The notion of continuity belongs, for our present purpose, to the middle class, although, as one can see from the recent example of the best-selling Italian novel, *Il Gattopardo*, it is also relevant to the aristocracy. The sense of continuity derives from a consciousness of the past which, in its narrowest interpretation, is tantamount to a sense of tradition and, in its broadest, to a desire for identity with the whole past of human history (the family of the novel becoming an analogue for the family of man), and for an assurance of continued identity in the future. Seen in this broad context, individual characters tend to be transformed into types or mythic prototypes, personal and typical identity fuse, mythical patterns emerge and themes take on universal breadth and significance. Continuity is here concretized in the cycle of generations of a family in a chain of birth, growth, decline, death and rebirth.

In each of the *romans-fleuve*, the crisis assumes a different form but in each case the perpetuation of the family and, beyond that, human continuity is threatened. *Les Thibault* shows us the rebellion of two sons against the father's efforts to preserve the family. Continuity is imperiled by the death of the father and the advent of war, so that the Thibaults seem doomed to disappear. Similarly, the Pasquier series dramatizes the efforts of three individuals to halt the disintegration of the family: Joseph Pasquier, the capitalist, endeavoring to give it new roots in property; Laurent, the idealist, attempting to nullify the deleterious effects of his father's extravagances and find new spiritual bases for family strength; Cécile, seeking harmony in the face of disorder symbolized by her broken marriage. In the case of *Les Aventures de Salavin*, which is not strictly a family novel, the crisis is still present but expressed in more general terms as the alienation of the individual within the group. Salavin's rebellion against loss of identity provokes the breakdown of the family.

In Lacretelle's *Les Hauts Ponts* and shorter novels like Gide's *L'Immoraliste* and Schlumberger's *Saint-Saturnin*, the family estate functions as an objective correlative of the desire for continuity. In each case, the property is menaced by a change of hands or dispersal. The threat invariably comes from within, from a rebellious or prodigal member of the family. Michel in *L'Immoraliste* performs the symbolically significant act of poaching on his own grounds and neglects the estate. The father in *Saint-Saturnin*, apart from indulging in similar acts of destruction, attempts to disperse the property. Sabine, wife of the owner of "Les Hauts Ponts," in Lacretelle's novel of the same name, precipitates her husband's bankruptcy and the loss of the estate by her extravagance and her sentimental attachment to a scoundrel. Mauriac's novels, a number of which tend to form a loose *roman-fleuve*, as the author has been ready to admit, also portray a collective crisis caused by rebellious elements who threaten the family fortune (*Le Nœud de vipères*) or the name and progeny (*Thérèse Desqueyroux*).

Insofar as these novels, through the pattern of bourgeois crisis, seek to record the social changes and present a panorama of society during those critical years, they may be said to continue the tradition of nineteenth-century Realism and Naturalism. Such, indeed, was the view of Georges Duhamel after listening to a reading of the first volume in Martin du Gard's series, *Le Cahier gris*. His assessment hits at the lack of significant innovation in the work: "Je me suis demandé, en écoutant votre lecture, ce que votre œuvre apporte de *neuf*. Eh bien, franchement, elle n'apporte pas assez. L'entreprise est courageuse, et, dans l'ensemble, réussie. Mais vous ne faites, en somme, qu'utiliser les acquisitions des bons romanciers français et étrangers du XIXᵉ siècle." [8] The Naturalist antecedence of the *roman-fleuve*, acknowledged here by Duhamel, suggests that these novels make little advance on those of Balzac and Zola. And, of course, there are superficial similarities: many of them attempt to provide the chronicle of an age; the fundamental structural pattern, as in *La Comédie humaine* and the *Rougon-Macquart*, rests on the all-pervasive rhythm of Decline and Fall, Rise and Fall, *Splendeurs et Misères*, representing the ebb and flow of fortunes and social tides. Characters recur from volume to volume. Already in Zola the family functions as a symbol of continuity and social decline is measured by the slackening of family ties.

But there exist other developments in the *roman-fleuve*, present also to some degree in Zola, which suggest that they are novels of transition, the most important of which is the shift from a social to an existential focus. The transitional character of a novel like *Les Thibault* appears particularly when it is linked with other novels of its period, those of Gide, Schlumberger and Mauriac, and with those that followed, novels by Sartre and Camus. Already in Zola, and even more prominently in Martin du Gard and his co-novelists, the Naturalist aesthetic is noticeably surpassed. Repetition and recurrence on all planes of composition (character, situation, image) are used so generally that there results both epic simplification and enlargement, images become symbols, and narrative patterns conform to the outlines of myth. One has only to take the obvious example of Zola's use of the single controlling symbol implied in the title of *Germinal* or the more complex shift to an epic and mythic dimension as he portrays the struggle between such forces as decay and vital energy, death and fertility, hereditary destiny and liberty of creation. In his novels there exist three distinct levels of understanding, the familial, the social and the cosmic.

A similar process of expansion and generalization occurs in the novels of Duhamel, Lacretelle and especially Martin du Gard, through the central function of a symbol of continuity, the family gradually serving as an analogue for humanity at large. Where, in the Naturalist novel, the emphasis remains largely sociological, in these novels of the Twentieth Century, in spite of their seeming similarity, man is no longer seen in relation to society alone but to broader humanity. The effects of hereditary determinism, for example, do not remain merely the object of scientific observation, they provoke a metaphysical response; there occurs a shift of emphasis from what Thomas Mann called "the bourgeois and individual to the mythical and typical." [9] This precisely is what happens in *Les Thibault* and this precisely is what is behind the debate over the novel's unity. By a curious coincidence, the continuity of the novel shows the same fissure as the human continuity that is the novel's main theme. But, clearly, "coincidence" is a word that has no relevance in this case, for the structural break results from the internal elaboration of the work itself; the seeming rupture in the composition of *Les Thibault* is organic to the very meaning of the work itself. Until this has been appreciated it seems to me that all accusations of structural disunity must await judgment.

At the basis of the rupture in *Les Thibault* there lies the change of plan which caused Martin du Gard to delay completion of his novel cycle, the circumstances of which bear re-examining. According to the detailed account given in the *Souvenirs autobiographiques et littéraires*, the hiatus after the publication of *La Mort du Père*, the sixth volume, was caused by a motor accident which gave the author time to have serious doubts about the direction his novel was taking. The original plan for the novel was drawn up in the spring of 1920 and consisted of the following:

> J'avais été brusquement séduit par l'idée d'écrire l'histoire de deux frères: deux êtres de tempéraments aussi différents, aussi divergents, que possible, mais foncièrement marqués par les obscures similitudes que crée, entre deux consanguins, un très puissant atavisme commun. Un tel sujet m'offrait l'occasion d'un fructueux dédoublement: j'y voyais la possibilité d'exprimer simultanément deux tendances contradictoires de ma nature: l'instinct d'indépendance, d'évasion, de révolte, le refus de tous les conformismes; et, cet instinct d'ordre, de mesure, ce refus des extrêmes, que je dois à mon hérédité. (*OC*, I, lxxx.)

130

Apart from the strong admixture of autobiography and the full scope afforded for psychological analysis, the plan appears tailor-made for a conventional Naturalist novel. The change it underwent following the accident of 1931 radically altered its dimensions, led away from the Naturalist prescriptions and transformed its social perspective into a mythic one. Particularly revealing in this respect is a comparison of the end of the novel as it now stands and the projected ending, which was to cover several more volumes. As we now have it, the climax of *Les Thibault* lies in the protracted description of Europe at war, with the *Epilogue* and Antoine Thibault's death as something of a prolongation of the catastrophe but situated on an individual plane. In the original plan, the World War appeared in a different perspective, and in fact was reduced in importance. Far from outweighing individual destinies, it was to figure as just another event in the history of the Thibault family and subordinate to such a history. Indeed, the cyclical pattern of the continuity of the family would have become fully rounded, with Antoine Thibault marrying Jenny de Fontanin, thus becoming, in effect, a father to his brother's child. The two brothers would in this way have been fused into a new incarnation of the father figure, especially if, as in the present version, Martin du Gard had shown Antoine persisting in his intention of adopting his father's name, Oscar. But the novel as we now have it carries a notably different emphasis. The cycle of generations receives incomplete development; the three pivotal moments of the novel occur at the time of the three deaths: the father's at the end of the sixth volume; Jacques's at the end of *L'Eté 1914*; Antoine's occupying the major part of the *Epilogue*. The last two merge into the universal death of a civilization through the World War.

The risk of disunity and imbalance as a consequence of the change of plan did not escape the vigilance of Martin du Gard but, if anything, he appeared to see this risk as considerably diminished in the new design for the work. As originally conceived, the novel would have benefited from an undeniable source of unity in the chronological movement of the generations of a single family; the change of emphasis must, therefore, in Martin du Gard's eyes, have necessitated the adoption of a new plan which in the light of his new purpose was superior to the previous one. Where this superiority lies can only be ascertained by understanding the role of the family in the final version of the novel. In fact, it now functions as a symbol and becomes the principal focus for thematic and structural patterns, whereas earlier it would have remained a loose framework for a series of detached episodes centering on the various members of the family.

The concern for racial continuity among the main characters remains constant from the first to the last pages. As early as the second volume, *Le Penitencier*, Antoine Thibault consciously voices it. Disturbed by his brother's rebelliousness, he attempts to initiate Jacques in the solemn responsibilities of preserving the Thibault line. In a fine burst of oratory, he emphasizes their representative status: "Frères! Non seulement le même sang, mais les mêmes racines depuis le commencement des âges, exactement le même jet de sève, le même élan! Nous ne sommes pas seulement deux individus, Antoine et Jacques: nous sommes deux Thibault, nous sommes les Thibault" (*OC*, I, 763). With this exhortation, and the vision it conjures up for the individual of a role which surpasses his time-bound existence, the horizon of the novel expands from the confines of the bourgeois and individual until it opens up perspectives of the mythical and typical. This enlargement receives particular stress in the *Epilogue*, where Antoine's concern for continuity, still basically rooted in the family context, now accretes added meaning and demands a broader understanding of the notion of continuity.

The *Epilogue* recounts Antoine's attempts to come to terms with his own dying. He notes the progress of his decline in his diary. It is not simply his scientific detachment that provides the platform for his resistance to death but faith in his own survival through Jean-Paul, his brother's son. In pages destined to be read by his nephew, he asks himself a fundamental question: "Au nom de quoi vivre, travailler, donner son maximum?" to which the ready reply comes: "Au nom du passé et de l'avenir. Au nom de ton père et de tes fils, au nom du maillon que tu es dans la chaîne . . . Assurer la continuité . . . Transmettre ce qu'on a reçu, — transmettre amélioré, enrichi" (*OC*, II, 989). However, this credo setting down Antoine's faith in the future does not rest solely on the knowledge that the Thibault family will continue to flourish through Jean-Paul for, with the approach of death, Antoine becomes detached from his personal destiny and is able to view it as part of the general destiny of mankind; he participates in a ritual moment of death and rebirth through the revelation that his death as a human event takes its place in the total human event of History. This, indeed, suggests why Martin du Gard submits Antoine's final moments to such clinical scrutiny. The diary serves the double purpose of minimizing, by means of the dispassionate notation of pathological details, the importance of the isolated phenomenon of a single man's death and of giving that death added significance in the light of the subject's perception of a more general decline in his own civilization.

A closer examination of the *Epilogue* will show how radically the dimensions of the novel have changed since the so-called break after *La Mort du Père*. The focus of the narrative, from being centered on the individual's vicissitudes within the family, has become phylogenic. The stage is gradually cleared for a confrontation, grandiose in its simplicity, between man and his destiny. Four years have passed since the events of *L'Eté 1914*; characters have disappeared (Jacques, Oscar Thibault); others, so important earlier, have faded into the background (Jenny, Daniel de Fontanin, Gise). Antoine, the last of the immediate Thibault family, becomes the center of the narrative. Through him man's final coming to terms with death is worked out and the tension of the moment is contained in the rhythm of the narrative itself — tension which, in the *Journal d'Antoine*, grows out of the alternating themes of individual decay and suffering and collective continuity, between the spectacle of pain and the quiet contemplation of that pain. The focus of the novel switches repeatedly from the individual's plight to broad visions of the eternal cycles of renewal evident in the progress of the human race (*OC*, II, 969). Antoine himself recognizes the double perspective of his journal when he states his intention of noting the advance of his disease as well as of exorcising certain demons from his past (*OC*, 11, 922). The sense of expiation, of undergoing a moment of tragic transformation, of sacrificing himself to a common cause, is inescapable when we read: "Tout ce qui m'accable de nouveau, ce matin, me semblait sans poids, sans importance; le néant, ma mort prochaine, s'imposaient à moi avec une certitude d'un caractère particulier, qui excluait la révolte. Pas exactement du fatalisme, non: le sentiment de participer, même par la maladie et la mort, au destin de l'univers" (*OC*, II, 972).

It is clear from the themes of the *Epilogue* that Martin du Gard has abandoned the preoccupations of the Naturalist novel. Given the function of the family as an expanding symbol of continuity, I think we are justified in reading *Les Thibault* archetypally and mythically. The unity of the novel must no longer be sought in the chronological tracing of the lives of individual characters but in the underlying structures which make the interaction of individual and typical, of individual and collective, an essential vehicle of meaning. The tragic archetype is the chief of these structures and is the one which explains the general movement of the novel towards the final confrontation between man and death. But this central archetypal pattern is accompanied by others which also depend for their logic and elaboration on the necessary expansion of the second part of the novel through the more specific enlargement of the function of the family symbol.

How, specifically, does this expansion operate? If we take the theme of revolt as an important and representative example we can trace the expansion of the central symbol through a series of correlatives until, in the *Epilogue*, family tyranny has become synonymous with all forces depriving man of his freedom. Very simply, this explains why during the course of the novel Jacques Thibault ceases to be a *révolté* and becomes a *révolutionnaire*, why what begins as personal, highly romantic rebellion against family repression in the name of self-expression and passive idealism emerges finally as resistance to social injustice, identification with a common cause and dynamic commitment to group action. Throughout the first six volumes of *Les Thibault*, the family, in the person of the father, is identified with various agencies of repression: the boarding school (*Le Cahier gris*), the reformatory (*Le Pénitencier*), L'Ecole normale (*La Sorellina*). By the time we reach *L'Eté 1914*, the family clearly represents capitalist society at large, a whole civilization whose collapse has already been heralded by the schisms among the Thibaults in the earlier volumes. Jacques makes these connections quite clear later when he tries to explain the pattern of his life:

> Ce qui a fait de moi un révolutionnaire . . . c'est d'être né ici, dans cette maison . . . C'est d'avoir été un fils de bourgeois . . . C'est d'avoir eu, tout jeune, le spectacle quotidien des injustices dont vit ce monde privilégié . . . C'est d'avoir eu, dès l'enfance, comme un sentiment de culpabilité . . . de complicité! Oui: la sensation cuisante que, cet ordre de choses, tout en le haïssant, j'en profitais! [. . .] Bien avant de savoir ce que c'était que le capitalisme, avant même d'en connaître le mot, à douze ans, à treize ans, rappelle-toi: j'étais en révolte contre le monde où je vivais, celui de mes camarades, de mes professeurs . . . le monde de Père, et de ses bonnes œuvres! (*OC*, II, 152.)

The transfer of allegiance which takes Jacques Thibault away from the family towards a second "family," the socialist action group, exemplifies the changes in society the novel attempts to portray. Jacques and his associates in Geneva strive to make good the failure in human relationships within the family by seeking a broader base for solidarity in political commitment.

From this one example of the kind of extension of meaning that takes place through an expanding symbol one is able to discern broad emotional configurations which correspond, the closer one looks at them, to the patterns of a central governing archetype. In her well-known study of *Archetypal Patterns in Poetry*, Maud Bodkin, with the concurrence of Gilbert Murray and C. G. Jung, examines the themes of tragic poetry and the patterns into which they tend to fall.[10] Essentially, she detects two movements in these patterns: the one of conflict occasioned by the attempts of an emerging ego to assert itself, and a counter-movement of atonement resulting in the merging of the ego with a greater power — "the community consciousness." This double action rests with notable regularity on a conflict of generations and dramatizes the underlying fantasy of the self seeking heroic stature in the face of a barrier posed for the emerging self-consciousness by the king/father figure. This pattern is clearly schematic and relies too heavily for our present purpose on Miss Bodkin's specialized vocabulary, but it is useful as a starting point in the elucidation of *Les Thibault*.

Inescapably, we find ourselves returning to a pattern of this nature in Martin du Gard's supposedly flawed novel. Fortunately, we do not have to speculate too loosely on the obsessional roots underlying the initial conflicts. For in the short novella written by Jacques, entitled *La Sorellina*, Martin du Gard has, by his own admission, attempted to give body to the fantasy of power entertained by the younger Thibault. As Martin du Gard says of *La Sorellina*: "Jacques est censé l'avoir écrite, en exil, d'après des souvenirs personnels et secrets, pour se délivrer de ses obsessions" (*OC*, I, xciv–xcv). Jacques's novella, which gives the volume its title, is a transparent parable of family life whose parallels with Jacques's own situation are neatly drawn out by Antoine as he reads it. The work provides a highly romantic account of a younger son's rebelliousness against his father. It is set in exotic Italian surroundings and conveyed in a breathless style of youthful exaltation. The elements singled out by Antoine for particular comment are a series of more or less developed portraits and descriptions of three interdependent relationships: the first between the son, Giuseppe, and his father; the other two contracted in defiance of the father and in-

135

volving, on the one hand, Giuseppe and his sister, and, on the other, Giuseppe and a young English girl.

Images of pain overshadow the first of these relationships, which finally resolves itself into a stasis of love-hate. The father is cast in the archetypal role of a repressive figure, the guardian of social values and institutions, the upholder of virtue, authority and the Church. Most striking is his complete identification with the society of which he is a monument. Metaphorically represented he emerges as: "Une force. Mieux, un poids. Non pas force agissante, mais force inerte qui pèse" (*OC*, II, 1176). The emergence of Giuseppe as an individual from the collective background produces a crescendo of hatred directed at the overpowering presence of his father: "Oui, haine et révolte, tout le passé de Giuseppe. S'il pense à sa jeunesse, un gout de vengeance lui monte. Dès la prime enfance, tous les instincts, à mesure qu'ils prennent forme, entrent en lutte contre le père" (*OC*, I, 1189). Expressed thus as a primal instinct, Giuseppe's passion can have only one outcome: the desire for the father's death and, in despair, his own destruction. In response, the father banishes his son, reducing him to a social pariah.

From this examination of the father-son relationship we must clearly conclude that Martin du Gard is indeed using the novella, *La Sorellina*, as a means of conveying Jacques's obsessions as well as extracting from the density of disparate events a psychological schema governing the multiple conflicts within the family situation. A further dimension is added by the two other relationships contained in the short story: both express rebellion in sexual terms, both contravene taboos, but the one depicts an attempt on the part of Giuseppe to liberate his instincts while the other shows him trying to excise them utterly. His incestuous feelings for his sister (reflecting Jacques Thibault's desire for Gise) indicate how impatient with any normal restraints his sensual drives have become, while his love for Sybil, the foreigner and heretic, takes on the aspect of a sublimation of the former love, reflecting, at the same time, a compulsion to rid himself of the dangerous attraction for his sister and to seek refuge from it by aspiring to a dream of purity. Giuseppe's solution to his dilemma amounts to a surrender to the prohibitions of society and to his own inhibitions, as he abandons both forbidden loves and leaves to seek a new identity abroad. This response closely parallels Jacques's own in that he too attempts to start afresh under an assumed name in Switzerland.

That *La Sorellina* lends itself to such schematic analysis is some indication of how patent a transposition it is of Jacques's obsessions and the workings of his subconscious. At the same time, we are forced to the conclusion that these obsessional patterns correspond to Martin du Gard's own, at least insofar as they provide a mold for his creative powers, especially in view of their recurrence in earlier works. *Devenir* (1908), besides containing a number of incidents found in *Les Thibault*, follows a familiar pattern of a quest for identity. The title stresses the theme of self-realization, while the dilemma of André Mazerelles foreshadows that of Giuseppe/ Jacques in *La Sorellina*. The subtitles *Vouloir!, Réaliser?, Vivre,* reflect the drama of will at work and point to Martin du Gard's re- current concern with the evolution of the individual in time, which leads directly into the theme of human continuity. Like his Thibault successors, André is torn between conflicting allegiances, between his atavism and what he calls his true nature ("ma nature à moi"). *Devenir* contains as a basic element of its structure a narrative within the main narrative, in the form of a project for a play to be written by André. Once again a work of the imagination serves to expose the underlying obsessions of the hero who begins to write at the critical moment of his rebellion and at the time he enters upon an illicit relationship with a sophisticated Russian woman. Through it Mazerelles attempts to come to terms with the conflicts in his own nature: "L'essentielle opposition des êtres d'action et des êtres de rêve, l'incompatibilité du terrestre et du mystique, le heurt incessant des générations entre elles" (*OC*, I, 113). Like Jacques Thibault, Mazerelles does not resolve these conflicts, but unlike Jacques, his life comes full circle and he abandons the quest, returns to the family, and dies in the bourgeois milieu to which he is indissolubly bound.

Jean Barois yields up a similar pattern. Again the hero's life is circular and reflects the general use of cyclical structures in the novel based on patterns of recurrence. The events conform to a classical topos, to what has been called the "battle of the individual" to free himself from his former self.[11] (Hence the original title of the work, *S'Affranchir*.) The recurrence of this sequence of events points beyond a personal preoccupation on the part of the author to the symbolic use of archetypal situations explanatory of human self-realization.

"The archetypal pattern corresponding to tragedy may be said to be a certain organization of the tendencies of self-assertion and submission. The self which is asserted is magnified by that same collective force to which finally submission is made; and from the tension of the two impulses and their reaction upon each other, under the conditions of poetic exaltation, the distinctive tragic emotion and attitude arises." Thus Maud Bodkin (*Archetypal Patterns in Poetry*, p. 23) characterizes the forces which in various permutations constitute the basic psychological texture of tragedy. Whether we accept the exact formulation or not, especially in view of the proliferation of theories of the tragic, is largely immaterial since what we have here primarily is a working hypothesis suggesting at least that the patterns that we have found to be insistently recurrent in Martin du Gard may be groping towards a novel with broader dimensions than may at first appear.

Examination of the text at close hand will, I think, yield up the kind of organization that these psychological patterns would inevitably promote. *Les Thibault*, being firmly centered on a quest for identity, quickly falls into a series of character situations in which the individual strives to see his way clear to freedom and self-realization. Overall, the ten volumes move through a parabola initiated in the individual, reaching its apogee in the group and community and its final definition in the individual once again. The interplay of the urge to self-assertion and the resolve to submission, contained particularly within the logic of the conflict between the generations, achieves its most tragic impact, as well as its greatest structural significance, in the individual's confrontation with death. In the change of plan for *Les Thibault*, Martin du Gard wrote a new dimension into his novel: in the rhythm of the narrative as we have it in its final form, the stress falls on the deaths of the three Thibaults; and in the existential questions posed and the solutions found or refused at those moments lies, perhaps, the coherence of the work.

Oscar Thibault's demise concludes the first sweeping movement of the novel. In it is contained the definition of his life; he is fixed once and for all in the role which society has forced upon him; at the same time, as Antoine goes through his father's private papers and letters, we glimpse the shadows of a life that was still-born; finally, in the long agony that precedes his death, we witness the erosion of values which fail in the end to protect him from the anguish of existence.

From the earliest pages of *Le Cahier gris* Oscar garners his reputation from the extensive public services he has performed, especially in works of philanthropy and moral preservation. The monument to his role in society is the Pénitencier to which he commits his own son and which, labelled with his own name, stands for all that is repressive and authoritarian. The spirit of Oscar Thibault reigns over the institution as does his image: "Un buste en plâtre de M. Thibault de grandeur naturelle, mais qui sur ce mur bas prenait des proportions colossales décorait le panneau de droite; un humble crucifix de bois noir, orné de buis, essayait de lui faire pendant sur le mur opposé" (*OC*, I, 682). The irony here could not be more fierce; it exposes the pretentions of Thibault in supplanting God as the arbiter of morals and justice and indirectly shows to what degree he has become petrified and forbiddingly dehumanized in his moral attitudes. In many respects Oscar is the institution. The only conduits for his feelings, his loyalties and ideals are those that lead into the narrow channel of social respectability. But it is at the moment of his death that the full extent of his capitulation to external forces becomes apparent.

Several of the themes explored in *La Mort du Père* assume particular importance in view of the fact that it is after this volume that the break in composition occurred; they therefore appear as so many loose threads which will be tied into the broad fabric of the narrative of *L'Eté 1914*. First of all, the progress of decay is accelerated: as a motif it forms part of a growing sense of degeneration which appeared as early as *Le Pénitencier* with the death of Maman Frühling, made a considerable advance during the volume *La Consultation*, in which Antoine almost literally struggles with the forces of death, and culminates in the extensive imagery of decay applied to a whole civilization in *L'Eté 1914*. Jacques's and Antoine's deaths, as we shall see, round out the movement. Although *La Mort du Père* represents a climax in the development of the novel, it is only a subsidiary one, a secondary stress in the rhythm of tragic action. The volume begins with a reminder of the pervasive atmosphere of decay and thereafter several scenes emphasize the finality of death, the void beyond, and, in the Abbé Vécard's visitations, the inadequacy of religion, especially in its glib formulas, in providing solace. Although solicited by Vécard's high-sounding assurances, Oscar Thibault turns from the promises of resurrection in an afterlife to seek purely human comfort in memories of his childhood; significantly, this is the rebirth he yearns for.

In his final moments it is noteworthy that Thibault senses the failure of his endeavors at achieving immortality: the insistence with which his last wishes aim at preserving his name, the childish fear, the temptation to blaspheme, all these responses inform us of his uncertainty and, more importantly when we compare him to his sons, of his failure as a man, his inability to achieve heroic stature. His last displays of energy are mere paroxysms of self-assertion in extremis, for his whole life has in fact been one of submission. In touching counterpoint to the slow subsidence into oblivion, marked by the gradual fixation of his features into a public mask, sounds an occasional echo from his past which suggests that once he was different: in passages from his letters and private papers that are sifted by Antoine, we are able to cull intimations of a love-affair, and a residue of affection, ill-expressed, half-concealed, for his wife. The private emotion has clearly sunk to the bottom and been obscured by the public persona. For there is in the first movement of *Les Thibault*, as there is in the novel as a whole, a double perspective: the public and the private, the general and the particular, man as individual and man as representative. And this is something that is carried over from volume to volume, nullifying the so-called break in composition, and it is carried through the theme of continuity.

The central question of existence nagging at Oscar Thibault as he confronts death is the one of continuity; the same question that will preoccupy both Jacques and Antoine in the second and third 'movements' of the novel. Oscar's solution has been to graft himself onto the body politic and civic by means of his devotion to its institutions, his championing of its causes, and his immersion in its principles. His funeral arrangements confirm this interpretation of his faith in the future of the society he has served; representatives of the country's institutions attend his interment, but in every respect Martin du Gard has chosen to emphasize the dominion of death in the scene. In a winter landscape the tributes of Oscar's half-dead contemporaries ring with hollow phrases tracing the deceased's contributions to the civilization of his time, celebrating his status as a representative — "un représentant."

The reactions of the two brothers on their return to Crouy (the location of the Pénitencier) are revealing inasmuch as they prepare us for the later developments: Antoine, while sensing his loneliness and the failure of his father, nonetheless identifies himself with the Thibault line; Jacques, on the other hand, finds only confirmation of the nothingness of existence and the urge to set fire to the Pénitencier, in order to obliterate the last grim vestiges of his past. This symmetrical playing off of one brother against the other is characteristic of the whole volume — which tends, perhaps to its detriment, to fall rather neatly into schematic patterns, thereby emphasizing the fact that we have reached a moment of summation, the drawing up of a provisional balance sheet. The title of the volume, with *Père* now capitalized to indicate the archetypal nature of the father's role, clearly stresses the phylogenic importance of the event and might be taken from a handbook of psychology. In the evolution of the Thibault family the event occupies a crossroads. The resistance of the sons to the authority of the father has culminated in the ultimate act of defiance as they do everything to terminate his life, for different reasons on each part, certainly, but with equal determination: Antoine sees the time has come to replace his father and is ready to assume the mantle of head of the family; Jacques wishes merely to consummate his rebellion. The outcome of the conflict of the generations, already foreshadowed in *La Sorellina*, Jacques's wish-fulfilment fantasy, is the killing of the father.

It is now clearer why one is tempted to call the three parts of *Les Thibault* "movements" for, in a profoundly organic way, they are linked together, not by the mere sequence of the narrative but by the way they are interrelated according to their themes. This interrelation explains the structure and its fundamental unity: the first six volumes lie under the sign of the father and represent a preliminary statement; *L'Eté 1914* is marked by the sign of Jacques and constitutes a development; the *Epilogue* is Antoine's and shows a movement of recapitulation, a return to the key of the first part. Or, if we wish to view the novel dialectically, the world of the father explored in the beginning states a thesis that is opposed by the world of the rebel Jacques and is finally reassimilated and renewed in the synthesis proposed in the *Epilogue*.

With the opening of *L'Eté 1914*, there is the airy sense that we have emerged from a dead world; there is a prevailing sense of renewal. The scene has shifted to Geneva, already associated with Jacques's original bid for freedom when he had fled the family stronghold. We find Jacques has taken his real name again — which, in the light of Martin du Gard's awareness of the importance of names, at once indicates that Jacques has, in some measure, come to terms with himself. Around him are the other rebels with strikingly similar experiences behind them: a pattern of rebellion against bourgeois oppression. As in the first six volumes, in *L'Eté 1914* the action un-

141

folds on two levels, the one universal, the other intimate, individual, intensely human. In the first movement we witnessed the constant interplay of individual and society; Oscar Thibault was human in his solitude, and in his fear of death, but dehumanized in his identification with social institutions. In the next movement, too, Jacques appears both as type and individual, merging with the others through the similarity of his experiences and silhouetted against the broad historical background by his intensely private love for Jenny de Fontanin. As the broad patterns stand out from the dense narrative of *L'Eté 1914*, it becomes steadily more evident that the threads left hanging at the end of *La Mort du Père* have been woven into the governing motifs which have changed the configuration of the novel. The process of expansion continues on several fronts, but always with the counterpoint of individual and universal serving as the touchstone.

Jacques has exchanged his defunct family allegiances for espousal of the cause of the more universal family of the International socialist movement; the sense of continuity is now historicist, with the millennium replacing the Thibault aspirations to immortality and endurance. Metaphorically, the spiritual foundations that once upheld the family are now transferred to the revolutionaries: fraternity is now the basis for political solidarity: religious terminology is applied to the fervor of the activists, seen as *apôtres* imbued with a *foi agissante* (*OC*, II, 33–34). *L'Eté 1914* is the most complex part of *Les Thibault*, the most interesting from the point of view of narrative technique, the most impressive in its handling, within the same framework, of abstract and emotional themes. It is also the keystone in the vast structure of the novel, for it is here in particular that *Les Thibault* becomes truly a novel about "origins and destinies," a mythic narrative.[12] With good reason Doctor Philip sees the situation of man as similar to that of Oedipus, for a tragic rhythm takes over in *L'Eté 1914* and only the death of the hero can appease the 'gods.' Given the complexity of these volumes, only those aspects which are immediately germane to our purpose will be examined and they are best seen through a limited number of structuring elements.

Overall there is a parallel to be seen with the first six volumes: the narrative begins with a vision of solidarity and ends with the death of an individual, and disintegration. (In this respect, the *Epilogue* breaks the pattern in a significant way, as we shall see; it contains a movement of reintegration and Antoine's death represents, if not a return to total harmony at least a perception of 'order.') The rhythm of impending doom is what gives the novel its unity in *L'Eté 1914*. This rhythm is created by a number of alternating themes: an abstract dialectic based on the different theoretical positions taken by the members of the socialist group, by Antoine and other 'techniciens,' by militarists like Roy and disabused humanists like Doctor Philip; the motifs of war and peace; the happiness of Jacques and Jenny as individuals and the overwhelming sense of chaos threatening the masses. Ultimately, the movement of the three volumes is towards the fierce agony of Jacques who as a new hero emerging from a dying society eventually becomes its victim. Jacques is the hero of *L'Eté 1914*, although one is tempted to say the novel as a whole has two heroes, Jacques and Antoine, or perhaps more properly, and more schematically, we should say that Oscar, Jacques and Antoine constitute a many-faceted Thibault whose heroic emergence the novel traces. After all if Martin du Gard saw Jacques and Antoine as two aspects of his own character, why not Oscar as well?

At all events, in the dialectic of self-assertion and submission *L'Eté 1914* portrays the heroic ascendancy of the individual after the story of Oscar's long submission in the early volumes. Jacques's quest is now heroic because of the universal dimension added by the constant presence of the socialist action group and by the background attendance of the faceless mass of common men, and by the conviction that Jacques is working for them, leading them towards a new society. For Jacques has truly assumed the status of leader; he is recognized as such by his companions; his intellectual superiority and mysticism confer this privilege upon him. In every respect, Jacques settles into his new-found independence; even his erotic drives find the positive outlet that was previously lacking.

But for the tragic action to be complete, the hero must fall and, for humanity to emerge renewed, there must be a cataclysm which swallows up the old civilization. Thus, the death of Oscar in *La Mort du Père* prepares us for the second major climax, the advent of war and the death of Jacques. The link between the two deaths is provided by the style: there may have been a break in composition but Martin du Gard's vision remains consistent and what disparity may exist is largely effaced by stylistic coherence. In particular, the language of organic decay which is established as a dominant in *La Mort du Père* now becomes an important source of imagery applied to the *body* of Europe, the body politic and, by ex-

143

tension, to civilization itself. The steady accumulation of images of disease, coupled with cosmic and diluvian imagery, produces the effect, by the end of *L'Eté 1914*, that we are witnessing the end of a world. Thunder clouds gather as Europe rolls steadily to its doom; oppressive heat and a feverish atmosphere grip Paris, emphasizing the concordance between cosmic phenomena and the affairs of men. This kind of coincidence and patterning in the events of the novel — like the coincidence of the death of Jaurès, with all its fore-shadowing of disaster, and the first intimacy of Jacques and Jenny, of which Jean-Paul is the hopeful offspring — suggests that the disparateness of naturalist technique has been replaced by the kind of stylization that makes us search for the significance of the events beyond what they immediately convey. Not that naturalism implies total lack of ordering and selection in the matter of fiction, but, in the case of *Les Thibault*, this ordering and selection is patently more stringent, more indicative of a tightly structured narrative.

Jacques's death belongs to this kind of careful ordering of events; there is much that is symbolic and archetypal about it. The sense of fatality, the feeling that individuals no longer control their own destinies, prevails throughout *L'Eté 1914* (especially in the imagery of crowds likened more often to elemental forces like rivers and floods) and enters an acute phase with Jacques's death. The mechanism — that "engrenage diabolique" so often mentioned — seizes Jacques and carries him along. From the moment he enters the aircraft — portentously compared to a giant bird of prey — Jacques's exaltation, his conviction that he is participating in truly momentous happenings, give the events apocalyptic coloring. Using recurrent patterns again, Martin du Gard makes it clear that Jacques's impending death will be of the same nature as those of Meynestrel, in despair at the loss of Freda, and Mithoerg, who has gone off to Austria to die violently. These men, the last remaining members of the Geneva cell of the International, have committed themselves to what has always been a barely concealed death wish; Jacques's last moments also carry all the marks of self-destruction. Like the tragic hero, he rises symbolically to great heights; he looks down from the plane, feeling delivered, viewing the ant-like activities of ordinary men, feeling in command of his destiny. He has chosen his death and, in that sense, has attained that existential freedom that he had sought for so long. But Icarus-like he falls and has, as a victim of society, a scapegoat, to expiate his excesses of pride and revolt. It is significant that the coup de grace should be delivered by a representative of social authority, a gendarme.

144

The existential questions raised by Jacques's death must remain unresolved, for, in spite of the hero's own sense of success, the dramatic irony remains too evident for us to see it as anything but a partial victory over the forces of oppression. It takes the experience of Antoine for the conflict of generations initiated in the very first volumes of *Les Thibault* to be resolved, and for the full return to a collective consciousness to be made. Throughout *L'Eté 1914* Antoine's likeness to his father provokes repeated comment on the part of Jacques; in the *Epilogue* Antoine fully takes up the father's role. Structurally, the *Epilogue* fulfills a crucial function: in the tragic pattern it shows the mending of the rent fabric of the drama, the return to stability and equipoise, the satisfactory accommodation within a single framework of the self-assertive and submissive impulses that govern the action of the principal characters. It hints at that purification and renewal through self-destruction that Doctor Philip mentioned as an organic necessity in civilizations, especially ailing ones, and Antoine perceives the positive outcome of war: "cette épuration de l'individu, cette formation soudaine d'une âme collective et fraternelle, sous le poids d'une même fatalité" (*OC*, II, 830).

The words "collective" and "individual" are juxtaposed again in those lines as in the *Epilogue*, we find, through the mediating function of the symbol of the family, that the novel continues to advance on two levels simultaneously. Significantly, the final movement of *Les Thibault* opens with a return to the ancestral home; Antoine, released temporarily from a clinic for gas victims, attends the funeral of Mlle. de Waize. One of his experiences in the family home during this time serves, again perhaps too schematically, to expose the subconscious strata underlying Antoine's feelings. One may object to what seems to be a deliberate use of dream psychology to throw light on the inner workings of the characters but, at the same time, one must see it as an indicator of Martin du Gard's awareness of the unifying substructure provided by such material. Antoine sleeps in his father's room and, conveniently for the reader, reveals through a subsequent account of his dream the logic behind his future actions, the logic of atonement for feelings of guilt associated with his father (*OC*, II, 813–818). Such atonement lies almost certainly at the back of Antoine's quiet resolution in face of death and it rounds out the pattern of self-assertion and submission that prevails throughout the novel.

A certain amount has already been said about the structural importance of the *Epilogue*, but to appreciate the positive quality behind Antoine's atonement closer attention needs to be given to the last of the Thibault deaths and, in particular, to Antoine's diary account of it. In one respect it points to the overall coherence of the novel as it counterbalances the famous *Cahier gris*, which was at the origin of many of the conflicts in the Thibault family. Jacques's diary betrayed the hidden spirit of revolt he had been nurturing; Antoine's records the return to a collective consciousness and loyalty to the family. The *Journal* allows a valuable glimpse into the mental workings of a dying man and from his recurrent preoccupations we are able to assess the final impact of the novel. The basic rhythm of the last pages derives certainly from the advance of Antoine's disease and is made the more inexorable by the certain knowledge of his death. But to see this as an inescapable irony nullifying any other expectations and justifying final pessimism seems to me a misreading. For one of the most important demands that the *Journal* makes on us is that we see events through Antoine's eyes, through the eyes of a doctor. His unflinching rationalism takes much of the sting out of the physical decay.

The themes of the *Journal* are few but reiterated: the determinism of the past, faith in the future embodied in Jean-Paul, meditations on death, meditations on continuity, the place of man in the cosmos. Antoine's solution to the existential dilemma that death poses, and that both Oscar and Jacques had found only unsatisfactory answers to, demands that he view his position with detachment so that his plight appears to him not restricted to the individual but generalized, as part of a universal *devenir* (*OC*, II, 920). Indeed, Antoine's meditations on continuity develop on three levels, and provide considerable confirmation of the mediating role of the family symbol in vouchsafing the unity of the novel. As the *Journal* is essentially written with Jean-Paul in mind and as a testament to the continuity of the family, it is paramountly important that the links between these three levels be apparent. There is Antoine's preoccupation as an individual with vital energy which he sees being channelled into the Thibault line; there is the lingering over the family past; finally, there is the attempt to view events in cosmic terms, to see the destiny of the Thibaults as merely reflecting the general destiny of humanity. He returns insistently to the suggestion, made by various friends and acquaintances in *L'Eté 1914*, that death is necessary for rebirth to ensue. This, of course, applies to humanity generally as well as to his own private situation. In an important passage (*OC*, II, 981ff.), Antoine attempts to foresee the future of Europe and predicts the breakdown of his worn out civilization, the death of old values, and using physiological metaphors to describe the struggle for life, he envisions the collapse of nationalisms and their replacement by a collective and fraternal spirit that will nonetheless leave room for individual freedom and survival. In his last moments, he feels his detachment from the world of the living but senses that it goes on in spite of him; his last words stress continuity.

What I have attempted in the foregoing analysis is to discuss the question, fairly limited in itself, of the unity of *Les Thibault*. In so doing I have been led into broader considerations affecting the development of the French novel at a given moment in its evolution. For *Les Thibault* is only, in the words of Mme Magny, "scindé en deux" if we continue to view it as a work of social realism. Such a view would imply an emphasis on events and social structures for their own sake. What emerges from the above analysis is a narrative relying for its coherence on recurrent patterns which take us towards archetypes and myths.

The disunity of *Les Thibault* has been mostly attributed to the seeming disproportion between the two halves of the novel, between the volumes composed before the accident of January 1931 and those belonging to the new plan, beginning with *L'Eté 1914*, which appeared in 1936. Once it becomes clear, however, that the considerable expansion of the scope of the novel, although certainly not foreseen before January 1931, is consonant with Martin du Gard's new concept of his work, then one is obliged to review and, ultimately, discount the criticisms. The expansion in *L'Eté 1914* rests firmly on the first part of the cycle. By making use of the mediating function of the expanding symbol of the family, Martin du Gard guarantees that the passage from the history of a social group to the History of mankind at a given moment can take place without rupture. The enlargement of the novel's structural dimensions derives organically from its thematic development.

However important the question of the aesthetic unity may be — and it is obviously paramount in determining the viability of the work — it also affects its status in the evolution of the genre. The close link with novels that follow it in time has been pointed out by many critics but, in technique, it has benefited little from such generous appraisal. But it is because of the techniques used in bringing about a new ordering of reality that the novel passes beyond the sociological viewpoint of Naturalism. Martin du Gard no

147

longer portrays the individual simply in relation to the family or society but has come closer to an existentialist perspective depicting man in History and man in the world. The themes of *Les Thibault,* in this broader perspective, take on added depth: revolt no longer appears as defiance of social laws but as a more positive desire to affirm one's identity and existence in the face of a deeper spiritual enslavement; social conformism gives way before a more positive and dynamic desire to participate in the activities of the human community at large; failure to do so results not so much in becoming a social outcast but in deep alienation and a sense of being at odds with one's time; the fatal movement of History holds out only slim hope for infinite progress and rather underlines the absurdity of existence. It is not therefore surprising, as critics have been quick to notice, that Camus should acknowledge the legacy of *Les Thibault*:

> les thèmes de Martin du Gard rejoignent notre actualité. Le chemin qu'il a suivi, avec une heureuse lenteur, nous l'avons tous refait au pas de charge, sous la poussée des circonstances. Il s'agit, en gros, de l'évolution qui mène l'individu à la reconnaissance de l'histoire de tous, et à l'acceptation de ses luttes. Sans doute, Martin du Gard garde ici encore un air singulier. Il se place entre ses prédécesseurs et ses pairs — qui ne parlaient que de l'individu et n'ont jamais donné à l'histoire qu'une place circonstancielle — et ses successeurs, qui ne font à l'individu que des allusions embarrassées. (*OC*, I, xvi).

To accommodate the vision that Camus detects in Martin du Gard required an enlargement of the resources of fictional technique.

NOTES

INTRODUCTION

1. *Nouvelles littéraires*, 14 March 1946, quoted by Jean Scheidegger, *Georges Bernanos romancier* (Paris: Attinger, 1956), 142.

2. The following abbreviations refer to those of Bernanos' works which are included in the Pléiade edition (*Oeuvres romanesques*, Paris, 1961): *MD, Madame Dargent; DO, Dialogue d'ombres; SSS, Sous le soleil de Satan; I, L'Imposture; J, La Joie; MR, Un Mauvais Rêve; C, Un Crime; JCC, Journal d'un curé de campagne; NM, Nouvelle Histoire de Mouchette; MO, Monsieur Ouine; DC, Dialogue des Carmélites.* The edition as a whole is referred to as *OR.* In addition, certain abbreviations refer to the writer's articles and polemical works: *GCSL Les Grands Cimetières sous la lune* (Paris: Plon, 1938); *NF, Nous Autres Français* (Paris: Gallimard, 1939); *LAA, Lettre aux Anglais* (Rio: Atlantica, 1942); *EH, Les Enfants humiliés* (Paris: Gallimard, 1949); *LPQF, La Liberté pour quoi faire?* (Paris: Gallimard, 1953); *CCA, Le Chemin de la Croix-des-âmes* (Paris: Gallimard, 1948), *FCR, La France contre les robots* (Paris: Club français du livre, 1955); *FSVS, Français, si vous saviez* (Paris: Gallimard, 1961). The notation *BPLM* stands for *Bernanos par lui-même*, ed. Albert Béguin (Paris: Seuil, 1961).

3. See, for example, *FSVS*, p. 35, and *LPQF*, p. 211.

4. Gaëtan Picon, *Georges Bernanos* (Paris: Marin, 1948), p. 107.

5. The images in the well-known preface to *GCSL* tend to support this statement. We might also consider the following, almost random examples: ". . . la monstrueuse enfance reniée, forte comme une bête, indomptable, avec un cœur de taureau" (*EH*, p. 93). "Il faut si peu d'eau croupie pour entretenir une mauvaise pensée" (*EH*, p. 112). ". . . ces régions de l'être où la mémoire individuelle ne se distingue plus de la mémoire héréditaire, se perd en elle ainsi qu'un ruisseau babillard dans les eaux noires et profondes" (*CCA*, p. 219). ". . . cette espèce de justice qui est à la véritable justice ce que le minéral est à l'être vivant organisé, le cristal à l'homme" (*LPQF*, p. 112).

6. This observation of frequency is based upon my own doctoral thesis, "Images and Themes in the Novels of Georges Bernanos: An Index with Commentary" (Harvard University, 1967). In the novels and short stories of Bernanos, there are well over 500 images of animals, about 375 of fire, light and their contraries, about 300 of water in various forms, about 200 of sickness and death, and 200 of various kinds of sensation. There are about 160 images of children. Among the less frequent categories are obstacles (100), roads (90), mirrors (40), circles (30), stones (20). Statistics of this kind can never pretend to absolute mathematical accuracy; for this reason, the figures have been quoted in round terms.

7. This combination of familiarity and incoherence, which is especially

149

apparent in *Monsieur Ouine*, is treated by W. M. Frohock in *Style and Temper: Studies in French Fiction, 1925–1960* (Cambridge: Harvard Univ. Press, 1967), pp. 45–61.

8. Henri Bremond, *Histoire littéraire du sentiment religieux en France* (Paris: Bloud et Gay, 1916–1933), XI, 405–408. This reference to Bremond is doubtless somewhat incongruous in an essay whose subject is Bernanos. There was little love lost between the two men, and it is probable that Bremond was the model for the apostate Cénabre. But the two men also seem to have had a certain respect for, or interest in, each other's works. Bernanos' friend Mgr Pézeril has told me that the novelist was thoroughly familiar with the *Histoire du sentiment religieux*. Bremond, on his side, expressed himself as being struck by the "divination étonnante" in Bernanos' portrayal of the mystic Chantal de Clergerie (*Nouvelles littéraires*, early June 1929, quoted by Henri Massis, "Coups de bec et bruits de plume," *Bulletin des lettres*, CLII [15 November 1953], 399–400).

9. The following examples seem especially similar to those cited by Bremond: "L'odeur que je veux dire n'est pas véritablement une odeur, ça vient de plus loin, de plus profond, de la mémoire, de l'âme, est-ce qu'on sait? L'eau n'y fait rien, faudrait autre chose" (*MO*, p. 1440). "Mais le rude maître n'était plus qui recueillait à mesure sa joie mystérieuse pour qu'elle n'en sentît pas le poids surnaturel" (*J*, p. 554). "Je n'ai rien vu, rien entendu, je ne pensais même à rien. Cela m'a comme frappé dans le dos" (*J*, p. 715). "Comme ces gelées vivantes, au fond de la mer, je flotte et j'absorbe" (*MO*, p. 1368). "Vous êtes dans l'ombre d'une aile gigantesque qui va se refermer sur nous" (*DO*, p. 48).

10. The following passage from *La Joie* seems explicable only in terms of a passage in Bremond. It marks the first appearance in the novels of the *tomber en Dieu* image.

"C'étaient les heures de jadis, si pareilles à celles de l'enfance, et il n'y manquait même pas la merveilleuse attente qui lui donnait autrefois l'illusion de courir à perdre haleine au bord d'un abîme enchanté. Au bord des Pyrénées, sur un sentier vertigineux, regardant par la portière du coche le gouffre rose où tournent les aigles, la petite fille préférée de Sainte Thérèse s'écrie joyeusement, 'Je ne puis tomber qu'en Dieu!' " (*J*, p. 552.)

The "petite fille" referred to here cannot be found in the biography of Saint Teresa of Avila, nor in that of Sainte Thérèse of Lisieux, in whom Bernanos was particularly interested. But she corresponds closely with Mme Jourdain, a wealthy young widow who helped the Spanish Carmelites establish their first foundation in France, early in the Seventeenth Century. Bremond describes the journey of the founders from Spain to France:

"On eut beaucoup de peine à passer les montagnes et à franchir les précipices qui se trouvaient sur le chemin. [. . .] Au bord de ces abîmes béants, Mme Jourdain disait avec allégresse: 'Je ne saurais tomber qu'en Dieu!' " (*Histoire littéraire du sentiment religieux*, II, 295). Since Bremond found this anecdote in a private publication of the Carmelites, it seems most probable that his work was Bernanos' source.

11. *DC*, p. 1672. In the face of the danger confronting her community, Sœur Constance laughs and says, "Mais nous, ma Sœur, nous ne pouvons tomber qu'en Dieu!" This young nun belongs to a category of childlike per-

sonalities, particularly frequent in Bernanos' later works. At the same time, she bears a certain family resemblance to Bremond's Mme Jourdain: both are Carmelite novices, and both manage to combine innocence and joyfulness with a kind of inner distinction.

12. Georges Poulet considers this metaphor to be a key to Bernanos' conception of the human condition: man is trapped in a hopeless predicament, as if in a lake of mud, and can only escape through the radical intervention of divine grace. (*Le Point de départ*, Paris, Plon, 1964, pp. 51–58.)

13. "Contribution au bestiaire de Bernanos," *Bulletin de la société des amis de Bernanos* (July 1958), pp. 9–23.

14. This *peur du flou* is treated at some length by Poulet (*loc. cit.*).

15. These metamorphoses into stone find an unexpected echo in a novel by the writer's son, Michel Bernanos: *La Montagne morte de la vie* (Paris: Pauvert, 1967). The work is concerned with a young sailor's voyage to unknown lands. It becomes apparent very early that the protagonist is engaged in a nightmare situation from which there is no issue; the only possible progression is from horror to horror, passively endured as dreams are. The voyage ends in the discovery of a mountainous desert, peopled by strange statues. In the last pages, the young sailor and his companion become like the statues and are changed into stone. The book ends in this way: "Le seul souvenir qui me reste, depuis des siècles que je vis dans la pierre, est le doux contact de larmes sur un visage d'homme," (p. 151).

16. This point is mentioned by Henri Debluë in *Les Romans de Georges Bernanos ou le défi du rêve* (Neuchâtel: La Baconnière, 1965), p. 59.

17. The letter already quoted is echoed in *Jeanne relapse et sainte* (Paris: Plon, 1934), p. 67.

18. "Twentieth-century Gothic: Reflections on the Catholic novel," *Southern Review*, I (Spring 1965), 391.

19. "The Hostile Phantoms of Georges Bernanos: *Sous le soleil de Satan* and *Monsieur Ouine*," *L'Esprit Créateur*, IV (Winter 1964), 208–221.

MALRAUX

1. Abbreviations and page numbers, cited in parentheses in the text, refer to Malraux's novels, as follows: (*LC*) *Les Conquérants*, (*CH*) *La Condition humaine*, and (*LE*) *L'Espoir*, all in the Pléiade edition (Paris, 1947); (*VR*) *La Voie royale* (Paris, 1961); (*TM*) *Le Temps du mépris* (Paris, 1935), and (*NA*) *Les Noyers de l'Altenburg* (Paris, 1948).

2. *André Malraux* (London, 1960), p. 62.

3. For a recent study of alienation in Malraux's novels, see Brian T. Fitch, *Le Sentiment d'étrangeté chez Malraux, Sartre, Camus et S. de Beauvoir* (Paris, 1964).

4. For literal references to the experience of grandfathers with passing circuses, cf. *VR*, p. 28, *CH*, p. 198–199, *NA*, p. 42.

5. The next sentence reads as follows: "Tous ces blessés étaient des soldats: il n'y avait pas d'affolement, mais un ordre farouche, fait de lassitude, d'impuissance, de rage et de résolution." As if frequently the case, Malraux's expository dramatizations of popular heroism offer information that strains

logic, and are notably less effective in their expressiveness than his imagistic style.

6. The nature of Malraux's art images, of which there are a very considerable number, is such as would require a study beyond the scope of the present one, and so they have not been taken into account here.

NATHALIE SARRAUTE

1. All references are to the following editions: Nathalie Sarraute, *Tropismes* (Paris: Gallimard, 1956); *Portrait d'un Inconnu* (Paris: Gallimard, 1956); *Martereau*, 3ème éd. (Paris: Gallimard, 1953); *Le Planétarium* (Paris: Gallimard, 1959); *Les Fruits d'Or* (Paris: Gallimard, 1963). The discussion here presented applies equally well to Mme Sarraute's most recent novel, *Entre la vie et la mort* (Paris: Gallimard, 1968).

2. Geneviève Serreau, "Nathalie Sarraute nous parle du 'Planétarium'," *Les Lettres Nouvelles*, 7me année, no. 9 (29 avril 1959), 29.

3. One sketch from the original edition (1939) has been cut and six new ones added to the edition here cited.

4. Nathalie Sarraute, "Rebels in a world of platitudes," *TLS*, June 10, 1960, p. 371.

GIDE

1. Almost any one of Gide's works could have been logically entitled *Great Expectations* (or rather *Les Grandes Espérances*). It is not surprising to find Gide on two occasions expressing admiration for the novel in which Dickens handles the theme of expectation with ambiguity and irony. References to *Great Expectations* occur in Gide's *Journal* entries for February 21, 1925 and December 25, 1943.

2. In *Portrait of André Gide* (New York, Knopf, 1953), pp. 129–130.

3. In my unpublished Harvard doctoral thesis, "André Gide's Abstract Vocabulary," I have attempted to clarify Gide's usage of 49 abstractions.

4. "*Lui*: Permettez: le maquignon qui vend un cheval sait fort bien ce que le mot 'cheval' veut dire; et celui qui l'achète le sait aussi.

Moi: Mais moins, peut-être celui qui parle de dévouement, d'honneur, de foi, de constance, de fidélité.

Lui: Evidemment le domaine concret est plus aisément saisissable." (*Attendu*, p. 172).

5. Reported by Professor Stephen Ullmann in "Glanures gidiennes," *Le Français Moderne* XXV (1957), 204.

6. Information on frequency is based on a comparison of the recurrence of certain of Gide's abstractions in 30 of his narrative, dramatic, and lyrical works with their frequency in the works of the 87 other authors tabulated in George E. Vander Beke's *French Word Book* in *Publications of the American and Canadian Committees on Modern Languages* XV (1929), 1–188. Among Gide's contemporaries who appear in the Vander Beke study are: Alain-Fournier, Barrès, René Bazin, Benoît, Bordeaux, Clemenceau, Duhamel,

Anatole France, Loti, C. L. Philippe, Proust, Romain Rolland, Rostand, and Schlumberger.

7. It should be explained here that the word "image" is being used in a broad sense — so as to include abstractions expressing sense impressions other than simply visual. Thus *soif* and *ivresse* with their implications of taste and touch are every bit as much image-conveying abstractions as the undeniably pictorial *déracinement* and *azur*.

8. It is in this sense that Pierre Guiraud in *Les Caractères statistiques du vocabulaire, essai de méthodologie* (Presses Universitaires de France, 1954) and Monique Parent in her *Saint-John Perse et quelques devanciers* (Paris, Librairie C. Klincksieck, 1960) have brought the term *mot-clef* into accepted usage in France. By the equally useful term *mots-thèmes* these two critics merely mean his most recurrent words.

9. Gide's other works — the autobiographies, travel accounts, and essays — will be used when they present examples of a word's special usage or lead to its clearer definition.

10. Dictionary definitions are from *Heath's Standard French and English Dictionary*, edited by J. E. Mansion (D.C. Heath and Company, Boston, 1960).

Wherever possible references are made to the *Oeuvres Complètes* (éd. Martin-Chauffier, 15 vols., Paris, Gallimard, 1932–39), abbreviated here to *O.C.* Titles are abbreviated as follows:

Beth.	— *Bethsabé* (*O.C.* IV, 219–237).
Billets	— *Billets à Angèle* (*O.C.* XI, 33–63).
Biskra	— *De Biskra à Touggourt* (*O.C.* III, 275–286).
Cahiers	— *Les Cahiers d'André Walter* (*O.C.* I, 5–175).
Caves	— *Les Caves du Vatican* (*O.C.* VII, 101–408).
Congo	— *Voyage au Congo* (*O.C.* XIII, 83–383).
Feuilles	— *Feuilles de route* (*O.C.* II, 1–53).
F.M.	— *Les Faux-monnayeurs* (*O.C.* XII, 17–550).
Grain	— *Si le grain ne meurt* (*O.C.* X, 27–454).
Hadj	— *El Hadj* (*O.C.* III, 65–95).
L'Imm.	— *L'Immoraliste* (*O.C.* IV, 1–171).
Isa.	— *Isabelle* (*O.C.* VI, 169–282).
Journal	— *Journal* (*O.C.* passim).
Lettres	— *Lettres à Angèle* (*O.C.* III, 161–247).
Mopsus	— *Mopsus* (*O.C.* III, 1–11).
Narcisse	— *Le Traité du Narcisse* (*O.C.* I, 205–220).
N.T.	— *Les Nourritures terrestres* (*O.C.* II, 155–229).
Pages	— *Pages inédites* (*O.C.* XI, 21–31).
Paysages	— *Paysages* (*O.C.* I, 245–250).
Poésies	— *Les Poésies d'André Walter* (*O.C.* I, 177–203).
Porte	— *La Porte étroite* (*O.C.* V, 73–241).
Prodigue	— *Le Retour de l'enfant prodigue* (*O.C.* V, 1–27).
Prom.	— *Le Prométhée mal enchaîné* (*O.C.* III, 97–160).
Renoncement	— *Le Renoncement au voyage* (*O.C.* IV, 239–340).
Roi	— *Le Roi Candaule* (*O.C.* III, 287–396).
Saül	— *Saül* (*O.C.* II, 231–407).
Symph.	— *La Symphonie pastorale* (*O.C.* IX, 1–87).
Tchad	— *Le Retour du Tchad* (*O.C.* XIV, 1–271).
Tent.	— *La Tentative amoureuse* (*O.C.* I, 221–243).
Urien	— *Le Voyage d'Urien* (*O.C.* I, 279–365).

Works not appearing in the *œuvres complètes*:

Anth. *— Anthologie du la poésie française* (Paris, Gallimard, Bibliothèque de la Pléiade, 1949).

Attendu *— Attendu que —* (Alger, Charlot, 1943).

Ecole *— L'Ecole des femmes* suivi de *Robert* et de *Geneviève* (Paris, Gallimard, 1944).

N.N. *— Les Nouvelles Nourritures* in *Les Nourritures terrestres* et *les Nouvelles Nourritures* (Paris, Gallimard, 1947).

Oedipe *— Oedipe* in *Théâtre* (Paris, Gallimard, 1947).

Pers. *— Perséphone* in *Théâtre* (Paris, Gallimard, 1947).

Thésée *— Thésée* (Paris, Gallimard, 1946).

11. *Op. cit.*, p. 129 and following. Note too that Gide arbitrarily alternates between the two spellings *dénuement* and *dénûment*.

12. In the not too convincing 1926 preface to *Les Nourritures terrestres*, *O.C.* II, 229, and the *Journal*, 24 mars 1935.

13. "Table rase. J'ai tout balayé. C'en est fait! Je me dresse nu sur la terre vierge, devant le ciel à repeupler." (*N.N.*, p. 194.)

14. Mrs. Sandra Newman, a University of Toronto graduate student, recently observed that Gide's works are far from "titillating," an opinion which is surely that of most modern readers. In general, Gide is less inclined to shock with sexual innuendoes than might be surmised from his reputation.

15. *Caves*, p. 164. In this case, Lafcadio is wearing rubbers! The interest which Gide takes in the significance of footwear can be judged as somewhat parallel to Flaubert's interest in hats, exemplified in his description of the young Charles Bovary's "casquette." The importance which Gide attributes to Lafcadio's "castor" reminds us of Flaubert, but I fail to see much or any significance in Gide's references to bareheaded people.

16.
> "Les plus douces joies de mes sens
> Ont été des soifs étanchées."

("Ronde de la grenade," *N.T.*, p. 127.)

> "Les plus grandes joies de mes sens
> Ç'ont été des soifs étanchées."

("Ronde de mes soifs étanchées," *ibid.*, pp. 168, 169, 171.)

17. "Je m'appris, comme des questions devant les attendantes réponses, à ce que la soif d'en jouir, née devant chaque volupté, en précédât d'aussitôt la jouissance. Mon bonheur venait de ce que chaque source me révélait une soif, et que dans le désert sans eau, où la soif est inapaisable, j'y préférais encore la ferveur de ma fièvre sous l'exaltation du soleil." (*Ibid.*, p. 114.)

18.
> "Certains jours je marchais au grand soleil,
> L'été, durant les heures les plus chaudes,
> Cherchant de grandes soifs à pouvoir étancher."

(*Ibid.*, p. 170.)

19. "— mais j'avais si soif et si faim que quelques grappes suffirent à m'enivrer." (*Ibid.*, p. 183.)

20. "Il y en a [des fruits] dont l'écorce tache les lèvres et que l'on ne mange que lorsqu'on a très soif." (*Ibid.*, p. 129.)

21.
  "Ils [les fruits] brillaient à travers le feuillage épineux
  Qui déchira nos mains lorsque nous voulûmes les prendre;
  Et notre soif n'en fut pas beaucoup étanchée."   (*Ibid.*)

22. "Notre soif était devenue si intense que, cette eau, j'en avais déjà bu tout un verre avant de percevoir, hélas! comme elle était nauséabonde." (*Ibid.*, p. 214.)

23. "Et la nature entière se tourmente
  Entre soif de repos et soif de volupté." (Ibid., p. 140.)

24. "Toute la terre flétrit de soif et de crainte et d'attente;
   Tant la soif est désir d'amour
   Et l'amour est soif de toucher, —"   (*Hadj*, p. 81.)

25 "J'étouffe ici; je songe à tout l'ailleurs qui s'entr'ouvre. . . . J'ai soif. . . ." (*Isa.*, p. 229.)

26. A study of Gide's hunger images (*faim*) would doubtless reveal a wealth of Freudian implications related to the theme of desire.

27. Gide uses this word family very often indeed: a total of 156 times in 30 narrative, dramatic, and lyrical works. Some even more frequent *mots-thèmes* are *attente* (699 occurrences), *bonheur* (533), *vérité* (529), *tristesse* (341), *joie* (335), *inquiétude* (256), *liberté* (167), and *plaisir* (157).

28. "La foule ne se possédait plus et oscillait comme en ivresse." (*Urien*, p. 299.)

29. Germaine Brée labels the fifth book of *Les Nourritures* "L'Evangile de l'ivresse" in her *André Gide, l'insaisissable Protée* (Paris, Société d'édition les Belles-lettres, 1953), p. 81.

30. "Nathanaël, je te parlerai de l'ivresse." (*N.T.*, p. 152.)

31. *Renoncement*, p. 318. In this work Gide even refers to turtles (p. 260) and a tree (p. 248) as intoxicated. These images help in re-creating the headiness of the North African atmosphere.

32. *N.N.*, p. 192. The same lines of poetry occur in *Perséphone* in *Théâtre*, p. 310.

33. "Eden! où les brises mélodieuses ondulaient en courbes prévues; où le ciel étalait l'azur sur la pelouse symétrique. . . ." (*Narcisse*, p., 210).

34. "On dirait des cloches de flamme, de grandes cloches d'azur emplies du parfum de l'amour et que balance le vent du soir" (p. 54).

35. "L'azur m'attire, ô poésie!" (*Thésée*, p. 70).

36. "J'ai vu dans les creux craquelés cette eau monter, lourde de terre, tiède, et qu'un rayon de soleil jaunissait" (*Mopsus*, p. 6.)

37. "L'air était presque tiède et l'azur lui riait à travers les rameaux déjà dépouillés des grands arbres." (*F.M.*, p. 484.)

38. Gide's earliest and most influential statements concerned with uprooting are to be found in the following sources: *A propos des "Déracinés"*, *O.C.* II, 435–444; *Feuillets 1898*, *O.C.* II, 469; *Le Renoncement au voyage*, *O.C.* IV, 309; *La Querelle du peuplier*, *O.C.* IV, 399–409; *Au service de l'Allemagne*, *OC.* IV, 433–440; *Supplément*, *O.C.* V, 277; *Nationalisme et littérature*, *O.C.* VI, 1–20; and *Journal sans dates*, *O.C.* VI, 84.

39. *Feuilles*, p. 14; *N.T.*, pp. 192, 202, 217, 221; *Saül*, pp. 320, 351; *L'Imm.*, pp. 44, 46, 50, 59; *Renoncement*, pp. 260, 324; *Porte*, p. 160.

40. "Jonathan, c'est pour toi que je suis descendu de la montagne où ta fragile fleur au trop ardent soleil serait fanée" (Speech of David in *Saül*, p.

NOTES

320); and see also: "Sous le soleil, ardent déjà, des buées s'élevaient" (*L'Imm.*, p. 50), as well as the synesthetic, "Et longuement l'œil interrogateur écoute comment un ton bleu passe au rose, puis du rose au fauve, à l'ardent" (*Renoncement*, p. 260).

41. "la ferveur de mon adolescence, je ne l'ai jamais retrouvée; et l'ardeur sensuelle où je me suis complu par la suite n'en est qu'une contrefaçon dérisoire." (*Journal*, le 16 juin 1931.)

42. *André Gide* (Paris, Editions R.-A. Correâ, 1931), p. 263.

MARTIN DU GARD

* All references to Martin du Gard's works, including autobiographical and prefatory material, are to the Pléïade edition of the *Oeuvres complètes*, (Paris: Gallimard, 1955). Quotations from the text are followed by the symbol *OC* and the appropriate volume and page numbers.

1. Claude-Edmonde Magny, *Histoire du roman français depuis 1918* (Paris: Editions du Seuil, 1950), p. 309.

2. Thomas White Hall, "A note on the so-called 'change in technique' in *Les Thibault* of Roger Martin du Gard," *FR*, XXVII (December 1953), 108–113.

3. Jacques Brenner, *Martin du Gard* (Paris: Gallimard, 1961), p. 78.

4. Denis Boak, *Roger Martin du Gard* (Oxford: Clarendon Press, 1963).

5. Graham Falconer in a review of Denis Boak, *Roger Martin du Gard*, *Modern Language Review*, LX (1965), 122–124. In his perceptive and complete reading of *Les Thibault*, Boak is hampered by the use of such traditional categories as the "historical" and "psychological" novel. As a result he is led into criticising the disunity of the novel. In two other recent critical works the problem is considered: I find myself on common ground on several occasions with Rejean Robidoux whose excellent *Roger Martin du Gard et la religion* (Paris: Aubier, 1964), treats the question less extensively while David Schalk, *Roger Martin du Gard: the Novelist and History* (Cornell University Press, 1967), is not directly concerned with fictional techniques.

6. H. Stuart Hughes, *Consciousness and Society* (New York: Vintage Books, 1961), p. 14.

7. Barbara Tuchman, *The Proud Tower* (New York: Macmillan, 1966), esp. chaps. II, IV.

8. Quoted in *Souvenirs autobiographiques et littéraires, OC*, I, lxxxvi.

9. Thomas Mann, "Freud and the Future," in *Essays,* tr. H. T. Lowe-Porter (New York: Vintage Books, 1958), p. 317.

10. Maud Bodkin, *Archetypal Patterns in Poetry* (London: Oxford University Press, 1965), chap. I.

11. Victor Brombert, *The Intellectual Hero* (Philadelphia & New York: J. B. Lippincott, 1960), p. 96. The whole of Brombert's chapter on *Jean Barois* is relevant to our present purpose.

12. This, according to René Wellek and Austin Warren, is one of the characteristics of myth. See *Theory of Literature* (New York: Harvest Book, 1956), p. 180.